STING WARS
BOOK 5 THE SOVEREIGN CODE

TAMAR SLOAN

HEIDI CATHERINE

SEQUEL HOUSE

CHAPTER
ONE
ECHO

Threads of awareness shimmer in Echo's consciousness. She concentrates, trying to bring them into focus. But the more she tries, the more they slip out of her grasp. Then they come rushing at her and she pulls back.

It's too much.

She doesn't want to remember what happened.

What was said to her.

What was done to her.

And who did it.

She groans, moving her face away from a hand that's slapping her.

"Echo! Wake up!"

"River," she whispers, her voice little more than a crackle. Her head is heavy, and her body aches. And that constant slapping is starting to hurt.

The assault on her cheek pauses and her face is gripped between a strong thumb and index finger. "Wake up! Echo!"

Her eyes flare open in anger. "Stop that!"

Chase's face hovers in front of hers. He breaks into a wide

1

smile and curses. Then letting his hand fall, he gives her a rough kiss on the cheek. "Welcome back. I thought you were dead."

More memories fight their way back like unwelcome intruders invading her mind.

Reed returned to the Dead Zone to make the Immunity. Which meant he needed Echo's spinal fluid. So, he injected her with queen bee venom. He scared her, just like he was meant to. But there's more to it. Something else her fuzzy mind is struggling to grab hold of. And she's glad for it.

"Stay with me, Echo." Chase grips her face again and she pushes away his hand.

"I'm right here." She struggles to sit up, seeing she's on the dirt floor of the LaB in the bunker.

Lifting her hands, she sees angry purple lines streaking across her wrists. Her fingertips go to the corners of her mouth, and she winces as she touches raw skin. Tears of confusion trail down her face, stinging as the salt mingles with her injuries. Reed hadn't just injected her. He'd bound and gagged her to keep her still.

She hadn't just been scared.

She'd been terrified.

"What happened to you?" Chase is crouched beside her, and she shakes her head, finding herself unable to explain.

"I'm not sure." Her voice gathers some strength, and she clutches at Chase's hand, needing her friend now more than ever.

Reed walks into the small room.

"Echo!" he gasps. "You're awake."

Fear ices Echo's spine and she throws herself at Chase, almost toppling him to the floor as she pins herself to his side. He puts a steadying arm around her, getting them both to their feet.

"What's going on?" he growls at Reed.

"I'm using the Code to make Immunity." Reed rubs his hands together and smiles. "Echo's fine."

"Then why is she scared of you?" Chase pulls Echo in closer to his chest.

Now that she's feeling safe, Echo's mind allows her to remember. And each of her memories comes sliding back with agonizing clarity.

She points at Reed. "He told me River's dead. That Oren killed him." These words sit like poison on her tongue as she struggles to come to terms with them.

Chase seems puzzled, rather than angry. "But Oren's dead."

She shakes her head, certain she's remembering correctly. "Reed said he's alive. That he killed River. And he's coming for us next."

Letting go of Echo, Chase stalks forward, grabbing Reed by his shirt collar and slamming him into the wall as he levels their faces only inches apart. "Is this true?"

Reed flushes red, shaking his head and putting up his hands. "I can explain! I only told Echo that to scare her. I needed to do it for the Immunity. Please, Chase! You're hurting me."

Chase keeps his grip on Reed, sneering at him with the same anger Echo saw when he held Daphne captive. And now Echo is afraid of both men in the room. Because while she may trust Chase with her life, that doesn't mean she trusts him with anyone else's. Especially a Green Born. Now's not the time for more death. They need answers.

"Chase." She goes to him, putting a hand on his arm and trying to pull him back. Her head spins with the sudden movement as a sick feeling builds in her stomach. "Let's hear what he has to say."

Chase gives Reed one more shove against the wall, then releases him. Echo drags in a deep breath, not wanting to empty the meager contents of her stomach in this small room.

Reed steps cautiously around the LaB, trying to get some distance from Chase who's taken up guard at the door. They've seen Reed run away before. Chase is taking no chances this time.

"Start talking," he growls when Reed remains silent.

Reed runs a hand through his red hair then pushes his glasses back on the top of his nose. "River's not dead. At least, not the last time I saw him. I mean, there's every chance that since then—"

"Enough." Echo holds up a shaking hand. "We don't need speculation. Just facts. Where did you last see him?"

"He was with Vern in the Green Zone," Reed answers quickly. "They went to the Sovereign graveyard to look for Flora."

Chase cocks an eyebrow to hear his girlfriend's name. "And?"

"I told them they were wasting their time," Reed snaps. "We all know she died in the fire. Going to the graveyard was foolish."

Echo narrows her eyes. "River's not stupid."

"Well, he did something stupid." Reed shrugs. "Oren's alive. That bit's true. He was pulled out of the fire the moment you left. That was River's first mistake. He should have known it takes more than an explosion to kill someone like his father. Evil scalds, but it seems it doesn't burn."

"Oren's not his father," Echo says, not wanting the guy she loves associated with that monster.

"What was his second mistake?" Chase asks, running short on patience.

"Coming back," says Reed. "Oren has death orders out on him. His guards were all briefed to kill him on sight."

Echo shudders. Oren may not be River's biological father, but he was still the man who raised him.

"Which is why I locked him in the Sovereign graveyard," Reed continues. "And Vern. It was for their own safety. I programmed the door to open at sunset, hoping by then they'd regain their senses and get themselves back here."

"Are you saying he's alive?" Echo asks.

"Echo," says Chase in a voice far gentler than the one he uses for Reed. "Sunset was hours ago."

Echo sits down on the chair that's been carved from dirt and plasters her hands over her mouth to stop herself from being sick. She glares at Reed, frustration bubbling in her gut.

"Hey!" He throws out his hands. "I'm on your side. You can trust me."

"Can we though?" Echo lets her hands fall to her lap and balls them into fists. "Because when you scared me last night, you did a pretty good job of it. As in, the *very best* job."

"I'm sorry," he yelps. "I needed to scare you. I really want this Immunity to work. You do, too. We're way out of time for any more mistakes."

"Don't you think leaving River and Vern in the Sovereign graveyard was a mistake?" Echo asks. "Why couldn't you have brought them here with you?"

"Echo." Reed shakes his head. "I thought you knew River. Do you really think he was going to listen to me, just because I told him to come back?"

Chase grunts. "River can be kind of stubborn."

"Fine." Echo wipes her palms on her trousers and stands up. "I trust you."

She doesn't mean these words, but she also knows she doesn't have much choice. The only other person qualified to make Immunity is Flora. And she's not here. She may never be here again. Which means it's all on Reed.

"Thank you," he says, not foolish enough to try to seal their truce with any kind of human touch.

"You have what you need from me." She stalks to the door, but Chase bars her exit.

"You can't leave," he tells her. "Why do you think I came back here in the first place?"

She shakes her head. "I don't understand."

"You're the Sovereign." Chase jams his hands on his hips. "We can't let anything happen to you."

She almost laughs. Growing up, she'd have loved nothing more than for Chase to be her shadow. But not now. She has to get into the Green Zone and find River. "You came here to guard me?"

"I came here to keep you safe," he corrects.

Anger boils inside her as she resists the urge to ask how safe he kept Flora. Echo doesn't need a minder. She needs the only thing that makes sense in this complicated world.

She needs River.

"Chase." She draws in a breath, trying to sound calmer than she feels. "Flora's missing. And now so is River. Don't you think we should look for them?"

"Flora's dead," he says without a hint of any emotion in his voice.

"You keep saying that." Echo puts a hand on his arm. "But don't you want to know for sure?"

He shakes his head, the gesture quickly morphing into a nod. "Of course, I do! But not at the risk of everything the Razers have worked toward all our lives. One of the reasons I fell for Flora was because of how strong minded she is. Or *was*. I have to trust that if she's alive, she'll come back to me. And you should do the same with River."

6

"But what if he can't come back?" she asks, not liking this answer. "What if he needs me?"

Chase shrugs. "Then he shouldn't have left."

Echo winces at the blunt harshness of this comment. She's never going to be able to convince him to come with her to the Green Zone. Which means she needs to wait for her moment to go without him.

Because just like she needs River, he needs her.

Their story isn't over yet.

TWO

RIVER

The golden orb of the sun sinking over the Green Zone feels symbolic. Sunsets are about endings. The day that existed has finished. It's...dead.

River wipes his hand down his face, trying to rid himself of the doomsday thinking, but then winces. He looks at his hand. It's bruised from hitting the glass wall over and over, hoping to break it. His nails are bloodied from trying to gouge away a chunk of cement from the ragged edge of the gaping wound in the side of the Sting. The hole that's giving him an unobstructed view of the death Oren is going to rain down on the Dead Zone. All River got was shredded fingers and dust. Nothing that would smash the glass.

None of it worked.

Escape is impossible.

He has no choice but to be an unwilling witness to what is to come.

River sits with his legs dangling over the edge, ignoring the dizzying drop below. He didn't need to study it for long to know it wasn't a way out of this prison. The smooth sides of the Sting leave nowhere to grip. The sheer height he's at would mean certain death.

Escape.

Is.

Impossible.

The netting over the Dead Zone is now a sheer shadow blanketing the ragged huts below. How long after nightfall will the Workers come? Their red and blue discs will be visible even from this distance as they land on the net, their jaws and claws working to create holes in the shield that protects the Dead Borns.

The holes won't have to be big. The weapons that Oren will control are smaller than River's thumbnail.

Yet deadly.

River resists the urge to look over his shoulder. Oren's wall of queen bees is on the other side of the glass, hundreds of little bodies twitching and humming within. Each little insect carries the ability to sting as many times as she'd like, injecting venom into bodies that have no way of fighting it.

It's a blessing to know the deranged man planning all of this isn't River's biological father. One that's tempered by the knowledge Vern, his real father, is trapped in the Sovereign graveyard. That Flora hasn't been seen. That his mother is in the Dead Zone about to be attacked.

And River has no idea whether Echo's alive.

Everyone he loves is either dead or about to be.

A fat tear trickles down his cheek and he swipes at it with the back of his hand, the slick feeling across his face telling him he just added blood to the salt water. Not that he cares. Nothing, not his battered hands, the hunger, the thirst, compares to the ache inside him. The grief. The regret. The helplessness that's burrowed so deep it's now part of his marrow.

River glances down, registering the ground hundreds of

feet below is now shrouded in darkness as twilight turns to dusk. For the first time in his life, he has an inkling of why someone would choose a quick death on their own terms rather than the pain of a life beyond their control. A life where they no longer feel like they can change it for the better.

With a sharp intake of breath, River scoots back from the edge. He stands, feeling the skin of his cheeks tightening as the tears and blood dry. He'd rather die trying to beat down the glass wall than give into those thoughts. As long as he's alive, he'll fight for those he loves. For what he believes in.

He turns and is about to take a step but stops. His gut drops, feeling like it just plummeted the length of the Sting.

The door to the Restricted Area is opening. Someone is coming in.

It's most likely Oren, here to gloat over the destruction he's about to wreak. River gave up hope it could be Reed the moment he was trapped in the Sovereign graveyard. Once again, he was naïve to trust his old friend. Seems River's heart is slow to learn that some people are just bad to the core.

Still, the person who walks through is the last person he expects to lay eyes on. Someone he never thought he'd see again.

River runs to the glass wall and slams his hands against it. "Flora!" He screams her name as loud as he can, and although it seems to pierce even the darkening clouds above him, he hates that she can't hear him.

His twin smiles, her eyes glistening with unshed tears. She walks forward, her steps almost hesitant, somehow looking smaller than he's seen before. She stops beside the central panel and presses a button. It lights up, pulsing softly among the rows of lifeless switches and controls.

"River," Flora says, her voice trickling through the speaker as she remains where she is. "You shouldn't have come back."

"You're alive," he gasps, his knees going weak. "I knew it. Blossom said she saw Oren inject you with the queen bee venom. I knew she was wrong."

Flora shakes her head, reaching out to clutch the control panel as if she needs the support. "He tried to kill me," she whimpers.

"Flora, lower the wall," River says, his hands curling into fists where they're still resting on the glass. He wants to hold her, to comfort her.

To show her that no matter what Oren did, she's loved.

Except Flora doesn't move. "Oren has no idea what he's dealing with." Her face tightens as she throws back her shoulders. "That I can take away everything he's ever wanted."

As the relief that his sister's alive abates, River looks more closely at her. Flora's hair is a mess of ragged spikes, her clothes are still streaked with ash. "Where have you been?"

"Hiding." She shrugs. "Thinking."

River glances at the button on the wall that will remove the barrier between him and his twin. "Lower the wall, Flora. Please."

She still doesn't move, almost seeming lost in her thoughts. As if part of her isn't here. For some reason, River doesn't want to think of where else her mind could be.

He tries another angle. Flora needs to realize what's at stake. "Oren's bred an army of queen bees." He points past her to the wall on his right. "He plans on using Workers to create holes in the Dead Zone net and then unleashing the queen bees on the Dead Borns."

Flora sinks to the floor, now pale as well as tear stained. "No one will survive."

"Chase is there," River says, his voice rising. "Along with Echo. And Oren believes she's not the Sovereign." As much as

River's tried to believe it's another lie, the risk Oren's telling the truth is too high. The thought of losing Echo...

River *has* to get back.

"She's not." Flora's words are soft yet laced with conviction. "Echo was never the Sovereign."

"Why didn't you tell me?" River wants to scream the words as desperation and frustration climb through him. But they come out as a whisper.

Fear and dread are wrapped around his throat, strangling him.

"I wanted to," Flora says, her gaze sliding away. "I wanted to tell you everything."

River has to resist the desire to slide down as the passing seconds weigh on him. He doesn't understand what's going on, only that he needs to fix it. "Oren wants to kill every Vulnerable in both Zones, Flora. We have to warn them."

"Oren's wrong," she says flatly. Yet still doesn't move.

River's glad something is finally getting through. "Yes, he is."

"We don't get to choose who lives and who dies." Flora finally raises her gaze to River. What he sees sends ice down his spine. "Just like we don't get to decide who should be saved."

The despair moving through his sister's dark eyes is like shadowy ghouls. As if monsters slumbered inside and have now woken.

"What are you saying?" he whispers.

"What are we fighting for, River? The Green Borns hate the Dead Borns. The Dead Borns hate the Green Borns. They kill each other. Turn their backs if one of them dies." Flora pushes her fingers into her hair and grips tightly. "Humanity doesn't deserve to be saved."

"No!" River's denial is swift and strong. "You don't mean that. There's so much good to fight for."

"Is there?" she challenges, even taking a step closer. "The man who we called father tried to kill me!"

"Flora, listen to me. I know what Oren did hurt you. I know it cut deep. But he's not like the rest of us. I love you. Mom loves you. Chase loves you."

Her green eyes flash. "Chase didn't come back for me," she states flatly. "His cause is more important to him. After everything I did for him."

River blinks, thinking of Rose, Clover, and Daphne. Was Echo right when she pointed out Flora had a personal score with each of them? Was that why they died? He shakes his head and opens his mouth, but Flora's hand snaps up.

"Don't try to convince me Mom's different. She chose to fake her own death so she could protect the Sovereign Code rather than be with her children."

River could point out that their mother did that so they had a future, but he can already see his sister has made up her mind. His mouth clamps shut, stunned. He's not entirely sure what he's fighting for here, but he's battling an enemy he didn't know existed. Flora's sense of betrayal is far deeper than he realized. And Oren's actions were the final twist of the blade.

Flora believes everyone she's loved has turned their backs on her.

Except him.

"I came back, Flora," he says, holding her with his gaze because that's all he has. The wall of glass between them feels a mile wide right now. "For you."

Her shoulders drop as the edges of her lips tip up. "I know you did. It means everything to me."

"Please, Flora." River presses his palm to the glass. "Lower the wall. We can figure this out."

"I already have," she says quietly.

Before River can try to decipher what she means, Flora presses another button on the control panel. The glass wall smoothly, silently begins to lower.

River lets out a sigh of relief. He opens his arms as he waits for the barrier to be gone. "I'll always take care of you," he promises.

Flora smiles, and for the first time, it's free of the darkness that she's been carrying since she stepped into the Restricted Area. No doubt the darkness that Oren's actions unleashed.

The length of glass disappears into the floor and River steps over it, his chest aching with the need to hold his twin. Somehow, he'll help her find peace despite the deep scar Oren left on her heart.

She takes a step forward. "I love you, River." Then another step. "I'm glad you came back. It proved to me you were always the ray of hope."

Flora breaks into a run and he stops, bracing himself so he can catch her, just like he always will. He lifts his arms in anticipation. They'll get out of here, free their father, and return to their loved ones. The hope that surges through his chest is inevitable.

Echo will be there. So will Chase.

They'll keep fighting for what matters.

Flora picks up speed as her smile grows into something beautiful. Something free. As if a weight has been lifted.

A heartbeat before his twin's supposed to crash into his arms, she sidesteps around River. Never slowing, she continues to run.

Straight past him.

River turns, his world slowing as he reaches out to grab her. All he clutches is a fistful of air.

Never hesitating, never looking back, Flora pushes off the jagged edge of the Sting and jumps.

She leaps into the twilight air, for timeless seconds seeming to be suspended, the shadows clinging to her in the ways River can't.

But they have as much power to stop this as he does. Flora plummets out of view, silently falling to the unforgiving cement hundreds of feet below.

"No!" River screams, running to the edge. He stops as his toes nudge the same nothingness Flora just embraced. "No," he sobs, staring into the darkness below.

He can't see his sister's body, but the truth is now lodged in his chest as irrevocably as the agony that accompanies it.

Flora no longer has to battle her demons.

She found peace.

CHAPTER
THREE

ECHO

Echo lies curled up in a corner of the bunker's crypt, pretending she's asleep. Chase is also resting, stretched across the exit like a snake. She can't believe he's preventing her from going to look for River. Or that he decided not to look for Flora. She knows how committed he is to his cause as a Razer, but to choose it over the girl he loves was a surprise. Perhaps he'd only ever been with her to further the cause—dating the daughter of his enemy may not have been the coincidence Echo assumed it to be.

Still, that doesn't mean she can't trust him. She wants the same thing he wants.

Immunity for all.

It's just that she wants to see it with River by her side.

Reed has her spinal fluid. There's nothing more she needs to do. Which makes Chase guarding her a massive waste of time. They should be searching for River and Flora, not resting like a couple of old people.

A cramp grips her middle and she curls herself tighter, aware of the way her body is still aching after her ordeal. She

16

hasn't felt as strong lately as she had in the time after her Confirmation. Almost like she's not herself. Which is likely due to everything she's experienced in that time. The running. The starvation. The fear. The harvests. She really shouldn't be so hard on herself. It's no wonder she's exhausted.

There's a loud sound at the entrance to the bunker and Echo sits up, taking a few seconds to realize someone is crying.

Chase leaps to his feet and turns to her. This could be just the distraction she needs to break free.

"Don't leave my sight," he warns, reading her mind.

She nods, glad that at least he's not stupid enough to expect her to stay in the crypt while he investigates.

The people they'd rescued from the Hive are gathered at the bottom of the stairs to the bunker. They look stronger than the last time Echo had seen them taking their rations from the Razers, brought in by the desperate Green Borns looking for safety in the Dead Zone.

Echo scans the faces, looking for who's making that awful sobbing noise, gasping when she realizes it's Nola.

"What happened?" Echo rushes forward, desperately hoping this has nothing to do with River.

Nola grips Echo's hand and drags her into the crypt. The others hang back, seeing they need some privacy. Echo has no doubt Chase has stationed himself outside the door.

"Nola, talk to me," says Echo, the moment they're alone. "What's happened? Is it River?"

Nola blinks at her with wide eyes. "I'm not sure."

"What do you mean?" Echo puts her hands on Nola's forearms, looking her directly in the eye as she tries to understand.

"I felt something," Nola whispers. "Something happened to one of my children."

Echo draws in a breath, unsure if this is good news or bad. "So, you didn't see anything? You...felt something?"

Nola casts her eyes down and nods. Then seeing the angry marks on Echo's wrists, her eyes spill over with more tears. "Who did this to you?"

Echo shakes her head. "That doesn't matter now. I'm okay."

Nola doesn't seem convinced, but she also doesn't have the energy to argue. Instead, she collapses into Echo's arms and sobs. "I really can feel it. It was like a jolt, then something severed. One of my children is dead. I know it."

Echo hates that she hopes it's Flora, but there's no denying this is how she feels. She's already mourned Flora's death. And if it's River...she can't bear thinking about that.

It cannot be River.

"Maybe they were just hurt," she says gently, wanting to reassure Nola, but not wanting to be dismissive of her fears.

Nola shakes her head. "Echo, I know it. I can feel it in my soul."

"I'm going to find out for you." Echo lets go of Nola.

"How?" Nola shakes her head, but the hope in her eyes is unmistakable. This poor woman has suffered enough in her life. She needs answers just as much as Echo.

"I'm going into the Green Zone." Echo keeps her voice low. "I need you to distract Chase so I can get away."

"How?" Nola wipes away her tears. "What do I do?"

"Tell Chase you have news about Flora." Echo nods, certain this plan will work.

Nola seems confused. "But he already thinks she's dead."

"He still has hope." Echo goes to the entrance. "He'd love nothing more than for her to walk back in the door. I'll ask him to come in here. You tell him you caught sight of her through the net. Keep him talking and I'll slip outside."

"We can try." Nola nods and Echo gives her a quick hug. She's always been drawn to Nola, and now she's certain she knows why. Somehow, when she met this strange woman riddled with scurge, she'd known she was important to her. Just like Nola knows something's happened to one of her children. Not everything in the world can be explained by cold, hard facts. Sometimes, intuition is the most valuable teacher of all.

Echo marches to the door. "Chase," she calls. "Can you come in here, please?"

Just as she suspected, he isn't far away. He immediately comes into the crypt, running a worried hand through his curls. "What's the matter?"

Nola rushes to him and slips her arms around him, sobbing into his chest as she subtly turns his back to the doorway. "I saw Flora."

"You what?" He pats Nola awkwardly on her back. "Where?"

Echo takes a step toward the door.

"On the other side of the net," says Nola. "I'm certain it was her."

Nola has Chase's full interest now. Whatever the reasons behind him choosing to date Flora and ultimately choose his cause over their relationship, Echo knows he loves her. It's only natural he'd want to find out where she is.

"What was she doing?" Chase asks.

Nola keeps her tight grip on Chase, her sobs becoming almost theatrical now. Or perhaps she's just letting her tears fall in exactly the way they want to. There's no doubt she's distressed by what she believes to be true.

Echo takes her chance. She moves silently out into the main chamber of the bunker. Without pausing, she heads up the stairs and out into the fresh air. It's dark outside. Well after sunset. And as Chase pointed out, that means River and Vern should have returned hours ago.

She runs through the scoring grounds, trying to get away before Chase notices her missing and comes after her. She's likely only got two minutes maximum as a lead. Which should be just enough.

When she reaches open space, she has to pause to catch her breath. Before she realizes what's happening, she's doubled over and heaving up the watery contents of her stomach.

"Urgh." She wipes her mouth and glances around. That harvest had taken so much out of her. Hopefully not more than she had to give. She needs her strength now more than ever.

Seeing what could be Chase's shadow in the distance, she pushes on. It doesn't matter how sick she feels, she has to find River. Nothing is more important than that.

She gets to the Betadome, disappointment slicing through her to see that Sledge and Tuff are guarding it. Don't they ever sleep!

Marching up to them, she gives them a curt nod. Tuff steps in front of her, blocking her way to the black door, which is still propped open with a net draped over the front. He shakes his head, the moonlight bouncing off his wrinkled face.

"No," he says.

"Chase sent me to pick some fruit," she tells him, injecting as much confidence into her voice as she can muster.

"That's odd," says Sledge, stepping up beside Tuff with his arms crossed. "Because he told us not to let you through. Especially if that was the excuse you used."

She curses, kicking at the hard ground with her toe. Chase knows her too well.

"Just let me through," she pleads. "I need to get to River. He could be hurt."

Tuff and Sledge continue to block her way.

"You're the Sovereign," says Sledge. "The Razers need you."

"Reed already harvested me," she explains. "He has what he needs from me. I'm no use to you now. It's okay to let me through."

"Good try." Sledge makes it clear he's not planning to budge.

"I'll pick you some fruit," she offers. "You can take it to Fray and Goldie. As much as you want. Just let me pass."

"No," Tuff grunts.

There's the sound of pounding footsteps and they turn to see Makk running up to them.

"Go home," Tuff grunts.

"Echo!" Makk pants, ignoring his father's instructions. "What are you doing here?"

"River needs me," she says. "He's stuck in the Green Zone. Except your father and Sledge won't let me get to him."

"Dad," Makk groans. "You have to let her in. Echo and River are a pair. They're always together. I hardly even recognized her just now without him standing next to her."

"Go home," his father repeats.

"You'd go in if it was Mom who needed you," Makk points out. "Let her in. I can go with her to keep her safe."

Tuff grunts, not bothering to form one of his rare words to tell Makk what he thinks of this suggestion.

"I can go alone," says Echo. "We're wasting time talking about it. Just let me through."

A humming noise starts up in the distance and Echo tilts her head, trying to get a direction on it.

Makk points above them as the noise grows. "It's coming from up there."

Looking up, Echo sees several large shapes crossing the clouds in the moonlight.

"Workers," she says with wide eyes. "But what are they doing out at night?"

"It might be Nectar!" Makk bounces on his toes.

"There's more than one," Echo points out. "It's not Nectar."

Several enormous Workers land on the net above them, their giant wings flapping to ensure the structure can hold their weight. Red and blue lights flash from their backs, sending colored shadows streaking across the dirt below.

"Why are they here?" Makk asks, not sounding as excited as he was a moment ago. "What do they want?"

Tuff looks from the net and back to his son. "Go home, Makk."

In the dim light, Echo can see there are a dozen or more Workers positioned around the net. Does this mean Oren really is alive? Because she can't think of anyone else who would have sent them here.

Tuff steps away from the door and makes a grab for Makk. It seems if he won't go home like he's being told to, he'll be forced to.

Makk waves his arms wildly and makes a strange, garbled sound. Echo knows what he's doing. He's making as much fuss as he possibly can to give her a chance to get into the Beta-dome while Tuff and Sledge are distracted.

She doesn't wait for an invitation. She shoves her way past Sledge and pulls back the netting. But just as she's about to slip through the opening, someone grabs her from the waist and forces her to the ground.

Pain shoots up her depleted body as a weight pins her down.

"I told you not to leave my sight," Chase growls.

She wriggles, trying to get out from underneath the first guy she thought she loved so she can run to the only one she's ever truly loved.

"Let me go, Chase," she pleads. "River needs me. And Flora needs you!"

"Flora. Is. Dead," he sneers. "And so is River. We need to forget about them."

"I can't," she sobs. "He's not dead. I'll never believe it. Not until..."

She can't say the words out loud. The thought of seeing River's beloved face without the spark of life behind his eyes is too much. She needs to hold onto the hope he's still with her.

"I need to get you back in the bunker," says Chase. "There are Workers on the net. It's not safe."

"That's even more reason for us to find out what's happening!" she says. "We won't get our answers in there. We need to go into the Green Zone."

He scoops her up in the same way Tuff had with Makk, treating her like a petulant child. He throws her over his shoulder and heads back the way they came.

Echo beats at Chase's back, howling with frustration. She should have kept an eye out for Chase. She should have been faster. And now River may be the one to pay the price for her mistakes.

With his life.

Chase may have chosen his cause over the one he loves.

But Echo will never make that choice.

CHAPTER

FOUR

RIVER

R iver welcomes the numbness that cements him to the spot. It freezes the grief spreading through his body, stopping it from completely overwhelming him. He remains at the edge of the Sting, unsure of how long ago he slipped into suspended animation but not really caring.

Flora's gone.

By her own choice.

And he wasn't able to stop her.

Light flickers at the periphery of his consciousness but he can't bring himself to turn his head. That would mean breaking the hold nothingness has on him. He can't face what's waiting for him beyond its veil.

A world where he's no longer a twin.

Blue flashes, then red. The pulsing dots move into his line of vision, floating through the night. He realizes it's the Workers, on their way to chew holes in the netting over the Dead Zone. The queen bees will be next.

Yet River still doesn't move. What's the point? How can he

save anyone in the Dead Zone when he couldn't even save his own sister?

He's going to have to watch their death, just like he was forced to watch his twin's.

A low, keening sound fills the air, not quite a wail, not quite a groan. And it's coming from him. River quickly clamps down his throat muscles, desperate to cling to the stillness. The numbness. To the void that's holding him together. Silence once more reigns, not even a breeze to dry the tears that he can't stop.

The world now holds one less heartbeat. It hears one less breath.

Because Flora's body is lying hundreds of feet below him. Dead.

River's armor of stillness cracks as he sways, solid floor and walls behind him, dark nothingness before him. This is how Flora felt. The deepest of despair. The darkest misery. With no way out.

No. She found a way out.

A faint sliding sound reaches from behind him and he finds himself instinctively turning. If that's the door to the Restricted Area opening, if it's Oren, River's finally found something to move for.

Vengeance.

Except the door remains closed. It's the glass wall containing the queen bees that's moving, inching its way down as it prepares to unleash the deadly insects. River stills again. He's free given that Flora lowered the wall before...she jumped. But the same words float through his mind.

What's the point? How can he save anyone in the Dead Zone when he couldn't even save his own sister?

The queen bees hum as the glass lowers, approaching the first row of cells. The trickle of fresh air fans the flames of their restlessness. Their desire to be free. So Oren can control them and enact his ultimate plan—attack the Dead Zone and everyone within it.

River's throat unclenches. The hold despair had on him snaps. There's something else worth moving for.

One word tumbles past his lips. "Echo," he whispers.

And then he's running toward the lowering glass and slamming his hand against the button beside it. The wall stops. Another punch and it raises back up, trapping the queen bees in their cells.

Oren won't be unleashing his deadly army tonight.

River frowns. His lip curls. Then he's hitting the button over and over. The glass smashes, digging into his hands, but he doesn't care. The wall around it cracks, the round case in the middle sinking with the force of his strikes. As the wires inside are revealed, River grabs them and yanks. They snap with a faint crackle and the small lights go out.

Oren won't be unleashing his deadly army any time soon.

Breathing hard, River steps back. He doesn't give himself time to think as he spins toward the door to the Restricted Area. He'll get Vern out. Then he's going back to the Dead Zone.

To his last ray of hope.

To Echo.

He's taken two steps when the sound of whirring stops him. River spins to face the gaping hole, heart thundering. Oren's sent a Worker. The mechanical bee that rises into view surges toward him, her silver disc illuminating the pale tiles around her.

"Nectar," River breathes.

She lands in front of him, waiting, and he has to swallow down the sob that climbs up his throat. Flora sent Nectar. Her parting gift.

She was planning on ending it before she entered the Restricted Area.

River climbs on, his chest aching. "To the Sovereign graveyard," he tells Nectar.

To River's surprise, she doesn't lift into the air and exit through the hole. She clatters to the door, steps through, and then enters the elevator. Inside, her front leg taps rapidly at the panel as the door closes. With a silent whoosh, they descend.

River remembers that Nectar was once one of Oren's Workers, just like the others. Who knows what her mechanical eyes have seen or her digital brain has stored in there. She clearly knows the code that will take them below the Sting to the Sovereign graveyard. This will be much quicker than having to fly to the hatch and through the tunnel.

The lift door opens and Nectar steps into an eerily silent Sovereign graveyard. River realizes the other Workers are still out there, creating the holes in the net. It's a stroke of luck he's going to make the most of.

He nudges Nectar toward the tunnel Vern was trapped in, hoping it's not too late. Surely Oren's been preoccupied with trying to kill thousands of people.

Nectar stops before the door. There are no sounds coming from the other side, making the silence feel like it's multiplying. "Aperta," River commands, hoping Nectar's programming still means she can open this door just like she operated the lift.

Her front leg extends, rapping on the panel beside the door. A moment later, it rises, revealing the blackness beyond.

River jumps to the ground. "Vern! It's me, River!"

There's no answer.

Please, no... He can't face another loss.

River steps closer. "Ver—" His voice cracks so he clears his throat. "Dad," he tries again, the word sliding over his lips with far more ease.

"I've waited a long time to hear that," says a raspy voice.

Vern appears, separating from the blackness of the tunnel, and grips River in a powerful hug. River holds him, relief bringing tears to his eyes. He pulls away before they can gain substance, though. The moment that dam breaks, nothing will be able to stem the furious flow of pain.

"We have to get back," he says. "We need to make sure they're okay."

Vern nods, squeezing River's shoulder before they both stride to Nectar. River leaps on then reaches out to his father and helps him up.

"To the bunker," River commands. To Echo. "Celer." And fast.

Nectar shoots forward then takes a sharp right, flying into the tunnel that leads to the hatch. River holds on tight, feeling Vern do the same behind him. The last time they tried to leave through the hatch it wouldn't open. The alternative is to go through the Sting, which isn't one River wants to consider unless they have no other choice.

The flight down the tunnel is fast and silent. River keeps his gaze straight ahead, not wanting to see the rows of dead bodies they're passing. Not when he's wondering if Oren will bring Flora's broken body here once he finds her. Nausea rolls through River's stomach. He wonders if his twin chose to die so gruesomely so it left Oren to pick up the pieces.

The hatch appears ahead. River focuses on it. Last time Nectar flew at it they almost crashed into the hard metal. They need to be ready for that.

Except the hatch opens as they approach, revealing a stretch of star-speckled sky beyond. Nectar smoothly slips through, leaving the Sovereign graveyard behind.

"That was easier than we expected," Vern says, clearly relieved. "It must be on a timer or something."

River doesn't answer, conscious that doesn't really make sense. Why would the hatch remain locked during the day?

Nectar's humming intensifies, bringing his attention back. It's time to get back to—

Workers with red and blue discs descend, surrounding them, their collective sound filling River with dread. Vern's arms tense around his waist, his body vibrating with tension.

There are at least a dozen deadly machines moving in.

They're going to have to fight their way out, no matter how outnumbered they are.

"Nectar, proeli—"

River never gets to finish the command. The Workers fly forward as one, contracting like a swarm. River yanks on Nectar hard, pulling her higher into the sky so they're not crushed. They'll fight from above, it's the only advantage they have right now.

Except when River looks down, they're not being followed. The Workers fly toward the hatch, falling into an ordered line as they descend into the tunnel. One after the other, they disappear inside, completely ignoring the additional Worker hovering above them.

"They're going back," River gasps.

"The mindless machines are simply following orders," Vern spits. "They've done their job and now they're returning."

Was that why the hatch opened? Would it have remained locked if they'd approached it only a few minutes earlier or later?

River doesn't take the time to wonder any further. "To the bunker," he says to Nectar again. "Celer."

She darts forward, the warm night air rushing against their faces as they hold on tight. River doesn't look back at the Sting and the devastating images it now holds. It feels like an eternity to get back to the secret entrance to the bunker, yet it approaches too fast. River's hands tighten on the strap as they descend. He's riding with this father, who has no idea that his daughter is dead. No one knows.

And he's going to have to tell them.

The hatch opens as seamlessly as the one to the Sovereign graveyard and River and Vern tuck low as they enter the earthen tunnel. The smell of damp soil fills River's lungs as he closes his eyes. He wants to be back in the bunker more than anything.

But he's already dreading it.

The instant they descend into the crypt, there's a gasp.

"River!" his mother cries out. "Vern!"

Nectar lands and the moment River's feet touch the ground, his mother grabs him. She clings to him, sobbing. "I was so worried."

He holds her tightly, closing his eyes when Vern wraps his arms around them both. His family is back together again. Yet it will always be one less than it was meant to be.

His mother grips his shirt as she pulls back to gaze at him through tear-filled eyes. "It's good to hold you again," she whispers. She looks to Nectar, then back. "Flora?"

River goes still, his heart shredding all over again.

"We didn't find her," Vern says heavily.

"I did," River whispers. He opens his mouth to say more, only to find he can't. A jagged boulder has lodged in his throat.

His mother's hand rises to cup his cheek, a terrible understanding settling in her eyes. A fresh wave of tears tracks down her face, these ones fatter, more steady. Ones that won't stop anytime soon. "I felt it," she chokes. "I was hoping I was wrong."

"She came to see me," River says, his voice hoarse. "She'd lost hope, Mom. She ended it herself."

She turns to Vern. "Our sweet girl."

A sob erupts from him as they fall into each other. River holds them as grief wracks their bodies so hard he wonders how they're still standing. His own pain wells up, powerful and devastating. Demanding to be acknowledged. For Flora's loss to be honored.

River steps instinctively back, realizing there was a reason he's held it at bay. If he falls apart without someone there to keep him together, he'll break so deeply he'll never be whole again. He can't ask that of his parents. They're fracturing themselves.

He needs Echo.

He glances around, realizing she's not here. "Echo, where is she?" His frantic eyes scan the crypt. "Is she okay?"

He knew there was a chance he's too late. That she's dead. Yet after losing Flora, it wasn't a thought he was willing to entertain.

If Echo's gone, too...

"She's in the LaB," his mother says, squeezing his shoulder in understanding. "Go to her."

He turns wordlessly, his body feeling like it's made of glass. He's surprised to find the LaB now has a door. And that it's closed. He frowns as a panicked voice reaches him from within.

"Hey! I thought you tied her up!" Reed cries out.

The sounds of a scuffle have him frowning deeper.

"I did. She—" Chase groans.

"Ow!" Reed yelps.

"I told you, I'm going to find River," Echo shouts.

River's heart jolts at hearing her voice. He reaches for the door, but it flies open before he can grab it. Echo skids to a halt as she realizes there's someone on the other side.

"River," she gasps.

E cho flies into River's arms. She clamps herself around him and he pulls her in so tightly it's impossible to tell where her body ends and where his begins.

"You're here," she breathes, hardly daring to believe he's come back to her.

He's shaking and it takes her a moment to realize he's also crying. Something happened while he was gone. Something terrible. So bad that he can't bring himself to tell her what it is.

"River?" She tries to pull back to look at his face, but he keeps her close, seeming to need her nearness as much as the air in his lungs.

She holds him, catching his tears in her hair as she puts together the pieces.

River went looking for Flora.

He was gone far longer than anyone expected.

Nola became certain one of her children had died.

Now River's back.

And distressed.

"You found Flora," she says quietly.

"She found me." He loosens his hold on her slightly.

"Where is she?" Chase asks.

River lets go of Echo. It's only now that she catches sight of his broken soul. His face is pale, aside from the dark rings beneath his bloodshot eyes. His hair is mussed. His shoulders stooped. He looks nothing like the River she fell in love with.

"Where's Flora?" Chase asks again, his voice rising as he grips River on the arm, forcing him to face him. "Why didn't you bring her back with you?"

"She jumped." River swallows and Echo's heart turns to ice.

"She jumped?" Chase grips River's other arm now. "Jumped from where, River?"

"The Sting." River casts his eyes down. "I couldn't stop her."

Chase holds River so tightly his knuckles turn white. "No."

River doesn't protest. Echo suspects he thinks he deserves the pain. Welcomes it, even. Which couldn't be further from the truth.

"It's true," River whispers.

Echo fights back tears of her own. She knew Flora was complicated. Understood that she harbored demons from her past. But to take her own life? That was something Echo had never seen coming. And clearly, nor had River.

She goes to Chase and tries to pry him off River before he hurts him.

"He's lying." Chase releases his hands and rakes them through his hair. "Flora wouldn't do that. She loved me."

Echo looks between River and Chase as sobs filter from the crypt that she can only assume are Nola and Vern.

"She did love you," River chokes out. "More than you loved her."

Chase's spine snaps up straight. "What did you say?"

"You heard me," River says forcefully. "You chose the Razers over Flora. And she knew it."

Echo gasps, stepping between them before a fight breaks out.

"This isn't Chase's fault," she says, defending the guy who only moments ago she'd sworn she despised. Now that River's back, being angry at Chase seems pointless.

"Are you sure about that?" River asks.

"Don't do this," she pleads. "I know you're upset and you want to blame someone, b—"

"No, Echo." Chase steps back. "He's right. It's my fault. I should've gone to look for her. Maybe if I had, she'd still be here."

Chase storms away, bustling past the people huddled in the bunker and heads for the stairs. Echo lets him go, knowing this is how he reacts to loss. It was exactly how he'd dealt with the news of the death of his family. First with his mother and sister when their hut collapsed. And later when his father chose to walk the same path Flora just had. This loss will be cutting him deeply. He needs time alone before he'll be ready to talk.

"Echo." Reed is standing in the doorway to the LaB. Echo had completely forgotten he was there. "I need you back in here."

"Get away from her." River steps in front of Echo. "In fact, get away from all of us. What are you even doing here?"

Reed holds up his palms. "I can explain. I locked you in the graveyard for your own good. Oren wants to kill you."

"And he nearly succeeded, thanks to you." River remains planted in front of Echo. "He cornered us in there and we couldn't get out because *somebody* locked all the doors."

Reed groans. "I programmed them to open at sunset when it would be safe for you to return."

"So, that's why..." River sighs, seeming too exhausted to finish his sentence, let alone this conversation. But something Reed said seems to have made sense to him.

Echo slips her hand into River's as she stands beside him. "Reed's making the Immunity using the Sovereign Code. He harvested me, which means he has everything he needs."

River looks at Echo properly for the first time since he returned. His eyes narrow as he takes in her injuries. First, the tender skin at the corners of her mouth. Then the purple marks on her wrists.

"Reed did this to you?" he asks.

"He was just trying to scare me," she says quietly, still unconvinced Reed needed to go to the extremes he had. But River's going through enough right now. Being angry with Reed won't help him. "I'm fine. Really, I am."

"I need Echo to stay nearby," says Reed. "I'm getting close to finishing."

River looks back at Echo's wrists. "Were Reed and Chase keeping you tied up?"

Echo shrugs, not wanting to lie. "I was pretty determined to go and look for you. But you're back now, which means I'm not going anywhere." She glances at Reed, making sure he gets the message. There's no way he's going to tie her to that chair again.

"We were keeping her safe." A flush rises to Reed's cheeks. "Just like I was trying to keep you safe in the graveyard."

River doesn't seem convinced. "Yeah, well if you could do a little less of that..."

"River, I really am fine," Echo reassures. "Come on. We need to talk. Let's step outside."

Reed opens his mouth to protest, then decides against it. He knows Echo won't leave now that River's back. And Chase isn't here to do his dirty work. He has no hope of trying to tie Echo up alone.

"Don't be long," he huffs, heading back into the LaB.

Echo leads River up the stairs and out into the darkness. They walk in silence through the scoring grounds, finding a bit of smooth dirt where they can sit in the warm night air.

River tucks his knees up to his chest and Echo snuggles in close to him, resting her head on his arm. This news of Flora has exhausted her even more. But at least her stomach feels more settled now that she's in the fresh air.

"I'm really sorry about Flora," she says. "I know how much you loved her."

"Yeah." This one word seems to be all River can manage for now.

"You know it wasn't Chase's fault, don't you?" she asks. River doesn't need another adversary in his life. The people who loved Flora need to come together at a time like this, not start some kind of blame game.

"I know," he says. "I'll talk to him later."

"Do you know why she did it?" Echo winces, fearing she's overstepped with this question. But she has to know. As much as River's finding it hard to make sense of what happened, so is she. Bringing Immunity to the people is going to be so much more difficult without Flora. Sure, they have Reed. But somehow that feels like second best.

"She said humanity doesn't deserve to be saved." His voice comes out on a croak. "But it's not true. There's plenty of beauty in the world. How could she not see that?"

Echo wishes she had an answer for that. "I suppose no two people ever see the same thing in exactly the same way. We don't know what it must have been like to see the world from Flora's eyes."

"She was my twin." River's words hang in the air. Echo

never had a sibling to be able to relate, but she does her best to try to understand.

"Everything about your past is connected to her," she says.

"And everything about my future is connected to you." River puts his arm around her. "I can't ever lose you, Echo."

"You won't," she promises, tilting up her face toward his. "It's you and me against the world. Always."

He leans down and kisses her, and all the things she knows are good in the world spark to life inside her. Humanity *is* worth saving. Because the connection she's feeling right now stems from that. She's witnessed enormous suffering in life, but she's also seen and felt things that are nothing short of wondrous.

"Always," River murmurs in response, spearing his hands in her hair as their mouths seek the comfort they both so desperately need.

Getting to her knees, Echo climbs on top of River so she can put her arms and legs around him. She kisses him with her entire being, trying to heal all his pain with each brush of her lips, each caress of her fingertips, each ragged intake of breath.

River pulls back, and she presses her cheek to the warmth of his, continuing to hold him with both her body and her heart.

"It's so quiet out here," River whispers.

Echo nods, then remembers the sound she'd heard outside the Betadome before Chase had forced her to the ground. Listening hard, she climbs off River's lap and sits beside him, concentrating hard on the noises of the night.

"I can't hear them," she eventually says.

"Who?" River seems confused.

"The Workers." She tilts her head, listening again. "They were on the net. Dozens of them. I'm not sure what they were doing, but they had to be here for a reason."

"Oh." The grimace is obvious in River's voice. "Oren sent them."

"So, it's true then?" She shakes her head. "He's alive."

"Unfortunately, yes," says River. "I saw him myself."

She pauses, not liking that her fears were confirmed. The world had seemed so much safer when Oren was no longer in it.

"But why did he send the Workers?" She squints, wishing the moon were fuller tonight so she could see his face properly. "Because whatever they did, it seems like they've gone now."

"He sent them to make holes in the net," River explains.

"He wants the bees to come in?" Echo is aghast. "But that will kill the Vulnerables."

"It's worse than that," says River. "He plans to send in his army of queens."

Echo feels the hope draining from her body. Oren isn't playing fair. But then again, he never has.

"I damaged the wall where he keeps them," says River, sounding a little more like the heroic guy she fell in love with. "Which will buy us a little bit of time. But eventually he'll fix it. And then..."

"And then we'll figure something out," she finishes. "Just like we always do."

He makes a noise that seems to indicate he agrees, then lapses into silence, and she knows without asking that he's replaying his final moments with Flora.

After a few minutes he draws breath to speak again. "I should have—"

"Don't." She refuses to let him finish that sentence. "You did everything you could at the time. I know that without any doubt. There was no way you could have predicted what happened."

"How do you know that?" he whispers.

"Because I know you, River," she says. "Which means I know you'd never let anything happen to someone you love."

She tucks herself into his side and lets the silence of the night take over.

Healing is going to take River time. Time that she's not sure they have.

But whatever happens, she's going to stick to her promise of keeping by this incredible guy's side.

Always.

CHAPTER
SIX

RIVER

River wakes to discover the soft glow of dawn illuminating the scoring grounds. He blinks, trying to rid himself of the gritty feeling in his eyes as he wonders why it's there. The answers hit him in a rush.

Flora's dead.

He returned without her.

And Echo's the one who comforted him as the grief lashed his soul.

Dirt crunches underneath him as he shifts, realizing they must've fallen asleep out here. The last thing he remembers is them curling up as they lay down, Echo holding him as if she'd do it for as long as he needed her to. His whole body feels dry and desiccated after the tears he shed.

River reaches out, wanting to thank her, only for his fingers to brush over more dirt. His head snaps from side to side, confirming the fear gripping his gut.

Echo's not beside him.

He sits up in a rush, his heart thudding. "Echo?"

She's several feet away, bent over as she tries to muffle the

41

sounds of her retching. He jumps to his feet and shoots to her side. "Echo! Are you okay?"

She reaches out to him as she straightens, trying to smile. "Maybe it wasn't such a great idea to eat those soft pears."

River frowns as he registers how pale she is. "You've had soft pears before." He's seen people eat much worse in the Dead Zone. Mold seems to be a staple for some of the Dead Borns.

Echo wipes her mouth, turning away from the small puddle at her feet. "The last harvest hit me harder than the others," she admits. "It's just taking a bit to bounce back."

River slips his arm around her shoulder, unable to wipe the concern from his face. Harvests are certainly an ordeal, but Echo was tired and drained as far back as their time in the Moon Zone. "You should be resting. Taking care of yourself."

"Because I'm the Sovereign?" she asks dryly.

River shakes his head. "Because I love you." He needs her.

Echo sinks into his side, placing her hand on his chest as a smile with a little more strength tips up her lips. "You're food for my soul, River." She looks up, then gives him a reassuring squeeze. "I feel better already."

"I still think you should rest some more." He slips his arm down to clasp her hand. "We'll go to the crypt. The sleeping mat will at least be a little more comfortable."

"I'm fine," Echo assures him.

River tenses, realizing this may be a battle of the stubborn. Echo's color is already coming back, but he's not taking any chances. "I really think you should—"

"River! Echo! There you are!" Reed exits the bunker and rushes toward them. His red curls stand up at odd angles and there are dark circles under his eyes. "I have news!"

They both tense. News hasn't generally been a good thing. River draws Echo in a little closer as if he can protect her from whatever's coming next. She may not admit it, but everything is taking its toll on her.

Reed grins. "I'm finished. I made Immunity."

River and Echo gasp simultaneously.

"Well, enough for fifty," Reed quickly clarifies. "But the vaccine is ready. We can protect people from bee venom."

River and Echo look at each other. They smile. Grin. Then clasp each other, holding their joy as tightly as they're holding each other. Everything they've fought for, every risk, every loss, brought them to this moment.

Immunity for all.

"Although that's assuming Echo's the Sovereign," Reed adds.

They separate, arms still wrapped around each other's waists. "We've been over this," Echo says, huffing in frustration. "How many times do I have to inject myself with queen bee venom to prove it?"

River stays silent, remembering Flora's words as they stood in what was left of the Hive.

She never was.

But Flora kept so much from him. Lied. Possibly even killed if the theory about Daphne and the other potential Sovereigns is right. And then left him before he could ask any questions.

Reed puts his hands up in a conciliatory gesture. "Okay, okay. I just wanted to check one last time."

"So there's Immunity for fifty people?" River confirms.

Reed nods. "I'm working my way through the files on Flora's computer." He winces at the use of her name. "Sorry, by the way."

River tightens his hold on Echo. "The fight for Immunity has taken far too many lives."

Which is why this next step is so important.

"Yes, it has," Reed agrees. "As I was saying, Flora seems to

43

have downloaded just about every database Oren had. I've found the one for the Dead Zone, and generated fifty names at random."

"Good idea," Echo says. "A lottery of sorts. It keeps it fair."

Reed nods again. "Exactly. Chase came back and went with Makk to collect them."

Echo shoots up straight. "Then we don't have long. The Dead Borns have been waiting for this for a very long time. We need to get organized."

River opens his mouth to object, wondering how he's going to get this beautiful, stubborn girl to slow down. She's done more than enough. But Reed grins as he shakes his head.

"I've got it all under control. The vaccines are waiting in the LaB. We'll bring people down two at a time to administer them." He waves an arm toward the net above them. "I even had Nectar repair the holes Oren's Workers made. She finished about an hour ago."

River's eyebrows shoot up. "Thanks."

Reed's gaze settles on him as he pushes up his glasses. "It was the least I could do. Oren's taken this too far."

"Yes, he has," River says, his throat tight.

"And I didn't want your faith in me to be misplaced." Reed ducks his head. "I think you believed in the good in me before I did."

A flush creeps up his freckled cheeks as he spins around and hurries back to the hatch, not giving River a chance to respond.

River blinks as he watches him descend into the bunker. "I told you," Echo says softly. "You have a good heart, River. And it makes a difference."

He turns to her, pressing a soft kiss to her forehead. "And what would make a difference to me is if you had a rest."

She arches a brow. "That's the angle you're going with?"

"If it works," he says, his lips twitching. "Did it?"

"Nope," Echo says flatly. "You heard Reed. There are fifty vaccines to be administered."

"From what I heard, you were terrible with a syringe."

Echo flushes. "A LaB was never the right place for me." She lifts her chin. "But I can help in other ways."

River clasps her shoulders. "What about a compromise? Once the fifty people are made Immune, then you rest. There's nothing we can do until we know it's worked."

Echo frowns, telling him he already knows what her answer will be. Which means they're about to disagree.

Before either of them can speak, the sound of gravel crunching has them both turning to see Chase approaching, several people trailing behind him.

The first of the fifty.

The first to be made Immune.

He indicates to a bare patch a few feet away. "The others will be here shortly," Chase tells them. "Why don't you sit while you wait, Afra?"

An older woman nods as she sinks to the ground, her bony body folding in as if her sore-riddled skin is barely holding her together. Chase smiles at her encouragingly before walking over to River and Echo.

"This can't take too long," he says quietly. "More and more Green Borns are arriving at the black door. Some were waiting beside it all night."

"Word has spread. They all seem to know about the rule of food for ten people for a week," Echo says. "We can let them in."

Chase rolls his eyes. "If one of them gets a whiff of the possibility of Immunity, they'll be here, demanding they have the vaccines. It'll cause a riot."

River's brow lowers. "We don't know that for sure."

Chase looks at him coolly. "I do. They think they deserve it more than we do."

River decides not to answer, conscious of the tension between him and Chase. They're both fighting for the same thing. Just from different perspectives. And ultimately, they both loved Flora, even if it wasn't enough to change the outcome.

Another group of people arrive and Chase directs them to join the others. River does a quick headcount, discovering there are fifteen people here. Most stand, a few sit like Afra, their bodies too weak even as they're about to receive the gift that could change everything for them. Echo greets most of them by name, and just that acknowledgement seems to ease the tension in their faces. Within minutes, more and more arrive, the ones most afflicted with the scurge leaning on those who have the strength.

Reed reappears with a piece of plastic with writing etched into it. River realizes it's the list of those who've been selected. Reed walks over to the group of Dead Borns and asks for their names.

"Afra."

"Sol."

"Tellus."

Each name is spoken with a mix of pride at being chosen and tense fear. Every one, male, female, young, old, lets out a breath when Reed nods and scratches their name off with a piece of wire.

"Leif."

River jolts as he recognizes his old friend. Leif steps forward, his shoulders back, showing nothing but pride.

Except Reed frowns as he scans his list. "Sorry, Leif. You're not on here."

"Check again," Leif says. "Of course, I'm on the list."

46

"He wasn't one I was sent to collect," Makk pipes up as he skips over. He grins at River and Echo, clearly enjoying being part of this. Turning back to Reed, he holds his fingers up, ticking them off one by one. "I had Sol, Danu, Acker, Ilana—"

"Thanks, Makk," Reed says, tapping his list. "We know who you were sent to collect." He turns back to Leif. "And it wasn't you because you're not Dead Born."

Leif scowls. "Aren't you the ones saying it shouldn't matter where we were born?" he demands. "And have you forgotten what I sacrificed so this vaccine can exist? I volunteered to be put in the Hive!"

River walks over. "We only have fifty vaccines, Leif. A lot of people are having to wait."

Leif turns his furious gaze on him. "After everything I've been through, I deserve that shot."

River clenches his jaw. Leif is proving Chase right.

"Everyone deserves it," Echo says, joining River. "That's why we chose people at random."

"Easy enough for the Sovereign to say," Leif sneers. "Why don't we harvest you right now so I can be just as sweet and selfless as you."

River steps between them. "That's enough, Leif," he says through gritted teeth. "We're sorry you weren't chosen. We'll keep moving forward as fast as we can."

As he says the words, River wonders what that will mean. Does Echo have to be harvested again? And if so, how many times? Considering how much the last one took its toll...

Leif lurches forward, shoving River out of the way. "I'm going to tell the others what you're doing here," he spits. Joining his brother who's waiting at the edge of the crowd, they stride back to the village.

Echo grips River's arm, but he's already decided he won't follow. "Everyone's going to find out anyway," he murmurs.

"Like I said, we need to be fast," Chase grunts.

River turns away, knowing he's right. He has something else on his mind, anyway. Something that's making him far more uneasy. Echo's last harvest produced enough Immunity for fifty. How many more will it take?

"Let's do this," Echo says.

She tugs his hand, and they turn their back on the bunker, facing the Dead Borns who are watching them cautiously, as if they're worried their precious gift is about to be taken away from them.

River gives them a reassuring smile, focusing on the task at hand.

The first doses of Immunity.

Chase steps forward. "You all know why you're here. We have fifty doses of Immunity, and you were randomly selected."

Afra smiles, revealing toothless, puffy gums. "Best luck of me life," she says.

"It's important you understand there are risks," Chase continues, his gaze roaming over their dirty faces. "Lives have been lost. We've done everything we could to make sure we've got it right, but there are never any guarantees."

A few Dead Borns glance at each other. River holds his breath, realizing Echo's doing the same. They're asking a lot of these people.

They're asking for faith.

"It's the closest I'll ever come to living longer than the next full moon," Afra grunts, painfully coming to her feet. "Where do I need to go?"

A murmur of agreement ripples through the people surrounding her.

Chase nods at Reed, and he slips back into the bunker. No doubt preparing for the first injections.

Chase raises his arms. "Those who would like to trial the first doses of Immunity, please step forward."

The Dead Borns move instantly. As one. With determination.

Collectively, they take a step toward Chase, their faces now only filled with pride. Any whisper of fear is gone.

River and Echo draw in a breath simultaneously. They glance at each other, smiling. "It's happening," he whispers.

Echo nods, her dark eyes shining. "We did it."

All the pain and loss weren't for nothing.

A faint cry has them both spinning to face the Dead Borns. River's gaze falls on Afra, assuming she's collapsed.

But the old woman is upright, looking stronger than ever.

Chase turns to the bunker, and River realizes it's the direction the cry came from. His blood goes cold, thinking of his mother and Vern inside.

Except it's Reed who shoots out, his face white. "The vaccines." He grips his hair, dropping to his knees. "They're gone."

CHAPTER
SEVEN
ECHO

"How can Immunity be gone?" Echo asks.

River vibrates with fury as he looks across the crowd of people gathered in front of the bunker. "Who took it? This isn't a game."

"Nobody move," Chase shouts. "Razers! Capture anyone who tries to leave the area."

Sledge, Tuff and Jupiter lead the charge as the Razers circle the crowd of Vulnerables. Makk runs around them, his keen eyes darting as he looks for a sign of anyone concealing the precious syringes.

"Hands on your heads," Chase commands as he begins searching people one by one.

"Why would we take it?" Tellus asks as he lifts his hands to his head and Chase pats him down. "We were already chosen for Immunity. This makes no sense."

"I bet it was Leif," says Blossom, her distrust of Leif stronger than ever. "He was right here."

"As much as I can believe that, it can't have been him."

Chase looks in the direction of the village where Leif had only just disappeared. "He never went anywhere near the bunker. We saw him arrive, then we saw him leave."

"Could Oren have taken it?" Echo asks River. "Maybe he came through the tunnel while we were all out here."

River's eyes open wide with concern. "Nola and Vern are in the crypt."

Echo takes River's hand, and they scurry down the stairs of the bunker. Echo's heart pounds. She can't bear the thought of anything happening to either of River's parents. But if they were standing between Oren and his relentless determination to sabotage their every step, then anything could have taken place.

River runs into the crypt and Echo hears his sigh of relief just as she catches up to him. She lets out a breath of her own.

"Mom!" River cries. "Dad. You're okay."

Nola is sitting in her beloved chair while Vern stands beside her. They both look surprised at the fuss River's making.

"Why wouldn't we be okay?" Vern goes to River. "What happened?"

"Did anyone come down the tunnel?" Echo asks, rushing to the corner of the room and looking up. The dirt doesn't look like it's been disturbed. Everything looks the same as when she'd last seen it, with the black cloth pulled across the exit.

"Nobody," says Nola. "We've been here the whole time."

"Did you hear anyone in the main chamber?" River asks.

Vern shakes his head. "No, although I'm not sure we would have with these thick walls. What's going on?"

"Someone came in and stole the Immunity Reed made." River balls his hands into fists. "It's all gone."

"Why would anyone do that?" Nola hauls herself out of her chair.

"Reed could only make enough for fifty people," says Echo. "He chose names at random for the first batch."

"It was the fairest way." River nods. "Maybe someone who wasn't chosen took it."

Vern grunts. "Trust your gut, son. What was your first instinct when you came in here?"

"That Oren had something to do with it," River says. "But if he didn't come through the tunnel, then I don't see how he could have."

"Maybe someone took it to him." Vern lowers his voice and looks toward the door. "Maybe the same someone who locked us in the Sovereign graveyard."

"Reed?" River mouths. "But..."

"I don't trust him," Vern growls quietly. "Look at what he did to Echo. There's something wrong with that guy."

Echo looks down at her bruised wrists. There's no doubt Reed had been more brutal than he'd needed to be with her during her harvest. But she's only just started to trust him again. She's not ready to start questioning all that again. Not when Reed's the only one who can make the Immunity for them now that Flora's gone.

"You should listen to your father," says Nola. "Reed could have made the Immunity, then snuck it out to Oren."

"Why would he have chosen the fifty names then?" Echo asks.

"It was a cover up," says Vern. "I'm telling you, I don't trust that guy."

"Nor do I." Nola crosses her arms, keeping close by Vern's side.

Echo looks to River who seems just as confused as she is. What Nola and Vern are saying makes sense. But there are also many other explanations. Ones that don't mean the one person they're relying on to save them is a traitor.

"It's probably wise not to trust anybody," River says on a sigh. "But we don't really have a choice with Reed."

"Echo!" comes Reed's voice from the main chamber of the bunker. "Where are you?"

"In here!" she calls back.

"Do you think he heard us?" River whispers.

Echo shakes her head, then nods as Reed appears in the doorway.

"I'm sorry Echo," he says, seeming genuinely distressed. "But I'm going to need to harvest you again. Just in case we can't find that first batch. Chase isn't having any luck with his search out there. It's just completely vanished. I don't understand how. I worked so hard on it."

Echo nods her agreement, reminding herself that the discomfort of being harvested is a small price to pay to save so many lives. Nobody said being the Sovereign was going to be easy.

"No." River's voice is firm. "Nobody's touching Echo. Not until we're sure the Immunity's really missing. She still hasn't recovered from the last harvest."

Reed pushes his glasses up on his nose. "We can wait until tomorrow, but no longer than that."

"I said no." River glares at Reed. "Tomorrow's too soon."

"It's okay, River." Echo puts a hand on his arm. "I'm feeling much better now than I did when I woke up. I'm sure by tomorrow I'll be fine."

River grimaces, clearly hating the dilemma. Then he turns to Reed. "You're not doing it without me there. Understand?"

Reed nods.

"And you're not tying me up," Echo adds, shuddering at the memory of how helpless she'd felt. "You can find some other way to scare me."

"Fine." Reed chews on his lip. "I'll give that some thought

while I get the other ingredients ready. I've been wondering if there's another way to do this. There are other emotions that cause the body to produce adrenaline other than fear. But however we do it, we're almost out of serpentwood, so we can't afford to lose this next batch."

Vern steps up to Reed. "How are you going to make sure that doesn't happen?"

"What?" Reed seems genuinely puzzled. "I didn't lose the last batch. Someone took it."

Vern extends two fingers and points them at his eyes then turns his hand to point them at Reed. "I'm watching you."

Reed's nose crinkles. "Watch me all you like. I'm on your side." He sweeps out of the crypt, heading back to the LaB.

"I won't let him do it to you." River puts an arm around Echo. "It's not happening. You're not strong enough."

"Echo *is* strong enough," says Nola, seeming puzzled.

Echo nods her agreement, glad to have Nola's support. "I'll be fine."

"Mom, she's exhausted." River continues to hold Echo protectively. "Haven't you noticed her lack of energy since the last harvest? And she threw up this morning. I'm really worried about her."

Nola tilts her head to study Echo. Her brows shoot up as if something just occurs to her. But before Echo has the chance to ask her about it, Jupiter comes running into the crypt, panting.

"River!" Jupiter says, trying to catch their breath. "We need you. Now."

River puts a hand to his chest. "Me? Why?"

Jupiter nods. "There's a woman in the Betadome making a fuss. She says she knows you. Would you come and talk to her please? She's stirring up all the bees. We need to sort this out as quickly as possible."

"I thought you were looking for the Immunity?" Echo asks, confused.

Jupiter nods. "Chase and Tuff patted everyone down. Nobody had it. They've gone into the village to ask questions and continue the search. I went back to help guard the Beta-dome, but it's erupting into chaos over there. I really need some backup."

"I'll go," says River immediately.

"Me, too." Echo takes a step toward the door, but River pulls her back.

"You stay here and rest," he tells her. "Vern can come with me. We'll be back before you know it."

"Like last time?" Echo cocks a brow, and River's face falls.

"That wasn't our fault," says Vern. "We can take Nola with us to keep us safe. If anyone tries anything, she can yell at them."

Nola rolls her eyes at his teasing. "I'd like to stay here and talk to Echo if that's okay. We have some secret women's business to discuss."

Vern pulls his face into a grimace. "Now that sounds terrifying."

"Umm," says Jupiter. "We kind of need to hurry. Please, River."

"Okay." He gives Echo a quick kiss on the forehead. "Give me fifteen minutes. If we're not back, you have permission to come looking for me."

"Deal." Echo goes to Nola who puts a motherly arm around her as Jupiter urges River and Vern from the room.

As soon as they disappear, Echo's hand instinctively goes to her middle.

"Are you okay?" Nola ushers her to her armchair and forces her to sit down.

Echo waves a hand at her. "I'm fine. I've just felt a bit crampy this morning. I can't seem to keep any of my food down. I think it was that pear I ate last night."

"Echo." Nola squats in front of her and takes her hands as she looks into her eyes with a strange expression.

"What?" Echo tries to sit forward but the softness of this well-worn chair seems to swallow her up, keeping her held down.

"Have you really not worked it out yet?" Nola asks.

"Nola." Echo sighs. "What are you talking about?"

Nola seems to find her question amusing, which is annoying given she's talking in riddles. "When was the last time you had your cycle?"

Echo pauses as she thinks about this. She's been so busy ever since Confirmation that she hasn't really stopped to think about anything like that. Besides, in the Dead Zone with bouts of starvation so common, her cycle's never been a regular occurrence.

"Just before Confirmation," she eventually answers, wondering how this is any of Nola's business. But as the words leave her lips, she realizes what Nola's really asking her. Her jaw falls open as her hands fly to her belly.

"I don't want to pry," says Nola. "But could there be any possibility that... Did you and River..."

Echo nods at her. "We did. Twice."

"Well, once is technically all it takes." Nola laughs, seeming pleased with the news that's still having trouble sinking in for Echo.

She blinks at Nola, wondering how she could have been so naive. She's been feeling so tired lately. And nauseous. Her chest has been hurting and stomach cramping, without any sign of her cycle for weeks now. It's so obvious, yet she couldn't see it until it was pointed out.

"I'm pregnant," she whispers. "I'm having a baby."

Nola leans in and kisses Echo on the cheek. "You're having my grandbaby."

Echo lifts a hand to her damp face, realizing Nola's crying.

"Yesterday, I lost a daughter," says Nola, her tears continuing to fall. "Today, I've gained another daughter. And a grandchild."

"Oh, Nola." Echo sits forward and throws her arms around her friend's neck. "And you're just like a mother to me. We've lost so much, but we found each other."

"Which is why we have to protect you, my girl." Nola touches her fingertips to Echo's cheek, then stands. "I'm not letting you go anywhere near Reed again. You're too important."

"But Immunity." Echo shakes her head. "Nothing's more important than that."

Nola looks her sternly in the eye. "Are you saying Immunity is more important than your baby's life?"

"Without Immunity, my baby will have no life." Echo splays her fingers on her stomach, feeling for the life that's growing inside her.

"The baby won't survive another harvest." Nola paces near the door. "You need to rest. Immunity's going to have to wait until after the baby's born."

Echo sits back in the chair and groans. Nola's right. Another harvest could kill her child. They're lucky the last one didn't end her pregnancy. It seems this baby's just been hanging on by a thread.

While she never thought anything would mean more to her than Immunity, she's just discovered there's something that does.

Her child.

River's child.

A child she's never met, but already knows she'd die for.

The problem is that she can't possibly ask everyone else to do the same.

How can she save the rest of humanity at the expense of her child's life?

CHAPTER

EIGHT

RIVER

The sight of the Betadome sends alarm spiraling down River's spine. He and Vern pick up their pace, even if it means more distance between him and Echo. He hadn't realized it was this bad.

People are milling around outside the silver netting, both Dead Borns and Green Borns. Those arriving from the Green Zone tip their sacks of food onto an ever-growing pile. The people of the Dead Zone guard it as they hand out fruit and vegetables to their fellow Dead Borns. Both sides glare and snarl at each other, one grudgingly gifting food, the other taking it, neither liking that they're part of any of this.

Vern is tense as he glances around. "I'll stay here and help with the rationing."

River nods, realizing there's something far more concerning. People are moving inside the Betadome.

Sledge and Fray stand at the black door covered in netting, checking every sack that's offered to them by trembling hands. The line snakes back through the verdant trees, a track now compacting and crushing the lush grass.

"There are too many in there," River murmurs, memories of his Confirmation rising in his mind.

The more people in the Betadome, the more movement. More noise. More Vulnerable pheromones rising into the air.

River strides past scurge-riddled Dead Borns and horror-filled Green Borns, stopping beside Sledge. "There are too many," he hisses.

Sledge cuts him a glance. "I'm pretty sure they've said the same about us."

"No," River says, urgency making his voice climb. "There are too many people in the Betadome. The bees—"

Sledge grabs the sack of the next Green Born standing on the other side of the door, opening it to inspect it. He grunts, passing it to someone behind him, and lets the young man through. The Green Born practically runs, shoulders hunched and head tucked in as if he's expecting to be swooped at any moment.

River steps around so he can look Sledge in the eye. "We need to check people and their sacks on this side of the Betadome."

"River?" a shaky voice asks from within the Betadome. "River! It's me, Astrea!"

She's tucked as closely against the netting as she can be, as if she can squeeze through the tiny holes if she tries hard enough.

"Astrea," he says, his heart clenching.

The old blind woman is a friend of his mother's. In fact, his mom visited Astrea three times a week in her hut not far from the Sting to make sure the elderly woman had everything she needed.

Astrea straightens and the lines in her face lift with her smile. "River!" she gasps. "I told them I knew you."

Sledge grunts as he lets another Green Born through, passing the sack to a Dead Born waiting behind him. "I also told her it won't do any good."

Astrea presses her hands to the silver netting, her face twisting with desperation. "Someone took my sack."

Sledge snorts. "Like we haven't heard that story countless times."

River steps closer to the door as he drops his voice. "She's blind, Sledge. Some desperate soul probably did exactly that."

"Blind people die young in the Dead Zone," Sledge hisses. "They can't fend for themselves. And she's lived far longer than anyone here ever has."

"Please," Astrea begs. "I'm a good person. I've never hurt anyone."

Which is true. Astrea is a gentle soul who did everything she could to make sure she wasn't a burden. She used to weave sacks for the Green Zone. Possibly some of the sacks being used by her fellow Green Borns to carry the food that will save their lives.

"You also didn't help," cries someone from behind River, making him wince.

"Please," Astrea moans, shuffling closer to the line. "The others can't hear it yet, but the bees are becoming agitated."

River instinctively glances up. Although there are no swarms visible, he believes Astrea. She's always had excellent hearing.

And there are far too many people in the Betadome.

"Get out of my way," a woman hisses as she elbows Astrea. "Here, I have turnips. They'll last far better than the pears Koa just gave you."

Sledge takes the sack, inspects it, then lets the woman through. He acts as if Astrea doesn't exist.

River frowns. This isn't unity. This is being as selective as Oren was.

Sledge leans in, his gaze turning hard. "She comes in without a sack and we'll have a stampede as every other desperate soul demanding the same treatment. There'll be a riot. We won't be able to keep them out." He glances up. "Or the bees."

River clenches his jaw, knowing Sledge is right. And the paintings capturing what happened at the Moon Zone was a testament that there isn't enough for everyone.

He just hopes Chase has found who stole the first vaccines. Immunity is the only way forward.

Astrea lets out a low moan as she sinks to the ground, clamping her hands over her ears. "I can't listen anymore."

Without giving himself time to think, River shoves past Sledge, past the Green Born who's holding only a half-full sack, and into the Betadome.

He squats beside Astrea, slipping a hand under her elbow. "I'll help you find a sack and some food," he says in a low voice.

Astrea's face snaps up to his with a gasp. "River," she whispers.

"Yes, it's me. Come on, we need to be quick."

He can already feel his lungs shrinking. But he can't just stand back and refuse Astrea's plea for help. He realizes they're fighting for unity as much as they're fighting for Immunity.

Astrea's sightless eyes dart past River, staring at something beyond him. "I can hear them," she whimpers. "You have to go, River."

She tries to push him, not taking her unseeing eyes off the heavens above them, but River's rooted to the spot. Now he can hear it, too.

And so can every other person inside the Betadome. A buzzing that's becoming louder and louder by the second.

"The bees!" screams a woman. "The bees!"

"Stay quiet, you fool!" a man hisses.

Someone darts past River. "They're coming!"

"River," Sledge shouts. "Get out, now!"

River spins to see him standing by the black door, one arm extended as he pushes at the Green Borns crowding in. A man tries to grab his hand but Sledge shoves him, making the man stumble. He staggers backward with a shrill cry.

A cry that's an instant beacon for the superbees.

"Shut the door," River cries out, knowing it's too late.

Knowing he wouldn't have exited, leaving everyone else behind.

Sledge does as he's told, the black door slamming shut, keeping the Dead Zone safe.

And cementing the fate of everyone in the Betadome.

Humming eclipses River's hearing as totally as the looming shadow of the swarms descending on them. "Remain still!" he shouts. "We need to calm the bees!"

But it's too late.

Panic has taken hold of the Green Borns. Screams pierce the air, high-pitched and terrified. Some bang on the black door, demanding entrance. Others run for the green door, seeking the protection their old home once afforded them. A few crouch down, their hands covering their heads, eyes squeezed tightly shut.

Each and every one knows their Immunity was a lie. Most of them are as Vulnerable to the bees as everyone Dead Born they ever ignored, denied, and shunned.

"You should've run," Astrea moans, curling up into herself. "This is our punishment."

River does the only thing he can. He drops down beside the old woman and wraps himself around her. If he can save one life...

The humming is now a furious roar. All that fractures it are the sound of cries and screams and pleas for mercy. But nothing pierces the gloom. The shadows of the swarms are absolute, casting River's world into semi-darkness.

He thinks of Echo, glad she's safe in the bunker. Glad she's not here to see this.

Yet wishing he could've told her he loves her one more time. The dream he had in the Moon Zone unfurls in his mind, the endless viridescence that extended as far as the eye could see. Echo, smiling, beautiful. The child by her side...

So much of it was a pipe dream, but his solace is knowing Echo's strong enough to make some part of that dream come true—she can make Immunity a reality. Who knows what else will be possible after that.

Somewhere to his left, a scream turns to a gurgle. Someone else's sobs are abruptly cut off. The buzzing grows so loud it swallows it all.

The first sting has River gasping as the burn pierces his back. The second has him wincing and pulling tighter around Astrea. Bee after bee lands on him, tiny legs brushing his bare arms. Several climb up his neck and onto the exposed side of his face. Below him, Astrea whimpers and shivers, even the hands clamped over her ears unable to block out the thunder of thousands of bees intent on killing.

River freezes, waiting for the avalanche of stings that will follow. He can already feel his throat clamping up. This time, no serpentwood can stop what's coming.

Astrea cries out and he curls around her more tightly, trying to keep her still. She jerks again, this time screaming. River opens his eyes a fraction, trying to understand how seeing is even possible. Surely his face should be too puffy by now.

A bee crawls over his nose, landing on Astrea's shoulder. Its wings flutter as its stinger flicks down, piercing the old woman's skin. Over and over again. With each one, Astrea's cries increase, an agonizing mix of pain and terror. River reflexively brushes the insect away, his thundering heartbeat almost as loud as the bees themselves.

Astrea's exposed skin is instantly covered again with more bees. River draws in a sharp breath through his clenched teeth. The bees are crawling all over him.

To get to the woman he's trying to protect.

Astrea's wails turn to hoarse gasps. A twitch and a jerk, and they stop. "So...sorry," she wheezes.

Then goes still.

River's breath saws in and out of his lungs as he pulls back. A silent denial rips through his mind. Astrea's dead. And somehow, he's here to witness it.

Her body uncurls as the bloating spreads and he shuffles backward, nausea a serpent in his gut. Astrea's face is puffed and purple, her sightless eyes bulging in the face smoothed of wrinkles.

The mass of bees lift now that their work is done, acting as if River's not even there. He registers that he can hear his harsh breathing. The bees everywhere are ascending to the treetops and their hives, their fury washed away now that the threat is gone.

His gaze roams over the interior of the Betadome, unblinking as he's faced with the aftermath of thousands of furious superbees. This is so much worse than his Confirmation. There are far more people. There's no adrenacure.

And no one would have chosen to be in here if they weren't desperately fighting to stay alive.

Now each and every one of them is dead.

Distended, bloated bodies litter the Betadome. Some cling to each other, others have collapsed beside both doors, many have fallen where they were stung. The sight is horrific. Devastating. Incomprehensible.

"River," says a quiet voice behind him. "Come out. Please."

He turns to find a pale Echo standing at the black door. She extends her hand, her dark eyes liquid with the same pain he's feeling. River goes to her, picking his way around the purple, open-mouthed bodies. The moment their hands touch they slip out of the Betadome and Sledge slams the door behind them.

"You survived," Echo chokes, throwing her arms around him.

River holds her tightly, his shock wearing off enough to realize she's right. Everyone else who was stung, died. But he's here, holding his girl.

Echo buries her head in his chest. "You're a true Immune."

He blinks, acknowledging she's right. The Immunity he had at Confirmation wasn't a result of the water in the Green Zone. "What a way to find out," he whispers, pressing his nose into her hair and breathing deeply.

She pulls back, one hand cupping his cheek while the other slips to press against her stomach. "We need to talk—"

A gasp ripples from the crowd surrounding the Betadome. Dead Born and Green Born alike were forced to watch the devastation that was just wreaked on the other side of the silver netting. Now every pale face is angled toward the green door.

River spins around, instinctively stepping in front of Echo. His knees were weak a moment ago after the horror he witnessed, but now every muscle is locked and straining. A Worker is entering the Betadome, someone riding it in a white suit. The giant metal bee picks its way into the verdant garden, the person sitting on it confident that either the carnage has passed, or that their suit will protect them.

River instantly knows who it is.

The Worker stops, swollen bodies littered around it, and the man raises his arms.

"See how the Dead Borns treat you?" Oren demands.

CHAPTER

NINE

ECHO

Oren's face is only just visible though the white suit he's wearing to protect himself from the very threat that just exterminated dozens of his own people. The black mesh disguises the melted features that River described to Echo after seeing him in the Sovereign graveyard.

Oren steps down from his Worker and holds up his hands for quiet. The Green Borns who sought safety in the Dead Zone come closer to the net, drawn by the magical power he still seems to hold over them.

Echo remains beside River. She trusts Oren about as much as he does. Nola stands to their side with Vern, silent tears running down her cheeks for the blind woman River had gone into the Betadome to try in vain to save.

"A tragedy has occurred today," Oren says, looking around at the dead surrounding him. "Many unnecessary lives were lost. Lives of people I dedicated my life to caring for."

River straightens his spine at this blatant lie and Echo takes his hand.

"They'll see through him," she whispers.

But looking around at the way the Green Borns are clinging to Oren's every word with reverence, she's not entirely sure this is true.

Chase marches forward. "You just stood back and watched your people die. That's how well you care for them."

Oren keeps one hand raised as he responds. "The only reason my people had to look for safety here was because your heartless rebels destroyed my ability to make Immunity for them. Immunity that enabled my people to build a peaceful and sustainable community without a cloud of fear hovering above them."

"Immunity was a lie," Jupiter calls out.

"At least in the Dead Zone we'll tell your people the truth," Sledge adds. "We can keep them safe better than you can."

Oren's eyes flash with anger. "You can only keep them safe with the net that the Green Zone has provided you with. A privilege that's about to be revoked."

There's a gasp as the people take this in.

Makk steps forward, pulling back his shoulders. "We repaired the holes you made in the net. We'll do it again if we need to. You can't hurt us."

Oren laughs as he swipes away a curious bee, an action that only draws several more to him. Echo knows he wouldn't be so flippant if it weren't for the suit that's keeping him safe.

"You didn't think the holes I made were the real thing, did you?" he sneers. "That was just a trial run. When my Workers return tonight, they'll be able to make three times the number of holes at three times the pace. And this time, my army of queens are ready to act. They're quite angry after someone locked them in their hive far longer than they were supposed to be."

River tenses beside Echo.

"If you do that, you'll be murdering your own people," Chase growls. "The same people you claim to care for."

"No." Oren's voice is harsh. "I love my people. You're the one murdering them by promising them safety when you can provide no such thing."

"Nor can you," Makk huffs.

"The Sting has been secured after the damage that was heartlessly done to it." Oren scans the distressed faces of his people. "And it's stocked full of food. I call on all Green Borns to come back with me and allow me to care for you again. Just as I always have. Leave here before this zone becomes exactly what its name implies. *Dead.*"

There's a gasp around the crowd as the Green Borns look at each other, trying to work out their next best move.

"What about me?" asks a voice in the crowd. "Will you care for me?"

Echo turns to see Cascade has stepped forward. It's a fair question. Oren's made it clear he won't welcome Dead Borns, but what about Green Borns who were declared Vulnerable at Confirmation?

"You may come." Oren smiles. "As long as you can make it through the Betadome alive. I'll even welcome any Dead Born who was yet to have their Confirmation, if they wish to give it a try."

"Over my dead body!" Makk shouts.

Echo winces. That was exactly Oren's point.

"He only wants Immunes," River says quietly. "He knows Vulnerables like Cascade don't stand a chance. Or Dead Borns. He'll even risk his precious Green Borns to find out if any of them are true Immunes."

"Like you," says Echo, still feeling enormous relief to have had this confirmed, even if it happened in the most horrific way.

"And Tuff," River adds. "And you. And most likely Makk. There may be others."

Echo nods. True Immunes do exist, even if they are rare.

"Will you give us suits to protect us from the bees?" a Green Born calls out.

The bees in the Betadome continue to scout for more victims, not satisfied with the massacre they'd only just enacted. And if Oren gets his way, their frenzy has only just begun.

Oren shakes his head. "I'm afraid the suit I'm wearing is the last one left that wasn't damaged by the Dead Borns."

"Liar!" Chase shouts. "We didn't touch your precious suits. You damaged them yourselves fighting over them."

"My people are peaceful," says Oren. "If they destroyed our suits, it was only because you pushed them to it."

River seems to have had enough. He turns to the people. "Don't go in there," he pleads. "It's a trap. He wants to see which ones of you are Immune and which are Vulnerable. We all know far more people will die if they enter the Betadome than those who will make it through."

"I made it through there yesterday." A Green Born man strides toward the black door.

"The bees were far calmer yesterday," says River. "You saw them just now. It's worse than Confirmation. Nobody survived."

"You did," the man grumbles. "Do you think you're better than us?"

"I seem to be a true Immune." River's cheeks flush. He's never wanted to put himself above anyone else. "We all know how rare that is. Please. Don't risk your lives to find out if you're the same."

Echo walks forward. "You need to listen to River. Oren wants you to go in there. He wants Vulnerables to die."

"I passed Confirmation," the man says as he forces his way through the black door. "And I barely drank any water the day before. I'm Immune. I know it."

"You can't know that!" River says as the man strides toward Oren. "Come back!"

"It's his choice," says another Green Born who's clearly contemplating her own options. "Leave him."

The bees sense an intruder and start heading his way as if drawn by a magnet.

Echo puts a protective hand on her stomach. This is the world she's bringing a child into. One that's filled with injustice and danger. She's not sure if it had been a conscious decision if she'd choose the same path. But she'd never wish away her child now. She hasn't even had the chance to tell River yet.

"Bring it on!" the man yells to the bees as he waves his arms around, infuriating them further. "You can't hurt me."

Echo's hands fly to her mouth. "That's not a good id—"

"Echo." River grabs her arm. "Look."

Leif and his family are approaching the door. His brother Glen has a pack strapped to his back, and it's clear by the way they're walking they intend to take Oren up on his offer.

"No, Leif!" River rushes over to him. "You're making a mistake."

"You promised us safety," Glen huffs. "If we stay here, we'll be dead by morning. Doesn't sound too safe to me."

There's a horrible scream inside the Betadome and Echo spins around.

The man who'd made his way back to Oren is writhing with pain on the ground as his face swells. Oren remains impassive by his side, neither helping the man nor providing him comfort in his last moments.

"See!" River shouts at Leif. "That will be you. Don't do it. Stay here. We'll figure something out with the net. We'll find a way to stay safe."

Glen stomps through the black door, quickly followed by both his parents.

"You need to stop them," River says desperately to Leif.

"No need." Leif steps away. "We're Immune."

He marches over to his family and Echo lets out a strangled cry as she realizes what's in the bag on Glen's back.

"They stole the vaccines!" she gasps. "The vials are in that bag. That's why they're so confident. We have to get them back!"

She goes to follow Leif into the Betadome, but Nola grabs her by the arm and hauls her back.

"Echo," she warns. "You have more at risk now than just yourself."

"It's okay," says River, misunderstanding. "I'm a true Immune."

Echo feels ill. Nola's right. She can't risk her baby. Her body has been so weak after the harvest, it can't tolerate much more. Even if the bee stings won't kill her, they would still put extra stress on her body. But how can she tell River that now?

Leif's family pick their way over dead bodies to get to Oren, while the Worker moves between them and the crowd gathered at the net. The other Green Borns near the door step back, waiting to see what happens before they decide if they're prepared to run Oren's gauntlet. They all know the safety offered by the Sting is useless if they die trying to reach it.

"River." Echo takes his hand. "Let's stay here for now."

"But..." River frowns. "We need to get the vaccines back. I don't want you to be harvested again."

"Then you go." She hates saying the words. But if she's going to be a mother, she already knows there will be far more sacrifices in her life to come. The baby must come first. Always. "I'll wait out here."

River nods, seeming both relieved and confused. Ever since he's known her, he's asked her to stay behind and keep safe. And she's never agreed. He must think she's far sicker than he'd realized. Or that something's wrong. When in fact something is right. Very right. She's having his child.

Her hand goes to the locket her father gave her.

Family.

When they get through all this, she'll have a family once more. That alone is worth protecting.

The hum of the bees rises as the deadly creatures spot their new target and prepare to strike. Leif and his family stand confidently as they wait.

Echo's gut clenches as River runs into the Betadome. So many people have insisted she's not the Sovereign. Even Reed wasn't convinced. And now they're about to find out. If Leif and his family die, then it can't possibly be her.

The angry bees swarm in a cloud made of gold and midnight. River doubles his pace as he launches himself at Glen, ready to grab the bag. But before he can reach him, Oren shouts something and his Worker spins around and takes the bag from Glen, tucking it inside the compartment in her belly.

River has too much speed to stop and just as he's about to collide with Glen, the Worker spins again, flicking him in the stomach with her back leg and sending him flying across the Betadome.

Echo yelps, clutching her own belly as she feels River's agony. That's exactly why she couldn't have gone in there with him. She hopes he understands when finally she has the chance to explain.

River gets to his knees and Echo lets out a sigh to see that while he's in pain, he's okay. He crawls forward, waving his arms to attract the bees who are paying him no attention at all.

The tiny creatures descend on Leif and his family and Echo reminds herself there's still a thread of hope. The bees could lose interest at any moment. And even if they do sting them, then it would have no effect on an Immune.

The attack begins and from the very first scream, Echo knows she was being naïve.

The stings are having an impact. Leif and his family drop to the ground and swat at the insects as their faces turn purple and swell.

River reaches Leif's mother and takes her by the ankles, dragging her toward the black door. Her skin is alive with shimmering movement as the blanket of angry bees moves with her, still ignoring River in the same way Daphne had treated Chase.

"Keep them away from us!" Sledge booms through the net. "Don't bring her any closer!"

River pauses, looking down at Leif's mother and seeing the futility of his actions. He lets go of her, his shoulders slumping in a picture of utter sadness. He goes to the black door, making sure no bees follow him through as he returns to the Dead Zone.

"Are you badly hurt?" Echo reaches out her arms.

"I don't understand," his voice breaks as he dissolves into her embrace. "Why didn't the Immunity work?"

"Because I'm not the Sovereign, River," she says, accepting what she's known is true since the bees swarmed toward Leif and his family. "It's not me."

"It is you," he says, holding her tighter.

"It can't be." She pulls back to look at him, wondering how long it will take him to accept it. "There's no other explanation."

"Reed did this." He shakes his head, stubbornly. "He botched the Immunity on purpose."

Before Echo has a chance to decide if that could possibly be true, Oren is at the net calling to his people.

"My offer still stands," his voice booms. "Come to the Sting before midnight. Or you'll all be dead."

TEN

RIVER

R iver watches Oren as he climbs back on the Worker and heads to the green door. He doesn't look back as he leaves the Betadome, as calm and cool as when he first entered.

As if he hadn't just offered people hope...if they're willing to risk their lives.

As if he hadn't just promised the deaths of thousands.

River's hands clench and unclench as he wonders if the Green Borns would be so willing to consider this if they could see how Oren looks now. That his outside reflects his rotten core. Few people would be taking cautious steps toward the black door as they glance over their shoulders, weighing up their options.

Possibly dying as they run through the Betadome to the safety of the Sting.

Or probably dying when Oren unleashes his queen bees tomorrow.

"You bastards," shouts a Dead Born, limping as he drags his sore-riddled foot. "You demanded we let you in, and now you're walking away, leaving us to die!"

"We brought you food," a Green Born hurls back. "You didn't exactly greet us with open arms!"

"You'd do the same," another spits. "You'd leave us behind if you had the chance."

River glances between the Green Borns, now congregating near the Betadome, and the Dead Borns, guarding the pile of food. Why can't they see that Oren's continuing to manipulate them, divide them, all so he can use them?

"We need to work together," he calls out, taking a step forward. "Risking your life so you can return to the Sting and leaving others behind isn't the solution."

"Staying here and dying sure isn't either!"

River's gaze falls on the middle-aged woman who shouted the words. Her arms are wrapped around two girls of the same height. Twins. His heart spasms as he thinks of how much it hurt to lose Flora. This mother is doing everything she can to protect her children. To allow them to grow up. Together.

Yet Flora died because she believed there wasn't a way forward. That these people weren't worth saving.

River refuses to believe that.

He takes another step. "If we fight together, we can win," he shouts. He has no idea how, but he has to believe it's possible. "It's the only way forward."

"Listen to him," Echo calls out, stepping up beside him, one hand pressed to her stomach. River suppresses a frown as pride swells in his chest. She's tired, exhausted, still recovering from the harvest, and she's still fighting, just like he is. "Oren is one man. We are many. Which is why he's trying to divide us."

She may not believe she's the Sovereign, but she hasn't given up. That's the definition of hope.

A few of the Green Borns glance at each other. The Dead Borns shift their weight uneasily. But no one openly disagrees.

Echo slips her hand into River's, interlinking their fingers.

"We are Dead Born and Green Born. The moment we saw beyond that, everything changed."

Cascade steps forward, her eyes flashing with fury. "The moment you two changed everything, people started dying."

River and Echo reel back. "That's not true!" River says, raising his voice so everyone can hear. "Oren's been killing all along, using the veneer of the Green Zone for years to hide his dark dealings."

"He's the one who led you to believe we're different," Echo adds. "That it matters which side of the net you were born on."

"Very few of us are Immune. Most of us are Vulnerable." River sweeps his arm to encompass the carnage of death inside the Betadome. "Do you need any more proof?"

"Or you're wrong," Cascade yells back. "Without you, none of this would've happened. Oren's the one who brought us peace. He can do it again!"

She spins on her heel and stalks toward the black door. River and Echo watch, shocked and disappointed as the Green Borns hesitate...then one by one, follow her.

The Dead Borns sneer, a few spit bloody globules into the dry dirt. "Cowards."

"Selfish bastards."

"This is what humanity has come to."

The last one has River wincing as the words slice deep. It's too close to what Flora said.

Cascade puts her hand on the door, glaring at Sledge who's still standing beside it. "We're going home. Where we belong."

Sledge curls his lip as he steps back. "Good riddance, if you ask me."

Cascade's shoulders tense, suggesting that despite her bravado, she's still conscious she's about to run a gauntlet. One littered with the bodies of those who didn't succeed.

"Wait!" River calls out, making several people turn to look at him. "Leave after dark. Bees aren't active at night."

His and Echo's attempt at unity may have failed, but more lives don't need to be needlessly lost.

Thoughtful expressions morph across the faces of the Green Borns as they stop, glancing between River and the Betadome.

Echo turns to the Dead Borns. "Any of you can go," she says, her voice climbing with conviction. "You heard Oren. The Sting is going to be the safest place as of tomorrow."

River realizes she's right. With Oren's queen bees, the Green Zone is safer for everyone.

Several of the Dead Borns blink. A few grin at the irony. A handful glance at the Sting uneasily. The idea no doubt feels like suggesting they go to the moon.

Cascade huffs. "Fine." She sits down beside the black door. "We'll go at night."

The other Green Borns follow suit, various shades of relief coloring their faces.

"You heard Oren. Dead Borns aren't welcome," Cascade adds. "We need Immunes, not more dead wood." She smirks at her play on words, looking pleased with herself.

Echo lifts her chin. "I'm Dead Born." She levels her gaze at Cascade. "And Immune."

Cascade draws in a sharp breath, anger making her skin flush pink, but Makk speaks before she gets a chance.

"So am I," he says proudly. River looks at him, shocked even as he realizes he shouldn't be. "Yep, been stung a few times," Makk continues, pointing his thumb into his chest. "How do you think I used to get messages to Dad?"

Tuff reaches out to grip Makk's shoulder but doesn't say anything. Although the action says it all. This is a father whose son has fought alongside him.

Cascade crosses her arms. "Do what you want. Oren won't welcome you."

River turns away, not bothering to question the blind faith from the girl who Oren so easily turned his back on, just like every other Vulnerable. At least no one will be running through the Betadome again today.

"Well, you aren't getting any of this," shouts the Dead Born with the foot encrusted in scabs. "I'll need me strength to get to the Sting."

He loads his arms up with fruit and vegetables from the pile, triggering several other Dead Borns to do the same. Once it starts, the avalanche is unavoidable. More rush forward, snatching as much food as they can, unwilling to miss out.

Chase and the Razers leap forward, trying to maintain some order, but the people's hunger and desperation and panic are stronger than the Razers' numbers. Within minutes, the food will be gone.

River and Echo glance at each other, the same sadness reflecting in their eyes. It feels like they've taken too many steps backward. After thinking they'd made significant leaps in the right direction.

River grits his teeth as he takes Echo's hand. "We need to talk to Reed," he grinds out.

If Reed had done his job, they would've had the promise of Immunity. It could've changed the tide.

River breaks into long strides only to slow within a few feet as he realizes he's dragging Echo. "Sorry." He looks back, his concern from earlier returning. Today was the first time she wasn't there beside him, fearlessly facing bees and Oren and any other enemy. "I'm worried about you," he admits.

Echo keeps walking, now the one tugging him along. "You're always asking me to stay behind. For the first time, I did, and now you're worried?"

River falls into step beside her. "I know. It's just that... something's wrong, Echo. Something you're not telling me."

She squeezes his hand. "I spoke the truth, River. When we chose each other, we changed everything." Her face softens. "And it's not death we've created."

He suppresses a confused frown, but no matter how hard he tries, he can't make sense of what Echo just said.

"We'll talk after we've spoken to Reed," she says, glancing over at the scoring grounds they're approaching. "We need answers."

River's spine stiffens as he acknowledges she's right. Leif and his family are among the dead in the Betadome, when they shouldn't be. They entered with all the confidence of someone who had injected themselves with the Immunity vaccines.

And yet, they were as Vulnerable as everyone else in there.

River and Echo enter the bunker and go straight to the LaB. With each step, anger bubbles hotter and hotter within River. Did Reed play him with all that talk of being grateful that River believed in him? Did he take advantage of the fact River wanted to believe his friend was on their side?

The moment they enter, River stops. Reed is sitting at the bench, his head in his hands, his back curled as if defeat has settled its immense weight on his shoulders. River shoves away the pang of empathy. It could all be part of Reed's act. Part of Oren's ultimate manipulation.

"Tell me the truth," River demands, stopping with Echo in the middle of the LaB. "Did you screw up the vaccines accidentally or on purpose?"

"I didn't screw up Immunity," Reed says, his voice so quiet River has to strain to hear it. He looks up, his eyes haunted and face ravaged. "I know who the true Sovereign is. Who it was all along."

River has to resist taking a step back. "What are you talking about?"

"Oren was right. It was never Echo." Reed waves toward the computer sitting in front of him. Flora's computer. "Your sister knew the truth all along. She'd hidden it under a file labeled *Vindicta*."

"What does vindicta mean?" Echo asks quietly, sounding as if she's not sure whether she wants to know the answer.

"Two things," River says, his throat tight. "Deliverance." He swallows. "Or revenge."

A shudder rips through Reed. "It's the latter," he says flatly. He stands slowly, as if he's aged a century. "Flora knew all along. She knew who the Sovereign was."

Echo gasps, sounding shocked although she was the one who suspected that Flora was lying and manipulating them. Echo was right. Flora knew that Rose, Clover, and Daphne were never the Sovereign.

River opens his mouth, finding his throat is too tight to speak. If Flora knew, it means Reed now knows. They finally have what they've been searching for so long.

And yet he looks devastated.

River clears his throat. "Who is it?"

Reed straightens, looking like it takes great effort. His gaze connects with River's, his eyes as hollow as his voice. "It was Flora."

River blinks. Then blinks again. Yet the information can't seem to get past the shock protecting his mind.

Echo shakes her head. "But Flora reacted to being stung during her Confirmation."

Reed shrugs. "My guess is she was allergic to something and took whatever it was to fake it."

"The medication," River whispers. "When we were kids,

she cut her foot and it became infected. She reacted to the antibiotics she was given and ended up in the infirmary."

Reed nods, his shoulders sagging. "Flora was the Sovereign."

River staggers back, his hand in Echo's the only thing stopping him from collapsing.

Was.

Flora *was* the Sovereign.

She knew, and yet she chose to die.

Their final conversation takes on a whole new, ominous tint.

I can take away everything Oren's ever wanted.

Flora chose to punish their father by taking away the one thing he's killed countless people searching for—the soul carrying the Sovereign Code. The body holding the DNA that could produce Immunity.

Humanity doesn't deserve to be saved.

Simultaneously making a decision that shreds River so totally he almost cries out. Flora took Oren's ultimate wish away—saving humanity. Because it didn't deserve to be saved.

"I'm sorry," Reed whispers, his gaze dropping to the floor. Without looking at them again, he hurries past and exits the LaB.

River drops to his knees, no longer able to support his weight. "Everything... Everything's gone."

There's no Sovereign.

No Immunity.

And Green Born or Dead Born, humans are all fighting to save themselves.

Was Flora right? Was this fight all for nothing?

Echo slips to her knees before him, her face impossibly soft despite the news, conviction making her eyes shimmer. "Not everything."

"How can you say that?" River rasps brokenly. "We've lost. There is no Immunity for all. There never will be."

"We fought for what we believed in, River. That's what counts."

An hour ago, River may have believed that. But now...the words feel empty. Hollow. They fail to spark hope.

"Echo..." he starts, only to find he can't finish. How does he tell her they've failed?

That there's nothing worth fighting for.

Her hands cup his face, keeping his gaze on hers. "When we chose each other, we created something beautiful."

He wants to believe her. He really does...

"River, I'm pregnant."

The air is forcefully pushed from his lungs. Everything in his chest bottoms out. His gaze drops to Echo's belly. "A baby?" he whispers.

Of everything he's been told, this is the hardest to process. To bring into the realm of reality.

Maybe because it's a reality he naively never imagined.

Maybe because now that he's heard the words, there's nothing he wants to believe more.

Echo nods, tears tracking gently down her cheeks. "Our baby."

River's hands drop to carefully, reverently cup her flat stomach. Among this storm of devastation, they've forged life.

They've created hope.

"Our baby," he repeats in a choked whisper.

"Oren's the enemy. Not the bees." Echo's thumb strokes his cheek. "He's the one who's killing and destroying. We have to make everyone see that."

"Unity is the answer," he breathes. "Peace is the way forward."

Peace between people.

Peace with the bees.

Echo places her palm over his hand, over her stomach. "That's how we'll have a future."

"I love you, Echo," River says, the words coming from deep within his soul.

He doesn't give her a chance to answer as he presses his lips to hers. He kisses her sweetly, tenderly, deeply.

Gratefully.

He has something worth fighting for.

A world for his child. A world where tomorrow is possible.

CHAPTER

ELEVEN

ECHO

"Our baby."

Echo smiles as River rests his hand on her stomach.

It doesn't matter how many times he says those two words, he can't seem to process them.

"Our baby," he says again.

Echo stretches out contentedly, thinking of an animal she'd heard of once that would make a purring sound when it was happy. That's how she feels now. Which is ludicrous as they have approximately nothing to be happy about.

Apart from their baby. That news is a rainbow in a storm woven from the darkest of clouds.

She turns to River on the sleeping mat in Nola's old hut. Jupiter has been staying here recently, but they'd generously offered to vacate it for a few hours, sensing Echo and River needed some alone time.

There's just so much to absorb. So much has happened. And so much is yet to come.

"So, are we sure Reed's telling us the truth about Flora

being the Sovereign?" Echo asks, still finding it hard to believe his twin kept such a huge piece of information from them.

"It fits with everything she said before she died." River pulls Echo closer. "I didn't fully understand what she was saying at the time, but it all makes sense now."

"She knew she was the only one who could save humanity." Echo nods. "And she decided we weren't worth it."

"Is it wrong that part of me understands why she came to that conclusion?" River chokes back a sob. "We endured a lot of hurt being raised by Oren. I don't think she knew how to process it all."

"It's not wrong," Echo soothes. "It's natural that you understand. You knew Flora better than anyone."

There's so much more she wants to say about this but doesn't. It won't help River if she questions how Flora could possibly have held this information back while sending them on the fool's errand of searching for a Sovereign who was never going to be found. Daphne hadn't needed to die. Nor had Clover. But it's Rose's death that hurts the most. She'd been so trusting. So sweet. Surely, seeing Flora and Chase in a secret tryst hadn't been a crime worthy of punishment by death? Flora had even risked Echo's own life, even if she'd lost the nerve one time and killed the queen bee before it could sting her. If only Echo had taken the time to show Flora all the beautiful things in life. Like the niece or nephew Flora will never see born.

"Do you think if she knew about the baby it would have made any difference?" Echo asks.

"I don't think so." River strokes her stomach gently. "She wasn't thinking clearly about anything. I doubt even a baby would have changed her mind. It may have made her more determined."

"I think that's why she fell in love with Chase," says Echo.

"He'd have been the first person she met who saw the world in the same way as she did. Broken."

"She thought Chase didn't care," River says quietly. "He didn't go looking for her."

Echo sighs. "He did care. A lot. He's just carrying around so much of his own pain. He lost his whole family. It was hard for him to face the idea of losing Flora, too."

River plants a gentle kiss on Echo's forehead and she tries to reclaim the happiness she'd been feeling only moments ago.

She lies still, listening to the sound of hammering and banging coming from the village around them. The Dead Borns are barricading themselves in their homes as they wait for the onslaught. Some are waiting by the black door for night to fall, preparing to take their chances in the Green Zone in the hope they can find a way into the Sting. Others are roaming the streets, trying to decide what to do.

Her hand goes to her locket, and she pulls it out of her shirt to study it. "I want to give this to our child one day."

River nods. "And you will."

"Our plan will work, won't it River?" Echo asks, needing reassurance, even though she thinks they've done enough.

Before they came to Nola's house, River sent Nectar to dig new chambers in the bunker so they can fit more people safely inside. But digging will take time. And they don't know how many people will trust them enough to agree to take the refuge they're offering.

"Of course, it will work," River reassures her. "Once that hatch is closed, the queens can't get in. The Razers will have brought all the food in by now."

Echo sits up and opens her locket, tipping the strange seeds into her hand.

"When my father gave me this, I had no idea what was inside," she tells him. "He wanted me to wait until I was in the

Green Zone to open it. He said what was inside would bring me luck."

"Well, you did meet me." River grins.

She laughs. "My Confirmation was the luckiest day of my life. Not that I knew it at the time."

"Why didn't you plant them?" River asks. "You had plenty of opportunity."

"I didn't want to plant them in the Green Zone." She shrugs. "When I saw what was inside, I made myself a promise to plant the seeds in the Dead Zone once the soil had a chance to regenerate. That's when I'll pass the locket to our child. When the world truly is a better place. Except, now I'm not sure that's ever going to happen."

River sits up beside her and leans in closer to look at the seeds in her palm.

"They look like serpentwood seeds," he says, frowning. "Is that a little yellow dot on the side?"

Echo laughs. "If only. There's no way Dad would have gotten his hands on any serpentwood. I'd never even heard of it until I got to the Green Zone."

"One day we'll find out what they are," River says. "When you plant them in the Dead Zone and give the locket to our child."

She smiles, believing with all her heart this dream will come true. Tucking the seeds back safely in her locket, she notices River looking at her with a look that's endearingly familiar, yet not one she's seen for a while.

He reaches out and strokes her cheek with the back of his hand.

"I love you, Echo," he says. "Everything's going to be okay. We've made it this far, haven't we?"

She nods, trusting him completely. She'd follow this guy to

the end of the Earth. Which now that she thinks of it, is exactly what she's done.

Pressing her lips to his, she hopes this tells him just how much she loves him, too.

He responds instantly, then seeming to catch himself, he withdraws.

"You need rest." He scans her face. "We can't—"

She kisses him so hard this time that they fall down to the sleeping mat.

"We can," she tells him between kisses. "We must."

"Well, if we must..." River's hands go to the hem of Echo's shirt and he skims the bare skin of her back. "But the baby..."

"Is too young to need a sitter," she finishes.

This seems to seal it for him. His gentle touch grows firmer and soon he's clawing at her shirt, trying to lift it over her head. She helps him, removing it and throwing it across the hut, the need to feel skin on skin growing alongside her desire for this gorgeous guy. She's tied herself to him with all her heart, it feels right to give herself to him in body, too.

River's clothes are soon in a crumpled pile beside Echo's and she trails kisses along his jawline, then heads down to his neck, feeling his back arch as she urges him to climb on top of her.

"I don't want to squash the baby," he says.

She laughs, certain that isn't possible. Her belly hasn't even begun to swell yet. But it makes sense that River would be feeling so protective. He's always been like that. With Flora. With Echo. And now with their child. River loves large. And when he does, he'll do everything in his power to keep those close to him safe.

She gets to her knees and crawls on top of him, biting her lip as she looks down at him. He reaches for her, putting one hand on her stomach and the other on her cheek.

"You're the most beautiful girl in the whole world." His hand moves from her waist to her heart. "Everything about you is good."

"River," she murmurs, loving what he's saying, but knowing now isn't the time for words. She wants him to show her how he feels with his touch. She takes his hand and slides it from her heart a little further down her chest.

He moans and she leans forward, kissing him like there's no tomorrow. Which there may not be. But they have now. And that's all she cares about. Because she'll store this moment away in her mind and bring it out when she needs it most. River has given her the strength and courage to come this far, and she can draw on what they have to go even further.

As they join as one, everything in the world feels right, even though in reality it couldn't be more wrong. But, together, they can make the world a better place.

Echo. And River.

None of this makes any sense without him. They were born as two different people in two very different zones and, somehow, they became halves of the same whole.

River moves with Echo in a rhythm built on tenderness. They know this could be their last time together, yet somehow it feels like the first. Because while River makes love with the same passion as the other times, there's a layer of gentleness that's completely new. He's not just expressing his adoration for her, he's sealing their future together as a family.

She trails her fingertips across his body, noticing he's slimmer than when she first met him. But this only makes him more appealing. Because the layer of muscle his body's shed has been an act of love. It shows his sacrifice for everything he cares about. His constant need to put everyone before himself.

She presses herself to him, shrouding him with her nakedness and feels him shudder. Covering his face with kisses, she gives into the intense feeling of oneness. It's powerful. All consuming.

And so beautiful it takes Echo's breath away.

As the exquisite feeling abates, she collapses on his chest, humming with tender joy.

"I love you, too," she whispers, repeating the words he'd said to her at the very beginning.

They hold each other. Both completely silent. Completely still. As if a single sound or movement will break the magic spell they've cast over this falling down hut.

A scream rings out in the village.

And just like that, the moment is over.

More screams follow, each one more terrified than the one that came before.

Echo and River don't have time to mourn the end of their time together. They don't even have time to speculate on what might be going on outside. They scramble to their feet, get dressed, and crawl out through Nola's half-sized door, blinking in the afternoon sun as they take in the chaos in the street.

"Look." River points up, his face white.

Echo squints, trying to see what has his attention.

There's a Worker directly above, hovering over a giant hole in the net. It flies a little further down and begins work on another hole.

"But it's too soon," says Echo, even though it should come as no surprise that Oren has launched his attack early. When he'd blown up the Alphadome, the bomb had gone off a full minute before the timer had counted down to zero.

"We need to get to the bunker." River takes Echo's hand. "And we need to get there now."

A high-pitched hum floats through the air as they begin to

run. It grows in intensity with each step they take until it's a hurricane in their ears.

"The queens," Echo huffs. "They're coming."

TWELVE

RIVER

R iver can taste the panic in the air as surely as he can hear the dozens of queen bees buzzing around the net above them. A shadow falls over him and Echo as they run through the village and he doesn't have to look up to know what it is.

A Worker.

Creating another hole so the queen bees can infiltrate the Dead Zone.

People cry out and duck, running into huts, running out of huts, running past those who are frozen with fear and indecision.

They're the ones who've realized there's nowhere to run. Nowhere is safe.

Someone cries out inside the hut ahead. "What's the point?" screams a woman. "We have no door!"

"Mama," comes a pitiful wail. "I want my trousers back."

River and Echo stop simultaneously as a shirtless man steps out. "Just tear them up and shove the scraps into any holes you see," he says as he looks around wildly. "The only way the blasted insects can get in will be past me."

He goes pale when he sees the Worker directly above him, then swallows hard as he registers the smaller, far deadlier queens landing beside it.

River looks past the man, seeing a woman cowering in the center of the rickety hut, curled around two young children. Their father is bravely standing by the door, ready to protect them, thinking he'll be able to stop what's coming.

Not realizing that Oren has programmed the queen bees to exterminate everyone.

River grips the man's arm. "Take them to the bunker," he says urgently. "It'll be safe there."

The man hesitates, glances back at the woman and children, then calls out for them to hurry. As a family, they break into a run, heading toward the scoring grounds, the child on their mother's hip looking up at the Worker with wide, fascinated eyes.

A haggard woman shuffles past River, moaning and crying. Decimated by the scurge, she already knows what her end will be.

River grabs her by the shoulders and spins her around. "To the scoring grounds!" he shouts over her, telling any Dead Born who can hear. "Head to the scoring grounds!"

"Get to the bunker!" Echo calls out, leaping in front of a young man who was about to dart past. "It's safe!"

The exhausted woman breaks into a shuffling run, a wave of people overtaking her as their screams turn from panicked to desperate.

"Hurry! The bunker!"

"Safety!"

A man screams. "Another one!"

A second Worker lands above, blocking out the sun. The

skeletal woman trips and River leaps forward to help her, but she's already being scooped up by the young man who Echo stopped. He keeps running, carrying her with him.

The promise of somewhere safe from the queens spreads fast and people flock past River, running toward the scoring grounds. His eyes widen when he registers exactly how many Dead Borns there are. Hundreds. Maybe more...

"Come on," River says, taking Echo's hand, the same sense of desperation pounding through his veins.

He has no idea how much more space Nectar's been able to dig out in the bunker, but surely if they cram people in as tightly as possible...

They run, overtaking many of the Dead Borns who have little more than adrenaline to fuel them. River squints as he focuses ahead, his thumping heart sinking as he registers there's only one person standing near the bunker.

And that the hatch is closed.

"It's Reed," Echo pants as they pass the family they saw in the hut. "And he's alone."

River and Echo glance at each other, dread weighing down the space between them.

"Get out of the way," a Dead Born shouts as they overtake him. "Let us in!"

Reed sets his jaw, looking as if he just pressed his feet into the ground. "The bunker is full."

River and Echo reach the front of the crowd and skid to a halt. "It can't be," River pants, someone shoving him in the back. "There are too many people who still need shelter."

Reed keeps his gaze squarely on River, ignoring the growing mass behind him. "I wish I could," he says in a low voice. "We've let in as many as we can."

Echo glances back. "Surely you can—"

"No," Reed says sharply. "Not unless you want to risk the lives of everyone in there."

River realizes he's right. He can feel the tension of the hundreds of people behind him. The moment the hatch opens, it'll be mayhem as they fight to enter. The bunker won't be safe for anyone.

Someone jostles River again. "Of course you'd say that! You've filled the bunker up with other Green Borns!"

Reed shakes his head. "We let in anyone who arrived. Everyone's in danger, no matter whether you're Green or Dead Born." He sets his jaw. "The bunker's full. Overflowing. No one can move down there."

A scream has River spinning around, even though he knows why the terrified sound just pierced the air.

"The bees!" The people at the rear of the crowd, the closest to the village, surge forward. "The bees are coming through the net!"

Cries and shouts erupt as the crowd explodes into a frenzy of motion around River and Echo. Someone shoves Reed out of the way, knocking him to the ground as they dive for the hatch. One set of hands, then two, then three, heave as they try to pull it open.

"It's locked," Reed tells them, dusting himself off as he gets back to his feet. "You can't get in."

Another scream reaches them, this one far higher pitched than the first. It's abruptly cut off a moment later.

The queen bees have taken their first victim.

"No," gasps one of the men, straining even harder in his attempt to get into the bunker.

Another straightens, looking around frantically. "There's nowhere to go."

The far edge of the crowd splits and divides, like material unraveling as more sounds of panic fill the air. River's heart hammers against his ribs as he realizes what everyone else has.

It's only a matter of time before a queen bee descends on him.

And Echo.

"Find shelter where you can!" Reed shouts, waving at his arms for the crowd to disperse. "Kill any bee that comes near you!"

The Dead Borns scatter, their faces twisted with terror. River watches helplessly as a woman drops to the ground in the distance, wailing as she flaps desperately at the air. He can't see the queen bees from here, but the sharp end to her screams tells him everything.

Reed yanks out a length of cloth from his pocket. "I'm going to help," he says. "I'll hide as many as I can in the sturdiest huts." He lifts the length of material. "And kill any queens who get too close."

River nods, uncomfortable with the idea of killing bees after a lifetime of growing up in the Green Zone, even as he knows there's no other choice. Even as he simultaneously decides he'll be there, alongside Reed, saving as many people as he can.

Reed's voice drops low as he glances at Echo. "But first, I can open the hatch, one more time."

River realizes what Reed's not saying. He can open the hatch for one more person. For Echo.

He turns to her, desperate for her to take this chance to save herself. To save their unborn child.

"I can't, River," Echo says, her eyes begging him to understand. "This time it isn't just about saving Leif and his family back in the Betadome. It's about saving every life in the Dead Zone."

"But—"

Echo takes his hand and presses it to her stomach. "I'm Immune. And I need to fight for our baby's future. Like I have from the beginning."

River's breath whooshes out as he realizes he can't ask this of her. Echo's courage and determination are the reasons their baby exists in the first place. But even as he accepts her decision, his heart rebels at the idea.

Echo will be running into a swarm of killer queen bees. Even though she's Immune, one too many stings... He'll have to protect her. Somehow.

Impossibly, no doubt foolishly, they run back toward the village, Reed right behind them. Most of the Dead Borns have now scattered from the scoring grounds, the open area feeling far too exposed. The empty space is almost calm.

But the closer River, Echo and Reed get to the village, the louder the screams. The more panic they witness.

The more bodies they come across.

The first is the woman River saw earlier, lying in the dust, purple and swollen, her mouth and eyes stretched open. Beside her is the young man who carried her, just as purple and swollen. Dead. Executed for being Vulnerable.

Reed screeches and River and Echo spin to find him frantically swiping his piece of material in the air above his head. River yanks his shirt off as he steps in front of Echo, adrenaline replacing the blood in his veins as he registers the threat.

Not one queen bee, but two.

They circle Reed's head, the tiny lights attached to their backs flashing red. The lights that are receiving the instructions from Oren. Instructions to kill. Simultaneously, they dive, working in tandem as they attack from either side, aiming for Reed's throat.

Oren's programmed them to go for the jugular. To inject

their venom in a soft, exposed area of skin rich with blood supply.

River flicks his shirt out, the material knocking one of the queens to the side. Reed ducks, flapping his own piece of cloth as he leaps aside. The queens dart away, only to attack again, converging on Reed. Single-minded in their determination to kill.

River brings his shirt down in an arc, trapping the queen in the downward swipe. The material hits the ground and Echo stomps on it, the faint crunch of the electronic control making her huff in satisfaction.

"Got her," Reed hisses as he flicks the other queen onto the ground and grinds her into the dirt with the heel of his shoe.

River straightens, breathing hard although the scuffle only lasted a handful of seconds. Yet in that brief moment of saving Reed, the Dead Zone has descended into chaos. They're surrounded by pleas for mercy and running feet, the scent of panic and fear, the taste of dust coating his tongue as the mayhem disturbs the very ground. The sight of eyes more white than iris, the bloated, purple bodies that are dropping everywhere he looks.

It's all too much. It almost has River doubling over.

Screams. Terror. Pain.

It won't be long before the Dead Zone will house nothing but...death.

Even the sight of those fighting to survive is hard to take in. Dead Borns flick lengths of material, some even swipe lengths of wood as they try to end the tiny threats to their lives. For most, the queens are too fast, too small, too focused on spearing their stinger into their victim's neck.

Countless people will die if they try to kill the queens one by one. In the process killing the very insect that humanity so desperately needs to survive. Each queen bee was supposed to be the matriarch of her own colony. The mother of thousands of workers who will pollinate countless flowers, creating food and diversity.

And it will never work. The queens will kill every last Dead Born before they can kill them.

A shadow moves over River and he looks up, discovering a Worker hovering above, staring down with her impassive, glass eyes. With a horrified jolt, River realizes why.

Oren's watching this all unfold.

No doubt reveling in the destruction and carnage.

Proud that his ultimate plan is coming to fruition.

Another Worker lifts from the net, having finished creating a hole, allowing a ray of sun to infiltrate directly into the Dead Zone. River looks around, realizing there are dozens of them.

Pockets of light pierce the protective layer, creating narrow beams that land on the ground, the huts, the people desperately trying to stay alive. River draws in a sharp breath as realization hits him. There's a way to protect Echo and everyone else in the Dead Zone.

He spins back to Reed. "I need your glasses."

Reed doesn't hesitate, slipping them off and passing them to River. "What for?"

"Come on," River says to Echo. "I have an idea."

CHAPTER

THIRTEEN

ECHO

E cho looks frantically at River, hoping that whatever his idea is, that it's a good one. *No*, make that a brilliant one. Because the way she sees it, they're all out of options.

"Why do you need his glasses?" Echo asks.

"I need the lenses to start a fire." River holds up Reed's glasses and squints as he angles them, trying to catch the rays of the sun.

Reed blinks, trying to focus. "That's actually a genius idea."

There's a loud buzzing as a queen comes careering through the hole in the net above them. Echo turns to the nearest hut that's little more than a wooden roof being held up by four metal posts of odd lengths. Whatever fabric had made up the walls is long gone, along with whoever had lived inside. She grabs the shortest of the metal bars and yanks it out. The hut collapses and she leaps back, waving the bar in front of her.

"I've got this!" she yells. "You do what you need to do."

River nods, trusting her completely as he heads for the pile of rubble that was once someone's home, stopping only to pick up his discarded shirt he'd been using to swat the bees away.

A queen flies at River, and Echo swings the metal bar. The killer insect changes course to avoid her, and River quickly ducks.

"I've got it!" she shouts again, hoping she really does.

She swipes at the queen and it flies away, although they all know that won't be for long.

"Good one." River scrunches his shirt on top of the collapsed hut and holds up the glasses to the sun.

"Say that when I kill the little sucker!" she huffs, scanning the space around them.

Reed stumbles forward, waving his hands in front of him.

"Get on the ground," Echo shouts at him. "And stay still."

They can't afford to lose the only person they have left who knows how to make Immunity.

The sun streams through the net, and River works to catch the rays that are angled directly through the hole made by Oren's Worker.

"I just need a few more minutes," he pants from behind her. "It's working."

"I've got you covered," she tells him. "But hurry!"

Reed cowers blindly at Echo's feet, and she turns in a slow circle as she scans for the queen, keeping the metal bar clenched tightly in her hands. She feels like one of the Moon Workers trying to protect herself with a scythe. She's crazed. Confused. And desperate to survive no matter all the odds being stacked against her.

The queen darts out of nowhere, heading straight for Echo. She holds still as she focuses on it, her knuckles turning white as she swings the bar at what she hopes is exactly the right moment to knock this miniature beast out of the air.

But it isn't.

She misses again, and the bee swerves toward a new target. River.

He can't move or he'll lose all the progress he just made. Starting a fire is their last hope. If they can create enough smoke, it might just keep the bees away. Plus, it will make it harder for Oren to see what's happening.

Echo steps forward, draws in a deep breath and prepares to strike. The world feels like it's in slow motion as she watches the queen preparing to land on the bare skin on the back of River's neck. She swings the bar through the air and connects with the queen, making the tiniest *plink* sound.

It's the sweetest sound Echo's ever heard. Far preferable to the screams floating up from the village and scoring grounds.

The queen spins in the air and plummets. Echo leaps forward, hitting it again and watching as it splinters apart. The transmitter that Oren strapped to the insect's back is smashed and Echo crushes it into the ground, turning it to dust.

"How do you like that, Oren?" she asks, hoping that somehow he can hear her.

The queen is dead, but Echo doesn't have time to celebrate her win or mourn the loss. Ultimately, they need these precious creatures for their planet to survive. They're not the problem. They're the solution. Except...it's hard to think like that when the bees have been sent out to kill every last person she loves.

"Go, Echo!" comes a small voice.

She spins around to see Makk, hopping from foot to foot with a wide grin on his face.

"Why aren't you in the bunker?" she gasps, scanning for more bees. That queen was far from being the end of their troubles. There are dozens more.

"Razers don't hide!" says Makk, waving a long strap of leather like a whip. "We fight!"

"And what about the rest of the Razers?" Echo asks. She could sure use Chase's help right now.

"They're in the bunker." Makk turns sharply to the right and cracks his whip, knocking a queen straight out of the air. "Got him! I mean, *her*."

"Makk!" Echo can't help but be impressed by his perfect aim. "Help me protect River. He's starting a fire so we can make some smoke."

"That's a genius idea," Makk gasps.

"That's what I said." Reed squints up at them from his position on the ground.

"Reed!" Makk gasps. "What are you doing down there? You look different."

Echo swipes her bar to her left, but it's a false alarm and she hits nothing but air. "River took his glasses."

"Borrowed," Reed corrects. "River borrowed my glasses."

"I've got it!" River shouts as his bundled shirt flickers to life. He blows on it and the fire swells. "Quick! Bring me anything small and flammable that you can find."

Echo's heart surges with hope. She keeps a grip on the metal bar, scanning the rubble for both approaching queens and anything that will burn.

Looking at River's bare chest, Makk immediately tears off his shirt and throws it at his big cousin. "Use this!"

River catches the shirt. "Good one, Makk." He carefully feeds the fabric into the hungry flames then raises a brow at Echo.

"Not a chance." She glances down at her filthy shirt, even though she knows River was only joking.

"Echo!" Makk shouts. "Look out."

She ducks as Makk's whip cracks over her head, sending another queen hurtling to the ground. Cursing, she berates herself for not paying closer attention.

"River! Here!" Jupiter's approached, their arms laden with thick hessian.

"Perfect." River takes the fabric eagerly and adds it to his growing fire, which is now licking at the timber of the hut.

"Why aren't you in the bunker?" Echo asks Jupiter, wondering if everyone she cares about has opted to stay outside.

"No room." Jupiter waves their hand as smoke drifts over. "But Nola and Vern made it inside. And Chase."

Right. So, maybe not everyone Echo cares about is out here. But River, Makk and Jupiter are more than enough. She scans her surroundings, looking for more queens, however the smoke is already doing its job at keeping them back.

There's a scream nearby and Jupiter ducks away. Echo stays by River's side. She's not leaving him. Not for anyone. There's far too much at risk.

Now that the fire is safely growing, River goes to Reed and hands him his glasses.

"Thanks." Reed sits up and quickly shoves the glasses back on his face, instantly looking more like himself.

"We need more kindling," says River. "If we can grow this fire, we can keep everyone safe."

Reed scurries off in the same direction Jupiter had disappeared.

"You did it, River!" Echo gives him a hug. "You really are a genius."

He kisses her quickly, then pulls back, knowing they have work to do to keep these flames alive. "*We* did it," he corrects. "Pretty sure I'd be dead a few times over if you hadn't kept the queens away."

She smiles. "And Makk."

He turns, having been concentrating so hard on his task it seems he hadn't noticed his cousin's arrival. "You should be in the bunker where it's safe."

"River." Echo squeezes his arm. "It's lucky he was here. He's quite the crack shot with that whip."

Makk beams at the praise, then gets distracted by something over their shoulders. They turn to see Jupiter and Reed leading over a group of Dead Borns, each of them carrying something to add to the flames.

"We're having a bonfire!" Makk exclaims. "The queens can't get us now!"

As the group gets closer, a woman near the back howls and drops the plank of timber she was carrying.

"It got me!" she cries as she collapses to the ground. "Help!"

Those who surround her know it's already too late. They rush forward toward the fire, throwing their offerings onto the greedy flames.

Echo darts away from River. The woman might not be able to be saved, but nobody should have to die alone. She runs to her, waving her metal bar in case any other curious queens come to investigate.

The woman is purple and swollen, looking very much like Rose had before she died. Echo crouches beside her. The queen is on the woman's neck, continuing to sting her despite the task already being complete.

"I'm sorry." Echo takes the woman's hand, wishing there was more she could have done for her. For everyone who's dying at Oren's evil hands.

The woman's eyes bulge then close as they develop the glassy look Echo's become way too familiar with recently.

Sensing movement behind her, Echo looks up to see River.

"Get back!" she tells him urgently. "The queen's still here. On her neck."

River may be Immune, but so far, the only person they've found who can resist the deadly queens is Echo.

"Only if you do," he counters.

"I'm sorry," Echo says again, still talking to the woman lying before her. She takes her metal bar and brings it down hard, squashing the queen on her neck before the creature has a chance to fly away and take the life of anyone else. She looks away, not wanting to see what damage she did to the woman herself.

River puts a hand on Echo's shoulder and helps her stand.

"Stay near the fire," he says. "Please. We have to keep you safe. And the baby."

She nods, knowing she'd taken too big a risk.

The smoke drifts their way, too late to save the woman at their feet, but enough to keep them alive for now. River stoops to pick up the timber the woman had dropped.

"River." They turn to see Makk behind them. "What do we do when the fire dies out?"

"We won't let it die out," he says.

"Eventually it has to." Makk scans the Dead Zone. "We can't keep burning everything we have."

"We'll figure something out," says Echo. "We always do. Just like with the fire. River has bought us a whole lot of time with that idea."

"But what if there aren't any of us left to feed the fire?" asks Makk, looking down at the dead woman.

Echo's heart aches with sadness. Makk's normally their ray of shining light in all this darkness, refusing to give in to any of the challenges thrown at them. But even he can see how dire this is. She goes to him and takes his hand, steering him away from the woman and back to the safety of the fire.

"We won't let Oren beat us," she says. "I promise."

Makk pulls back his shoulders, these words seeming to be the fuel he needed to keep his own fire burning bright.

"We're Razers," he says, taking the timber from River and throwing it onto the fire. "We're fighters!"

"That's the Makk we know and love," says River, putting his arm around Echo. "The fearless Razer!"

"I'm a fearless Razer!" Makk repeats.

More Dead Borns have seen the blaze and are gathering. The flames leap higher and higher, twisting and multiplying in hues of blue, orange and gold. The heat is intense but the crowd stays close, each puff of protective smoke feeling like a mother wrapping a blanket around her children.

The screams in the distance begin to punctuate the air less frequently. It seems the queens are running out of victims as people have either already succumbed or have gathered near the safety of the flames.

The Dead Borns get to work dismantling the huts that are close by, throwing the materials on the fire and cheering as the flames continue to build.

"We need to keep control of the fire," River calls out to them. "Don't let the village catch alight. Try to contain it to this area."

"Burn the village down!" cries a man. "It's not safe anymore. We have nothing to lose!"

"We have our hope to lose!" says Echo. "And we can't do that. River's right. Let's keep the fire contained. We can find a way to fix the holes in the net and kill the rest of the queens."

The man laughs and points above their heads. "Maybe you should look up."

Echo does as she's told and lets out a gasp. The flames have reached so high they're almost touching the net.

Jupiter lets out a cry and tries to smother some of the smaller flames. "Quickly! It's getting too high!"

"Everyone stop!" Echo shouts, trying to help Jupiter. "Stop adding to the flames."

"Those flames are keeping us alive!" a nearby woman protests, throwing a bag of torn up rags onto the fire.

"Let the Dead Zone burn!" the man sneers, throwing on a large plank of wood.

It's turned into a frenzy now that they have no hope of stopping.

There's a roar as the flames gobble up their latest offerings and the fire leaps up, catching the net and burning a hole even bigger than the Workers had managed to create. The flames spread quickly from there, moving across the net at impossible speed as it consumes the delicate fibers, one section at a time before it moves onto the next.

The hexagonal shapes that have kept the Dead Zone safe all of Echo's life are turning into ash. It's a sight she never thought she'd see. One she never wanted to see. An unwanted tear slides down her face as she accepts the ramifications of their actions.

They needed the fire to keep them safe.

But now the fire is doing the opposite.

Because without the net, they've turned the Dead Zone into something else...

The Extinction Zone.

FOURTEEN

RIVER

River watches with horror as the determined flames shrink, becoming ants crawling over the net above him, eating away at the shield that protects the Dead Zone. The gaping hole grows, inch by inch, allowing more and more light to enter.

Bright sun pours down over the fire, beams piercing the ashen smoke, illuminating the desolation that's always defined this side of the Betadome. It's the brightest the Dead Zone's ever been.

Yet all it's doing is highlighting the harsh reality everyone here is now faced with.

"They're dying off," Makk says, letting out a breath.

River realizes he's right. The flames are too small to maintain momentum. The net doesn't provide enough fuel to keep them going. The edges of the crater that's over a yard wide turn gray, then black.

A piece of timber drops as the bonfire devours the fuel the Dead Borns are piling on it, sending up a shower of sparks. Echo gasps and Makk groans as the tiny sparks rise on the waves of heat, twisting and twirling in all directions, then hitting the barrier above. They stick, then flare with excitement as they discover just what they need to not only survive but thrive. The hungry process of devouring a new breach in the net begins all over again, in a dozen new places.

Reed groans. "We're doomed."

"May as well take everything down with us," sneers the man with the crazed eyes.

"No—" River tries, but the man shoves past him, reaching down to pick up a piece of wood sticking out of the fire.

He lifts his torch high above his head. "More!" he screams. "We need more fires!"

The man darts away before River or Echo can stop him, carrying his flaming piece of wood like a beacon. He stops beside a nearby hut, kicks it, then runs to the next. He's looking for the location of his next bonfire.

"He's right," shouts the woman who agreed with him. "More fires mean we can keep the queens away."

River grabs her hand before she can follow, wincing when she looks at him in fury. "Please," he says, his voice low and urgent. "This isn't the answer."

"I sent my son to the bunker." Her fury morphs to desperation. "I don't want his heartbroken face to be the last time I see him."

River's heart twists. This woman wants to get back to her son. She wants to survive. "Working together is the answer. That's where our strength is."

Her gaze drops to where his hand is wrapped around her wrist, clearly weighing up what she's going to do. River releases her, acknowledging she has a right to make her own choices.

A wailing scream has them both spinning to look in the direction it came from. The direction the man ran in. He's waving his torch around in a panic, slashing it through the air like a sword.

Echo grabs River's hand. "No..."

The man screeches again, spinning one way then the other, the whoosh of the torch slicing through the air apparent even over the roar of the fire.

"Get them away from me!" he screeches.

Because it's not one queen who's attacking him. It's not two. It's at least ten.

Oren is coordinating his weapons.

The man turns to run back to the bonfire, but the queens contract, their tiny red lights forming a circle that lowers and constricts, becoming a halo around his throat. As if a thread has been tightened, they snap closed, becoming a necklace of death.

He drops, dead almost instantly. Already bloated before he hits the ground. The torch rolls away, snuffing out in the dirt.

River finds he's holding Echo's hand far too tightly. He loosens his grip, realizing she's clutching just as hard. He was holding her back in case she decided to try and help the man. She was probably doing the same.

A twitch of movement beside River has him reaching down to grab Makk. "It's too late," he says heavily.

"And Oren's decided to target us." Echo glances up at the Workers hovering in the smoke, watching everything calmly like the emotionless machines they are.

River wonders if the man controlling the beasts, the man he believed was his father, is exactly the same. Oren can't do this and have a heart.

The queens that attacked the man rise into the air and spread out. But don't leave.

They're waiting.

The woman moans. "We really needed that piece of wood."

River turns back to the fire, registering that it's already shrinking. The wood is thin and dry. Each piece practically combusted on impact.

An older man throws his shirt on the fire, revealing a back riddled with sores and scabs. The woman moans again, her fingers tangling in the edge of her threadbare top, clearly thinking of doing the same thing.

Fury flashes through River, burning far hotter than the bonfire ever will. They're trapped. The fire that's their only protection is dying. And more queens are arriving, forming a circle around the Dead Borns huddled beside their last line of defense.

River looks up, hating the Workers watching this like some sick entertainment. Hating that they've run out of options.

Hating Oren.

Furious, River grabs a piece of wood and hurls it into the air. It spins, one end ablaze, flying straight toward the nearest Worker. The timber hits her underside with a clang, the flames brushing the smooth, black metal, then drops straight back down several feet away.

The only response is for the Workers to move as one, ascending several feet higher so they're out of reach.

Even the burst of fury was futile.

The woman sinks to the ground, still wearing her top as if she decided it wasn't worth it. "We really needed that piece of wood too."

River's hands form hard fists. She's right.

Time is the only thing they can guarantee themselves. And for that, they need to keep the fire alive. He doesn't look at Echo as his gaze roams the huts nearby, calculating which is the closest.

Makk moves and River instinctively clamps his hand on him again. "You're not going anywhere."

"We need more wood," Makk hisses. "And I'm fast."

Echo points to the hovering queens just beyond the veil of smoke. "Not faster than them."

"You were going to go," Makk says, narrowing his eyes at River.

River sighs. "That's not the point."

Echo slips her arm through River's, then clamps her hand around his. "And now he's not," she says firmly.

"Which I knew would happen," Makk says, rolling his eyes. "And why I need to get the wood."

River tightens his grip on Makk in the same way Echo just did with him. "Not happening."

"Stop treating me like a kid," Makk mutters, crossing his arms.

River almost smiles, even as he wishes his cousin didn't feel the need to grow up so fast.

"River," Echo says, her body tensing.

His own body freezes as he doesn't know where to look next. From every angle, the queen bees just simultaneously moved a few inches closer.

They're tightening the noose as the fire dies down.

"Now will you let me go get some wood?" Makk asks, feet shuffling with impatience.

"There's even less chance now," River states flatly.

"And you had zero chance before," Echo adds.

The woman shoots to her feet, her face pale and eyes wide. "The queens! They're coming closer!"

The others around the fire gasp and cry out as they realize what River and Echo already have.

Reed frowns. "I'll go," he says, hunching his shoulders.

"No," River says sharply. "Oren won't spare you just because you were once loyal to him."

Reed huffs. "Of course he won't." He glances back at the

fire, his gaze scanning it. "I'll take a piece of wood. Just like... that guy did."

The dead one.

River opens his mouth to point that out, but Reed raises his hand to silence him. "You have Echo and the baby. Makk has a whole life ahead of him." He closes his eyes for a moment. "And I owe these people."

River snaps his mouth closed, unsure how to respond to that. He understands the drive to try and make things right. But Reed's chance of surviving a desperate run to the nearest hut to get more wood....

Makk tugs on River's hand. "River, I—"

"You're not going, Makk," River snaps, the tension inside him pulling infinitely tighter.

His cousin tugs even harder. "Look!"

River follows where Makk's pointing, squinting as he peers through the smoky haze. He draws in a sharp breath as he registers what it is.

"Chase!" Makk says, bouncing up on his toes.

And it's not just the leader of the Razers. It's the Razers themselves.

And everyone else in the bunker.

They move toward them, Chase an apex at the front, Sledge, Tuff and Vern behind him, everyone else spreading wider and further back.

"What are they doing here?" Echo asks, shocked.

River shakes his head, wishing he wasn't seeing this. Chase and the others must have left the bunker and discovered there aren't any queens in most of the village.

"Get back!" Reed shouts, waving his arm. "The queens are here!"

Chase lifts a piece of wood that has material wrapped in a thick bunch on the top in response, breaking into a run.

"Go back!" River screams.

Echo raises her arms, waving them wildly. "We're surrounded by queen bees!"

Chase doesn't falter, doesn't pause. Sledge and the others spread out to flank him, holding their own sticks wrapped with cloth.

A faint whirring above tells River that Oren's registered the threat. A moment later, half the queen bees turn toward the approaching crowd.

And attack.

River and Echo break into a run simultaneously, remaining where they are no longer a choice. Echo picks up the pole she had, barely breaking stride. River sidesteps to pick up the charred piece of wood the man dropped.

The queens are fast, too fast, and they reach Chase and the others within a blink. He lifts his frail-looking club and swings. The thick end, dark with moisture, slices through the air as he keeps running.

Chase got the queen on the first hit?

Beside him, Sledge swipes at another. Tuff leaps as he brings his club down on another. None of them slow. Not one of the Razers hesitates.

River and Echo's steps falter, confused. Do the Razers not know the danger they're in?

Chase runs straight past them, his face set with determination as he lifts his baton high, focused on the queens surrounding the fire.

"River!" Vern calls out. He throws his baton to him. "We weren't going to sit by and let people die." His gaze hardens. "We're not Oren."

River catches his breath, instantly recognizing the smell, and judging by the way Echo just gasped, so did she. He knows it from his time in Eden. She knows it from the time Flora tortured Daphne.

The material on the end of the sticks is dipped in insecticide.

River's mother or father must've told the others that in small doses, the chemical is safe for bees. In large doses, it's deadly.

The Razers and Dead Borns flock around them and someone shoves another insecticide club in Echo's hand. The people further back are carrying pieces of timber, lengths of material, anything they could get their hands on as they seek out queen bees just as valiantly as those with the insecticide.

River's head turns from side to side as he blinks.

They're watching unity in action. The Dead Borns are rallying, no longer willing to sit back and watch their own die.

Chase appears in front of them, breathing hard. "Come on," he says urgently, indicating they need to move to the front of the fray, closer to the fire.

Where the remainder of the queen bees are.

Chase darts away and they follow. Uneasiness climbs up River's spine despite it all.

"This isn't the answer," he says softly, not speaking to anyone in particular.

More death was never the solution, including bees.

Yet, he has no idea what is.

Chase swipes, then stomps on a queen bee with enough strength to send up a puff of dust. "It's not," he says through gritted teeth. "We're going to the only safe place left."

River's gaze is drawn to the east, to the tall spire that rises above the layer of smoke like a beacon. Chase is right.

The Sting is the only remaining haven.

Their last bastion.

It's time to go back.

CHAPTER
FIFTEEN
ECHO

E cho once believed nothing in the Dead Zone would ever change. Now she can barely recognize the place. Or the people.

Oren pushed them. And pushed them. Then pushed them some more.

And finally, he tipped them over the edge.

Homes have been torn apart for fuel. Belongings destroyed to be used as shields or weapons. And bodies scatter the ground in twisted mounds of wasted life.

Echo wants to give in to the defeated feeling consuming her, but she can't. She has a baby to think of, along with all the other broken souls who've managed to survive this far.

"The moment we've been preparing for all our lives has arrived!" Chase shouts, raising his baton in the air. "We're storming the Sting!"

"But Oren will kill us," a man protests. "He said no Dead Borns are allowed in."

"He's already killing us," Vern growls. "Open your eyes."

"That's right!" shouts a woman. "It's time to stand up."

Several others murmur their agreement.

Echo looks down at her hands. In one she has the metal bar she'd been using to protect herself. In her other is the club that's been doused in insecticide. She throws the metal one aside, having seen how much more effective the clubs are.

"If anyone has a better idea, speak now," says Chase.

The crowd falls quiet.

"Then let's move." Chase puffs out his chest, completely in his element. He's waited a long time for the Razers to lead their people from their downtrodden zone into one that promises safety. Ironically, it's not the Green Zone that's been razed to the ground, it's the Dead Zone. But Echo doesn't point that out. Chase has given up so much. And lost so much. He deserves to feel confident, even if it's misplaced. The chance of being able to successfully lead everyone to safety is even slimmer than Makk's chance of being allowed to collect more wood.

"Everyone, find a partner," River calls. "Put your back to them as we move. That way you can see in all directions."

This reminds Echo of when she and River had done exactly this when Daphne had attacked them in the darkness in the Extinction Zone. They can't risk even one of those queens sneaking up on them. While they must have killed at least half of them by now, it only takes one to cause total destruction.

"Good thinking." Chase nods at his former rival. "And kill as many of those little bastards as you can along the way."

Everyone pairs up and the large group of Dead Borns begin making their way toward the Betadome. They wave their weapons above their heads. Some have batons, others have planks they've set on fire, some have strips of thick cloth they're waving wildly in circles.

But they all have one thing in common.

They're angry. And they're terrified.

Chase has teamed up with Tuff. Vern has his back pressed firmly against Nola's. And Makk is fiercely protecting his mother. It's not even a question as to who Echo's partner is. From the very moment she and River were the final two teens left standing at their Confirmation, they've been a pair.

River struggles with something in his pocket for a moment, then gives Echo a kiss.

"I won't let anything happen to you," he tells her.

"And I won't let anything happen to you." She kisses him again, drawing in the warmth of being so close. She's said goodbye to this guy so many times, and somehow, each time they've managed to survive. They can do it again.

They turn their backs and begin their sideways shuffle away from the safety of the smoke toward the Betadome.

There's a scream as someone at the back of the crowd is stung. More screams ring in the air as the Dead Borns attack back.

"Got it!" someone grunts. "Die you little bi—"

"Keep moving!" Chase shouts. "No matter what."

Echo looks up and sees huge sections of the net have burned away, the embers moving across it like cancer. The sides are sagging now that they're no longer being supported by the canopy. It's only a matter of time before the whole thing comes crashing down. Then they won't only have Oren's queens to contend with, they'll have regular bees too. The harsh reality is that not everyone will make it to the Sting. But if they stay here, none of them will make it at all.

A queen circles above, just out of reach, pausing at intervals before orbiting again.

"It's looking for someone," Echo says.

"*Oren's* looking for someone," River corrects.

Panic surges through Echo's adrenaline-flooded body as she realizes who Oren's seeking. "Keep your head down."

But her warning comes too late.

The queen dives down toward River. Someone nearby lets out a garbled scream as they swipe at the air.

"River!" Echo gasps, spinning around.

He raises his baton, ready to strike. The queen anticipates his move and changes course, moving swiftly to the left like she was intending to do this all along. But Echo also anticipated it and she swipes hard with her baton, connecting with the queen and sending her spinning. As she hits the ground, River uses the end of his baton to finish the job.

He grins at Echo. "Teamwork makes the dreamwork."

She laughs, releasing some of the tension beating at her temples. They both know they're far from escaping danger yet.

"Keep moving," Chase orders. "And well done. That's one more down. But don't get complacent. There's still plenty more up there."

The group shuffles forward and the Betadome comes into sight. It's always looked like a precious gemstone set in a sea of misery, but now it's a glittering jewel. The silver net is perfectly intact, untouched by the fire. And the trees inside seem even greener against the soot blanketing the devastation they've just walked from.

As they get closer, Echo's traitorous mouth waters at the sight of the brightly colored fruit inside, each one a jewel of its own.

"Can you hear that?" River asks. "The bees..."

Echo listens harder and is reminded of Confirmation when Harsha had insisted that bees don't buzz. They hum. There's no doubt that's what they're doing right now. The humming grows with each step they take. It's a frenzy as these confused creatures work hard to locate the danger and protect their queen. The smoke may not have reached them, but the sounds of screams had been enough.

"We can't go in the Betadome." Nola reaches out and taps Chase on the back.

"We were never going in there," says Chase. "Why would we?"

Echo and River turn to look at each other.

"Do it, Tuff," says Chase.

Tuff smiles broadly. It's not an expression Echo is used to seeing on his face. It strips years off him. He marches forward with his baton that's burning brightly with fire. He goes directly to the section of net beside the Betadome and holds the flame against it.

"Burn it down!" someone shouts as more Dead Borns carrying torches run forward.

There's a commotion behind Echo as Makk cracks his whip, flicking a queen from the air and Goldie stomps her into the ground.

"Another one!" Makk pumps his fist and looks at the sky. "Come on! Come at me. I'm ready."

It's both endearing and heartbreaking that a boy his age has learned to become such a fighter.

Echo looks back at the net with wide eyes to see it's been set alight at intervals. The tiny flames scurry like spiders, turning the dark gray material to black, which then crumbles to ash and sprinkles to the ground in snowflakes of despair.

The Dead Borns beat at the net with their weapons, some tearing at it with nothing more than their fingertips. Small holes become large holes, which quickly become gaping sections of nothingness.

"Watch out!" someone calls as a large section near the top breaks away and crashes to the ground. The sparks set a woman's clothing alight, and she rolls on the ground to put it out before the fire consumes her just like it had the net.

"Is this a good thing?" River asks, his mouth agape as he looks directly into the zone he once called home.

Echo shrugs. "I think so. We're one zone now. Everyone's in this together."

"Let's hope the Green Borns see it that way." River runs a hand through his hair, leaving a black streak of ash on his forehead.

Echo reaches up to wipe it away. "We'll convince them. If anyone can, it's you."

There's a whirring sound and the people cower as a Worker descends.

"It's okay!" River shouts, catching a glimpse of silver on her disc. "She's the friendly one."

Echo realizes that's what River had been fiddling with in his shirt pocket earlier. He'd called for Nectar with his remote.

The metallic bee is covered in dirt from her efforts in the bunker. She tilts her head at River in the same way she used to look at Flora, awaiting her next command.

"I thought she'd be useful if we needed to break through the net," says River, putting a hand on his twin's companion. "Looks like we didn't need her."

Nectar lifts into the air, her front leg darting out and knocking a queen from the sky. Returning to the ground, she lifts the injured insect in one of her pincers and crushes her.

Echo gasps. "River, that was headed straight for you!"

"Seems we needed her after all." River pats Nectar on the back. Her glassy eyes shine, then she launches herself upward, swatting at the remaining queens circling overhead. One by one their small bodies rain down as the Dead Borns jostle, keen to be the one to crush them into the dirt.

Once Nectar has dealt with every last queen, there's more whirring and Oren's Workers that were hovering high above the net fly off, disappearing in the direction of the Sting.

"Where are they going?" Echo asks.

"I don't know," says River. "But I don't like it."

Before they can speculate further, Nectar flies at the charred remains of the net.

"Everyone, get back!" Chase shouts as Nectar works quickly to safely tear down a huge section of the woven threads that kept generations of Dead Borns safe.

A small piece of netting floats through the air and lands at Echo's feet. She picks it up, pocketing it as a souvenir, wishing her father were alive to see this. He was always proud of her. She's certain that wouldn't have changed if he could see her now. Touching her locket at the thought of him, she promises to continue to make him proud. She's going to plant the seeds encased inside this locket in the Dead Zone one day. This is only just the beginning of what's to come.

"It's so strange," says River, his eyes glued to space where the net once was.

Echo nods, not needing to ask what he means. Green Zone has met Dead Zone. There's no longer a barrier between them. Which means that while they can move freely between the zones, so can the bees.

"Onwards to the Sting!" Chase shouts.

"Wait!" Echo calls, going to stand at the front of the crowd beside Chase. "We need to move very carefully. Oren's queens may be dead, but a sting from a regular bee will kill almost everyone here. Do *not* stir up the bees. Don't swing your weapons. Don't wave your hands. Just a slow and steady pace. Now's not the time to find out if anyone's Immune."

She looks across the gathered crowd nodding their heads. She desperately hopes they can keep to their part of the bargain.

"Move on!" Chase commands. "And you heard Echo. Slow and steady."

He leads the way, walking with confidence. The people follow. For many of them, this is the first time they've stepped foot inside the Green Zone. They've never experienced what it feels like to stand beneath the canopy of the trees they've stared at all their lives. They keep to their end of the bargain, silent and awed, moving slowly as they take the path that will lead them to the Sting.

River holds Echo's hand and they walk at the rear of the group with Nectar marching loyally at his side.

"What do we do when we get there?" Echo whispers. "How will we get in? Oren will surely have locked the doors."

"Let's just get there first," says River. "Maybe we can use Nectar to break our way in."

Echo nods. "Whatever happens, we're getting in."

"Most definitely." River squeezes her hand. "No more zones. Just people."

"Just people," she repeats.

There's a shout ahead and a flurry of movement that has Echo wincing.

"Stay still," she calls as loudly as she dares.

The people go very quiet.

"There's a bee!" someone whispers.

Echo and River move forward. There's a woman writhing on the ground. Her face is purple and she's gasping for air.

"Keep walking," Echo tells everyone. "And stay calm! We're Immune. We can deal with this."

"But that's my sister," another woman sobs. "I can't leave her."

"Go," says River, squatting down to hold the dying woman's hand. "She wouldn't want you to risk yourself. We'll stay with her."

Jupiter appears by the sister's side. They wrap an arm around her and try to lead her away, but she struggles, breaking free and running back to her sister, throwing herself on top of her.

The commotion sends several more bees heading for them and Echo ushers the rest of the people away. "Please," she says, keeping her voice low. "Stay calm and keep walking. It's your best chance. Slow and steady."

The people nod, their eyes laced with fear but their bodies doing as they're told. They march forward to the Sting, desperate to get somewhere they feel safe. *Anywhere.* Even if it's in the heart of enemy land.

Chase cocks a brow at Echo to make sure she's okay.

"We'll catch up," she tells him.

Chase nods his understanding. Being Immune, they can move quickly without danger.

Echo turns back to River to see there are now two dead women at her feet, the bloated sisters holding each other in their last moments.

"That should never have happened." River closes the women's eyes then stands with clenched fists. He picks two flowers from a nearby bush and puts them on top of the sisters, then loops his arm around Echo. Her heart swells with love. It wasn't all that long ago River had thought of her people as Dead Borns. And now he mourns their loss as if they were his own.

She gives him a long hug and they hold still. Several bees hover around them, then seem to decide they're completely uninteresting and move on.

"We need to go." River kisses the top of Echo's head and they walk quickly to catch up to the others, Nectar gliding along beside them.

The path is clear and Echo's chest lightens a little when they don't find any more bodies along the way. The Dead Borns have finally learned to listen and work as a team. They've come so far since all of this started. She just wishes there wasn't still so far they have to go.

The Sting soon looms before them, but the scene isn't anything like Echo expected.

There's not a single Dead Born waiting at the front doors. Even Chase is missing.

"Where is everyone?" Echo asks. "Oren couldn't possibly have let them in."

"Unless..." River comes to a stop and swallows. "Unless they've all just walked into a trap."

CHAPTER

SIXTEEN

RIVER

River and Echo break into a run and he wonders if her heart is thudding as hard as his. There's no way Oren would've just let the Dead Borns walk into the Sting. He'd kill every single one of them first.

The sun glints off the glass doors, meaning River can't see inside. He squints as he works to inject more speed into his legs, even as he dreads what they're going to find. Having all the Dead Borns in one place is actually genius. Oren can exterminate them all in one fell move...

"Maybe they've gone somewhere else," Echo pants, her tone dubious.

There's nowhere nearby that would be safe.

The doors slide open as they stop in front of them, the shadows of the interior revealing the inside of the foyer.

It's full. Teeming. Overflowing with moving, frowning Dead Borns.

River and Echo stop in the airlock, stunned and breathing hard. Everyone who's made it this far is alive.

"Pax," River says over his shoulder to Nectar. The foyer is

130

large but is now overflowing with bodies. She'd never fit. She powers down, crouching beside the Sting.

The second set of sliding doors open, and they enter, trying to understand what's going on. The Dead Borns shuffle to let them in, their frowns dissolving as they register who just joined them.

"It's River," someone shouts.

"And Echo!"

"They'll know what to do."

River suppresses the urge to glance at Echo. She'd be as uncomfortable as he is with the smiles rippling through the crowd.

They've been fighting for justice.

They didn't expect to lead it.

Or be the hope to fuel it.

The crowd parts and Chase pushes through. "About time," he says, his features tight. "The elevators aren't working. And every other door is locked."

River frowns as he and Echo follow Chase to the elevators. Someone pats him on the back while a woman reaches out to Echo and gives her hand a quick squeeze. People shuffle out of the way, exposing the white doors that River used throughout his childhood. One glance reveals what River already expected —the hexagonal buttons beside it aren't lit up like they always have been. They're blank and dark. Dead.

"They're shut tight," Chase says darkly, watching as Sledge and Vern try to open it.

They have their fingers dug into the crack where the doors meet, teeth bared and necks straining as they pull back, trying to open them. Others are doing the same with the sets of elevator doors on the perimeter of the large hexagonal space. Reed is throwing his weight against one, grunting each time he hits the unyielding white.

Every elevator remains tightly closed.

"Oren controls all parts of the Sting," River says flatly. "We won't be able to access them."

"There's the emergency exit doors," Echo offers. "We've used them before."

Chase grunts, turning toward the nearest one. "Oren took care of those, too."

River and Echo follow, although he already knows Chase is telling the truth. River's still surprised when they discover the handles are gone. Oren not only locked the doors, he removed any way to open them.

River's hands form fists at his side. Turns out, Oren had no intention of letting the Dead Borns in. In fact, this was probably one of his sick mind games. Give them false hope by allowing them into the foyer. Then ensure they can't get any further.

Their options are to stay here and starve, or go out to the Green Zone. And die if they're not Immune.

That's Oren's goal. Let every Dead Born be stung, culling the Vulnerables. Leaving him with only true Immunes. The only ones worthy of living.

Chase crosses his arms. "We can get something heavy and break the door in. Maybe if we got a piece of metal, we could pry it open."

Which would mean going out to the Green Zone to find what they need.

They're doing exactly what Oren would expect them to, yet what other choice do they have?'

Echo's hand brushes River's. "We'll go. We're Immune."

River turns to her, a smile lifting up his lips. He'd been totally absorbed in the disgust at Oren's plans that he'd forgotten they have a way to thwart them. "Yes, we will."

Even Chase grins. "Well? What are you waiting for?"

River and Echo spin around and hurry back toward the airlock. Although there's no immediate threat, he can't shake the sense of urgency. There's only one certainty in this war for Immunity—Oren is unpredictable and single-minded in his plans for extermination of Vulnerables. That makes him dangerous in ways River can't even imagine.

The crowd parts as they make their way through the foyer, some even smiling encouragingly. The faith that River and Echo will succeed shines from several people's eyes. Others look like they're holding their breaths, too scared to hope, even as they already are.

"I'll come," Makk calls out. "I'm also Imm—"

River looks over his shoulder to see Tuff standing behind his son, his hand clamped over his mouth. Makk's shoulders drop on a frustrated huff and River's lips twitch. Seems Makk's learning what it's like to have a father around. One day he'll appreciate the gift.

Echo reaches the glass doors first, slowing as she waits for them to open. She takes one step. Two. Then reaches the doors themselves, her toes brushing the glass.

They don't open.

Frowning, River joins her, stepping back and forward again, knowing there's a sensor above.

The sliding doors remain closed.

Beyond them, the airlock is empty, the second set of glass doors also firmly shut. River glances above, his frown turning to a scowl when he registers the small red light above them. All his life that light's been green. He never knew it could be any other color.

No one has ever shut down the doors so no one can come in.

Or leave.

River presses a hand to the glass. "I don't like this," he says, uneasiness slithering up his spine.

"Why would Oren lock us in?" Echo asks in a whisper.

River doesn't know, but he also knows he doesn't want to find out.

A startled cry has them spinning round. The Dead Borns are moving in a rush, something making their eyes wide. River and Echo start to walk to whatever has fear rippling through the crowd.

They see it before they've taken more than a handful of steps.

A glass column is rising from the center of the foyer, just as a false ceiling is expanding from one of the walls, cutting off the rising sea of balconies above their heads.

Hexagonal and as wide as River's arms, the column ascends steadily, the glass thick and crystal clear. The Dead Borns continue to move back, giving it a wide berth as they stare at it, open-mouthed.

"It's empty," Echo says, sounding as perplexed as River feels.

The inside of the hexagon holds nothing but air.

Chase and Reed appear beside them, also looking uneasy. No one speaks as the glass column continues to rise, its rim now above the height of the crowd. Then one body length above. Then two. It continues until it reaches all the way to the top of the false roof, locking in as if it's designed to be here. Then it goes still and silent.

"I like this even less," Echo mutters.

River takes her hand, communicating his agreement with a soft squeeze. "Oren has something planned."

Echo looks up at him, and he wonders if she's aware that her other hand just came up to rest on her stomach. A potent mix of emotions swirl in her dark gaze. Apprehension. Fear.

And fierce determination.

Whatever comes next, she'll fight it.

River nods. They'll fight it.

A piercing, terrified scream has them turning back to the glass column. It's followed by a hoarse cry. Then a man dropping to his knees to their left with a defeated moan.

Echo grips River's hand so tight it hurts as she looks up. "No..." she gasps.

He also raises his gaze, his lungs freezing in his chest. Bees are pouring from a hole in the ceiling inside the column. Hundreds of bees. Thousands of bees.

More bees than River's ever seen in one place.

They tumble down, becoming a river of black and gold as their numbers continue to swell. They steadily fill the column, swirling around in agitated waves. Although the glass is thick, the steady hum coming from within is unmistakable.

"He wouldn't..." Reed breathes.

"He already has," Chase snarls.

The Dead Borns scamper as far back against the walls as they can. Some are sobbing. Children whimper. Several frantically try to get the elevator or emergency exit doors open. Even more run to the glass doors, banging their fists on them.

"Nectar!" River gasps, remembering the Worker is outside. "She can break through the glass." Just like she did in the Hive.

He sprints, Echo beside him as they push their way through to the airlock. River pulls out the small controller in his pocket as they go.

"Proelium!" he shouts. "Nectar, proelium!"

But she remains powered down outside the Sting, her silver disc pulsing gently as she slumbers, waiting for her next order.

The one River is screaming as loud as he can.

But Nectar can't hear him.

He yanks the controller out, pressing his thumb to the

button as he does. Nectar remains still. River lifts his arm high, pointing the controller at her, and presses it again.

Nothing.

He holds his thumb down, pressing hard enough that he worries he'll break the black square, then keeps it there.

Nectar remains unmoving. Even though she's the one thing that can break them out of the heinous trap they've found themselves in.

Echo slumps. "It can't reach her through the walls of the Sting."

"Or Oren's jammed the signal," Reed says, his voice heavy as he comes to stand beside River. "He's thought of everything."

"Look out!" Sledge roars, and they jump out of the way just in time as he propels himself at the doors.

Sledge hits the glass with a sickening thud, bouncing off and stumbling backward. He grunts, shakes his head, and tries again. This crash is harder, yet just as useless. His chest pumping in and out, Sledge walks further away this time. He's going to take more of a run up.

River goes to join him. It feels fruitless, the glass is as thick as the walls, yet they have to try. And maybe two people throwing themselves at the glass holding them captive might make a difference. Maybe it's not as impenetrable as it looks.

"River!" Echo cries out.

He turns, seeing she's pointing at the ceiling.

Because the cylinder is slowly, undeniably descending.

"We need to stop it!" he shouts, now running back toward the center of the foyer.

Echo joins him as he plasters his back against one of the hexagonal panes, slaps his palms against the glass, and pushes up with every fiber of his being. Seeing what he's trying to do, Echo moves to an adjoining one, pressing her back against it and hauling up. Reed joins them. Then Chase. And River's father and Sledge and Jupiter and anyone else who can find an opening around the column.

As one, they strain and heave. Groans fill the air, punctured by the squeal of skin sliding on glass as collectively, they push with all their might. The column groans as it meets resistance, even shuddering as it fights the opposition to its downward trajectory.

"It's working," River's dad gasps. "We've stopped it."

Even as River realizes they won't be able to hold this forever, he feels his knees bend as the column lowers.

They're losing.

It's coming down.

River pushes back, a roar climbing up his throat and exploding out of him as he adds his force of will to his desperate pushing. Echo moans at the strain, the tendons on Chase's neck look like taut rope.

The column drops another few millimeters, taking the people fighting its descent with it. Jupiter falls as their knees give out, then quickly scrambles up, throwing themselves against the glass to keep pushing.

Even though it's not working.

"A bee!" shouts a woman. "It's—"

She screams, but the sound is cut off with a garbled gasp. Panic explodes in the foyer, people running and screaming, even though there's nowhere to go. And no one to hear them.

Even though the noise sends the bees into a furious frenzy, faint pings sounding as they throw themselves against the glass.

"Got it," comes Makk's voice from the melee.

Except River doesn't feel relief. Within minutes, probably seconds, more bees will escape. Thousands more. And they won't be able to stop these with flicks of material and sticks and insecticide. There will be too many.

"Push harder," Chase screams.

Everyone doubles down on their effort, dredging up strength born of desperation. Born of the drive to live. Sweat trickles down River's temples as he pants, his eyes squeezed tightly shut, pushing oxygen into his muscles. He can't be a witness to mass murder. He has to try.

The column shifts another few millimeters, showing him how useless the fight is. He opens his eyes, wanting to look at Echo, wishing there was something to say.

He's sorry.

He loves her.

The world their child will grow up in will be born of death.

His gaze never makes it to her. The elevators catch River's attention and he gasps. His muscles go slack. His mind rebels.

The doors are opening. It has to be Oren, he's the only one arrogant and cruel enough to walk into a death trap of his own making, no doubt safely ensconced in a white suit.

He's here to gloat.

And to collect those who survive.

The Immunes.

CHAPTER

SEVENTEEN

ECHO

The doors to the elevator open. Echo has to work hard to maintain her position with her back pressed against the deadly glass column when she sees who it is.

It's not Oren.

It's not even a Green Born.

Or a Dead Born.

It's Lyra.

And she's brought a dozen other Moon Workers with her.

They march out of the elevator clutching their scythes. Fray and Cascade clamber to hold the doors before they close again.

"What the..." Sledge gasps from the other side of the column.

"They're from the Extinction Zone," River explains.

The Moon Workers scan the terrified faces in the foyer, who all take several steps away from the new arrivals.

"It's okay!" Echo shouts. "They're not here to hurt us."

Lyra gasps, seeming genuinely surprised to see her. "What are you doing here?"

Echo was about to ask Lyra the same question, but it's

taking all her effort just to hold up the column. It slips another few millimeters and a bead of sweat runs down her forehead. Her palms are also damp, making it nearly impossible to stop the inevitable descent. They can't let those thousands of angry bees go free inside this space! Even with the elevator working, they can only rescue twenty people at a time. She has to try harder.

Lyra runs up to the column, her eyes widening when she sees what it contains. Echo twists to look up, wincing as two bees escape from the tiny gap at the top. Makk is ready with his whip and the other Dead Borns hold still, desperate not to aggravate the bees further.

"We need help!" River pants. "We have to stop this thing from lowering."

"What do I do?" Lyra scans the column.

"Jam your scythe in the base," puffs Echo, hoping that might work. "Hurry!"

Lyra does as she's told. The pointed metal tip of her weapon slides into the small gap between the column and the floor, and there's instant relief in the resistance of the glass against Echo's slippery hands. Cautiously, she steps away, seeing River and the others doing the same.

There's a loud crack and Echo ducks as Makk's whip sails over her head, taking a bee down with it.

"Got another one!" he cheers.

Several other Dead Borns have taken Makk's lead and stand with thick strips of fabric ready to strike any stray bees out of the air. They've spent their whole lives hiding from these creatures but no more. They're ready to fight. To protect each other, and themselves. As long as the bees don't start escaping too quickly then they have a chance.

Chase turns to the room. "Everyone stay calm and keep back."

"I'll get the first load of people out of here!" Cascade shouts from the propped open doors of the elevator.

Echo looks around at the masses of people who need to be moved. Taking them one group at a time will take far too long. And there's always the risk of Oren disabling the elevator.

"Go one floor up!" she calls to Cascade, glad it's someone who knows her way around the Sting. "Head for the stairs and come back down. See if you can open the door from the other side."

Cascade nods, and a group of Dead Borns pile into the elevator. For a moment, Echo's afraid they might fight over who gets to go first, but the opposite seems to be the case. This group of downtrodden souls has finally learned they have a better chance if they look after each other before taking care of themselves. Echo's chest swells with pride to be a Dead Born.

The elevator doors close behind the people jammed in there and River lets out a sigh. Clearly, he'd harbored the same fears about Oren preventing their escape.

Echo turns to Lyra. "You got here just in time."

"We didn't come to save you," Lyra says, shuffling her feet.

"But you did," says River. "And we're so grateful."

Lyra shifts her hair in front of her face and averts her eyes from River.

"It's okay." He puts a hand on her arm. "I know who you are. You're Iris."

Lyra recoils at the sound of her original name, then scans the room. "Is my mother here?"

River hesitates, his face turning pale.

"She's not," says Echo, deciding that's a conversation for later. "These are Dead Borns. Oren destroyed our net. We're seeking safety."

"Doesn't look too safe," one of the other Moon Workers grumbles, his eyes still stuck to the column of angry bees.

Chase takes a step closer. "If you didn't come here to help, why are you here?"

"Hi Reed," says Lyra, using a shy voice Echo hasn't heard before as she bites down on her lip.

"Ah...hi." Reed furrows his brow, seeming confused.

Echo realizes they must know each other from when Lyra lived in the Green Zone.

"But you're not a Vulnerable..." Lyra frowns in confusion.

"Turns out we all are." Reed shrugs dismissively. "But we don't have time for that now."

"You didn't answer my question," Chase presses. "What are you doing here?"

Lyra looks at the bees as she speaks, not seeming to be able to meet Chase's gaze directly. "Things changed in the Moon Zone after Celeste and Luna came."

"It's River and Echo," River splutters as Echo suppresses a smile. "We don't go by those names."

Lyra nods. "Samir went back to his birth name as well. He makes everyone call him Ruff. I prefer Lyra. I don't want anything my mother gave me."

"Is Ruff here?" Echo asks, getting a flashback of him throwing Manu off the roof of the building.

Tuff steps in closer, clearly interested to hear what became of his brother.

Lyra shakes her head. "He's trying to turn the Moon Zone into a replica of the Green Zone. He even painted over our wall of memories. We don't Remember anymore. A group of us decided we had enough. The Green Zone may have cast us out, but they can't keep us out."

"Yeah!" the other Moon Workers repeat, banging their scythes on the tiles. "They can't keep us out."

"But they can keep us in," Vern mutters. "Or at least they think they can."

"Oren lured us here," River explains. "He locked us in. Then this column emerged, along with the ceiling."

One of the Moon Workers shifts uncomfortably as he stares at the bees. "Can we talk away from this thing?"

Chase checks Lyra's scythe to make sure it's secure. So far, the column appears to be holding tight. They move closer to the stairwell, hoping Cascade will emerge at any moment to let them through.

"How did you get in here, Lyra?" Echo asks, wondering if there's another exit they hadn't considered.

"Same way we were pushed out," a Moon Worker answers for her. "Through that creepy place with all the dead bodies."

Echo nods. Oren hadn't thought to secure the Sovereign graveyard. It's good to know he doesn't think of *everything*.

The door to the stairwell bursts open. Except it's Fray, not Cascade.

A relieved cheer erupts over the crowd as people head toward the door, not caring who opened it just as long as there's a way out of this death trap.

"Come on!" Fray calls, propping open the door.

The glass column groans as the metal blade on Lyra's scythe starts to warp.

Chase takes a scythe from one of the other Moon Workers and jams it in the gap on the other side. "This thing isn't going to hold for long. One way or another, these bees are coming out."

"I'm ready for them!" Makk shouts, flexing his bare torso. "Bring it on!"

His mother and father each put a hand on his back and firmly steer him toward the exit, despite his passionate protests.

"Keep calm," Chase instructs the crowd as people start pouring into the stairwell. "Remember, we have just as much right to be here as those Green Borns. They're no better than us!"

"Where do we go?" a man shouts back, directing his question at River and Echo.

"Spread out!" River calls back. "It makes it harder for Oren to attack."

Chase clenches his fists. "We need to find that evil scum."

"What we need is unity," says Echo firmly as they follow the last of the people to the stairwell. "The Dead Zone and the Extinction Zone are working as one. We need the Green Borns to join our side. Oren can't win if literally everyone in the world is against him."

"My mother would never turn on him," Lyra says quietly. "She chose him over me."

"Lyra." Echo draws in a breath, realizing they can't put off telling her any longer. "Your mother died."

Lyra's eyes fly wide open. "How?"

"Queen bee venom," she says, sticking to the necessary facts.

"Was it fast?" Lyra asks.

Echo glances at River, but Chase is the one who clears his throat.

"It was a painful death," he says. "Iris, I'm sorry but your mother wasn't a good person."

Lyra nods as she pulls back her shoulders. "She left me in the Extinction Zone to die. Her own daughter. She got what she deserved."

"Couldn't agree more," Chase says.

Reed puts a comforting hand on Lyra's back as he leads her into the stairwell.

Echo and River are the last to leave the foyer. They turn to look at the groaning column that's determined to sink down into the floor.

"Look!" Echo gasps.

A large crack has appeared at the base of the column and is spearing up the glass like a bolt of lightning. Two more cracks join it on either side and race to the top with breathtaking speed. The splintering sound is terrifying. Like a giant beast crunching on bones. The cracks quickly spread, obscuring their view of the frantic bees as the clear glass becomes a maze of jagged lines.

Echo winces as the glass blows out, shattering and raining down on the foyer. River presses Echo to his chest, and she finds herself with her hands protectively across her stomach, her first thoughts of her baby.

For two beats of her pounding heart, the bees circle in the shape of the tall spiral of the column. Then realizing the walls to their prison have vanished, they scatter in every direction, the hailstorm of glass morphing into one made of black and gold.

River hauls Echo into the stairwell, slamming the door behind her and heaving for breath. Not even an Immune could survive the sheer number of stings an army that size could deliver.

"Are you hurt?" he pants.

She shakes her head. "I'm fine. You?"

"Also fine."

Echo shakes her head, trying to process the enormous quantity of bees. She never expected to see so many of them all in one place at the same time. "They'll be right through the building in no time."

"That's what Oren wants," says River. "These aren't queens. Just bees. Only the true Immunes will survive."

Echo shakes her head. "He can't do that."

"He just did." River leads her up the stairs.

The others are far ahead and they walk quickly with no

idea what floor they might have gone to. They emerge on one of the residential floors only to find every door firmly closed. Echo knocks on the closest one.

"Open up!" she cries. "We need to talk."

"Go back to where you came from!" comes the reply from inside. "You'll kill us all."

"It's not us who's killing you," she pleads. "You must listen. Oren has released bees into the building. He wants to exterminate anyone who's not Immune."

"Then I'm definitely not opening the door," a man gasps. "Go away!"

"It's no use," says River, who had similar luck a few doors down. "We need to get to the open wall of the Hive to see if Nectar can hear us from there."

Echo squeezes River's hand. "Genius."

They head back to the stairs, passing a few Dead Borns on the way.

"Where do we go?" they ask, eyes darting around their strange surroundings.

"Look for food," says River. "And try to convince anyone you can find to join our side."

"Got it." The Dead Borns dart away. They may be frightened but there's the unmistakable glint of hope in their eyes. That alone has made the fight worthwhile.

Echo and River head up to the Hive, not surprised to find Reed already there, sifting through the burned shell of what used to be his beloved LaB.

"No sign of Oren," he tells them. "His office is in ruins. He must have set up a new one somewhere else."

Echo groans. The Sting is enormous. "He could be anywhere."

Reed nods. "Chase and the Moon Workers have gone to search."

There's a crackling noise and they all look up at a speaker box that's dangling from a wire in the collapsed ceiling.

"Hello, Dead Borns," says Oren's honey-coated voice. "I'm disappointed you didn't seem to appreciate the welcome gift I tried to give you upon your arrival."

"More like a farewell gift," River growls.

"But never mind," Oren continues. "Those little presents are flying around the building right now looking for you. And Green Borns....either stay in your rooms or help me to remove the filthy threat that's infiltrated our peaceful lives. Dead Borns don't belong here. You know I reward loyalty. I'll look after you. Like I always have."

"Sure you have," grumbles Reed.

"Oh, and one more thing," Oren adds. "If our new visitors don't leave the building before nightfall, I'm going to destroy the last of our serpentwood. And you know what that means."

The speaker crackles and falls silent.

They *do* know what that means.

No serpentwood means no Immunity.

No serpentwood means only the Immune can live.

EIGHTEEN

RIVER

River stares at the speaker, knowing the ramifications of Oren's ultimatum, but still resisting them. With no Sovereign, he's threatened the only way to create Immunity. By destroying the serpentwood.

And by pitting the Green Borns against the Dead Borns, he's trying to deepen the divide.

"What the heck do we do now?" Reed asks, spearing his fingers into his hair. "There's no way the Green Borns are going to let the Dead Borns remain in the Sting."

River takes the controller out of his pocket and turns to stride to the missing wall so he can see if he can call Nectar, only to pause. Then freeze.

This is the last place he saw Flora. This was where they had their final conversation.

This is where she took the remaining shred of hope of ever finding the Sovereign straight over the edge.

A hand presses to his chest a moment before Echo slips in front of him. "You couldn't have done anything, River," she says, her eyes soft with understanding. "She'd made her decision."

River swallows, trying to move the hard, jagged lump lodged in his throat. "How... Why would she choose that?" he whispers hoarsely.

"She was hurting." Echo's hand presses more firmly against his chest. Against his heart. "Sometimes it's hard to see past that."

He nods, understanding, yet not understanding at the same time. He just wishes Flora was still here. Mostly because she's his twin. Partially because now the unity they're fighting for is so much harder without the promise of Immunity.

Echo's hand slides down, her fingers clasping the controller in his hand. "I'll try." River releases it, glad for her understanding and compassion. He can't bear the thought of looking over the edge.

Echo walks a few feet away, facing the gaping hole and lifting the controller. Her hand tenses as she presses it, then waits.

Long seconds pass and nothing happens. Nectar doesn't appear.

"Yep, Oren's jammed the signal," River says heavily.

Echo returns to River, passing him the controller. "We'll need to wait until we're beside her so we can use a voice command." She glances at the elevator. "Right now, we need to help the Dead Borns."

She's right. Oren's trying to incite the war they've avoided until now.

They reach the elevators, only to discover the doors refuse to open. Oren has once again been a step ahead. River's lips twist. "The stairs it is."

He's just opened the door when Reed speaks. "The Dead

Borns are all over the place. How are we going to keep them all safe?"

River and Echo glance at each other, neither of them speaking. Because neither of them has an answer. The Sting is a massive building. Who knows where the Dead Borns have scurried to, especially now they know they're seen as a threat to every Green Born's future.

The industrial floors directly below the Hive are silent and still. The Green Borns abandoned them as they holed up in their rooms. The Dead Borns either haven't found them, or saw there's nowhere to hide among the machines to produce glass and metal and timber.

They continue to descend, and River's heart sinks with each floor they inspect. Just as he expected, each one is empty and silent. All that greets them are corridors of closed doors, their voices bouncing around the white walls as they wait for a response.

The Green Borns are ignoring them.

The Dead Borns are no doubt desperately trying to seek shelter.

"We'll keep checking every floor," Echo says, walking back toward the door to the stairs.

River follows, knowing there's no other choice. Their greatest threat is the Green Borns taking up Oren's challenge and leaving their rooms, becoming more than a fragmented, scared group of people. Their unity will be a threat to the Dead Borns, just like the Dead Born unity has become a threat to Oren.

And Oren knows that. Which is exactly why he issued his public threat.

They've just reached the door, Reed behind them, when it flies open. Echo and River reel back, bumping into Reed.

Makk beams from the doorway. "There you are! Do you know how many stairs I've had to climb looking for you?"

River tries to calm his thumping heart. "Makk, what are you—"

"I counted, actually. I didn't even know numbers went that high! So I had to make up some words just to—"

"Makk," Echo says, gripping his arm. "Why were you looking for us?"

His grin widens. "We've found food!" he says excitedly.

"Food?" Echo asks. "Where?"

River knows exactly where the Dead Borns are. Reed's grunt behind him confirms he's realized it, too.

"They're in the eating hall," River says to Echo. The level where the Green Borns would come together for meals.

Makk nods. "I call it the White Room of Plenty." He angles his head. "Is *everything* white around here?"

River steps past him into the stairwell. "Pretty much," he says, conscious that Echo commented on it when she first arrived, too. And now that River's been away, now that the Dead Zone has become more of a home than the Sting ever was, he can't help but notice it, too.

Oren's mission to keep the people of Green Zone calm has far more layers to it. He wanted compliance. He wanted peace because most were never truly Immune. He wanted everyone's mind to be as blank as each tile.

"So there's a lot of food in there?" Echo asks, looking more and more alarmed.

River instantly realizes why.

The Dead Borns will be in a frenzy. Any semblance of calm will be shattered by their lifelong desperate drive to survive.

Echo and River break into a run simultaneously. "This way," he says, leading as they descend a few more floors, then shoving open a door.

They burst into the large room that extends over an entire floor, then skid to a stop, Makk and Reed behind them.

The expansive room is familiar and alien at the same time. The eating hall where River's family would have most of their meals stretches out, everything as it always was. But that was back when River believed Oren was his father. When he believed his mother was happy. And when Flora was alive.

The rows and rows of white tables are surrounded by white chairs. A long bench extends behind them, the kitchens behind that. Even from here, River can see the crates of fruit and vegetables. The loaves of bread stacked on shelves. The barrels of preserved olives and mushrooms and asparagus beneath them.

And yet the Dead Borns are all sitting on the chairs, milling about, looking relieved to see River and Echo. Most are munching on a chunk of bread, a few are wiping the juice from a piece of fruit from their chin. A young man spits out the pit of an olive into his hand, looks at it, then pops it back in his mouth. The Moon Workers are here, too, leaning against their scythes and tools.

No one is fighting. Gorging. Panicking.

Chase appears from behind the long bench where River used to collect his food and walks toward them. "We each had something for now. While we decide what our next step is."

"That's…great," Echo says, sounding just as astounded as River feels.

Chase glances from the Dead Borns to River and Echo. "What do you think we should do next?"

The shocked feeling grows. The leader of the Razers is asking them?

"We need to hide," Goldie calls out, drawing Makk closer to her.

Other women and a few men draw their children to them, nodding in agreement.

Sledge crosses his arms. "We need to fight."

A few grumbles of assent ripple through the Dead Borns.

"We need to protect the serpentwood," Reed mutters, shifting his weight uneasily.

River and Echo move simultaneously, reaching to grasp the other's hand. "We need to unite," he calls out.

"The only way forward is to work together," Echo adds.

The Dead Borns don't object, simply stare back expectantly.

River draws in a deep breath, trying to keep the motion steady. "We need to convince the Green Borns of that."

That gets a reaction. The Dead Borns collectively shrink back.

"They'd never…"

"They hate us."

"They think we're the enemy!"

And Oren's only reinforced that.

"We have to try," Echo says. "Oren's one man. Together, we're many. A force to be reckoned with."

River nods, the proof this is possible staring back at him with every set of eyes in the room. The Dead Borns are here. They haven't fallen on the stacks of food behind them like starving animals. They want to work together. They want a way forward.

The door to the eating hall opens before River can answer, prompting Chase to leap beside River and Echo. He may be willing to seek guidance, but his suspicions are very much alive.

Cascade steps through, her eyes widening when she sees the area is full of Dead Borns.

River smiles. "It's okay. Everyone's safe. We're just—"

Cascade shoves the door open wider. "I told you they'd be here," she sneers.

Dozens of Green Borns pour in, fanning out as they form a line several people deep. Dread fills River's gut. It explodes through every other organ when he sees the Green Borns are carrying weapons. Some have garden tools. A few have knives. Far too many are carrying venom guns.

"Where did you get those?" Echo demands.

Cascade ignores her as she throws her arms out wide. "See? This is where they came. So the selfish fools can eat everything we've worked for."

"We've?" Chase gasps. "You've been in the Dead Zone."

"I'm Green Born and always have been," she snaps. She waves a sweeping hand toward the Dead Borns. "I was never one of them. I'm not some desperate, dirty leech."

River takes a step forward. "Cascade..."

A Green Born called Grove also takes a step, lifting the venom gun he's holding. To think he used to sit only a few tables away from River and his family in this very eating hall. Grove curls his lip in warning.

River stops, frustrated. The Green Borns need to understand that unity is the only solution.

Echo joins him, her hands clenched. "This is exactly what Oren wants. For us to fight. To believe we're enemies."

"Leave and there will be no fight," Cascade says, ensuring her voice carries through the room. "If you don't, we'll lose the serpentwood."

"Not unless we stop Oren first," River says, moving his head so he's speaking to Green and Dead Born alike. "He can't stop us all."

"Enough!" Cascade shouts. "We've spent too long trying to care for you, and this is how you thank us. You filthy creatures have taken enough." She moves closer to the Green Borns, her gaze roaming over the Dead Borns. "Leave or die."

The Dead Borns move closer together, their faces forming dark scowls.

"When will you see us as more than scum?" Jupiter cries out.

Fray punches her fist in the air. "We're not leaving!"

"You'll never order us around again," Sledge snarls.

A chair scrapes as someone picks it up. The Green Borns tense and tighten.

Inevitability hangs heavy in the air.

"No!" River cries out. "This isn't how it has to be!"

Yet it's a tide he can't stop. The Green Borns are the first to move. Grove lifts his venom gun, smiles.

And shoots.

CHAPTER
NINETEEN
ECHO

Echo watches the bullet loaded with venom sailing toward her in slow motion. Her instincts scream at her to move, but how can she in a room filled with Vulnerables? She's Immune, which makes her one of the few people here who can survive being shot.

Bringing her hands to her eyes, she winces.

And waits.

A sharp pain hits her and she sails backward, landing on the floor with a heavy thud. It takes her a few seconds to process that River's sprawled on top of her.

The sense of order that was present in the room only moments earlier shatters as chaos erupts. Echo can hear Chase shouting and the sounds of punches being thrown.

"I'm okay," she tells River. Her arm hurts where the bullet hit her but it's not so bad. Her biggest problem is her airway being cut off by River's bulk. He may not have eaten much lately, but he weighs as much as one of Makk's lellephants. "Can you move off me?"

Nola appears next to them, her face etched in concern as she shakes her son. "River! Wake up!"

Panic stabs Echo in the heart as she realizes he's unconscious. With Nola's help she rolls him off her and onto his back. Glancing up, Echo sees Vern circling them protectively while anarchy continues to rain down around them. Chairs are being used as weapons, tables are being flipped, scythes and shovels are swinging through the air, and pained screams are ringing out.

Looking back at the person who means the most to her in the world, she touches his cheek. "Open your eyes, River. Please!"

His lashes flutter and he groans.

"You were shot with venom," Nola tells him. "But you're fine. We need you to wake up."

"Shot?" Echo's hand goes to her arm where she'd felt the sharp pain. "I was shot."

Nola shakes her head, not removing her eyes from her son. "River pushed you out of the way. He took the bullet."

"The baby," River says. "Is it..."

"The baby's fine," Echo tells him, rolling up River's shirt where she can see blood. The bullet is lodged shallowly in his side. She plucks it out as quickly as she can, hating to see the pain it causes.

Nola quickly presses her sleeve to the wound to stem the bleeding.

"I'm okay," River says, trying and failing to sit up.

"There's a bee!" someone shouts.

"And another!" a woman gasps.

Echo gets to her feet and looks up. Oren's bees are coming through the air vents in the ceiling in a steady stream.

The panic in the room lifts to a whole new level as the

people shift their focus from attacking each other to protecting themselves from the deadly creatures.

"We need to get out of here!" Reed pants as he runs up to Echo. "It's not safe."

Echo's not entirely sure how safe it was before the bees found their way inside, but she finds herself nodding. River withstood being shot with venom, but there would be a limit to how much his body can take at one time.

Chase appears beside Reed, panting. "We're not leaving this room. That would be doing exactly what the Green Borns told us to. The bees will be all over this building. We're staying here."

"We can't stay here just to prove a point," says Echo, wanting to get River somewhere safe just as soon as she can move him.

"Unee. Choom," River mumbles, trying to sit up again. "Uneechoom."

"What's he saying?" Echo looks at Nola.

"Honeycomb!" Nola's face lights up. "He's saying honey-comb. They store some in the kitchen. It'll attract the bees and keep them away from the Vulnerables."

Echo's eyes light up. That might buy them enough time for River to recover and get out of here safely before he gets stung.

"I'll show you where it is," says Reed. "It's a good idea."

Echo looks down at River, not wanting to leave him. "But..."

"Go," Nola tells her, tears filling her eyes. "Let me look after my boy."

Putting a hand to her stomach, Echo nods, unable to deny Nola the same thing that's become so important to her—protecting her child. Especially when Nola was denied the chance of doing it for so long.

"I'll be as fast as I can." She gives River one last, long glance and takes off behind Reed as he leads her through the eating hall.

Chase shields them as they move, and Echo's horrified to see several bodies strewn on the floor. Some are clad in crisp white suits, some in dirty rags. There's even a Moon Worker lying sprawled at the base of one of the serving tables with blood seeping from a wound on his head.

They pass Lyra who has a Green Born in a headlock and Chase glances at Echo apologetically. Two bees are hovering dangerously close by to the scuffle.

"Help her!" Echo says. "Quick!"

He nods, running across to Lyra as Reed steers Echo through a set of double doors with hexagonal windows at the rear of the room.

The kitchens are expansive. Long white gleaming counters are lined with baskets of food, and shelves overhead are stacked with jars of preserves. Echo would have no hope of finding anything in here alone.

Two Dead Borns with bulging cheeks look up from a cupboard.

"We're collecting food for everyone in case we have to run," the woman says, pointing to a sack on the floor.

Echo nods her approval. She can't blame them for helping themselves while they work. This is more food than they've ever seen in their life. "Be quick. They could use your help out there."

"Come on." Reed takes Echo by the sleeve and drags her over to the far corner of the room. He stretches to the back of a row of jars and takes the largest one from the rear. Opening the lid, he withdraws a chunk of honeycomb. Part of it crumbles away as honey oozes back into the jar in glistening drops. Echo's mouth waters as the sweet scent reaches her.

"Take it," says Reed, shoving the jar at her as he reaches for another.

Hugging it to her chest, Echo races out of the kitchen, bracing herself for more death and destruction.

As she re-enters the eating hall, she's struck by how many bees are circling now. Everyone's in danger, Green and Dead Born alike. Many are hiding under tables with their heads in their hands.

"Stop!" Echo shouts as loudly as she can. Climbing up on a table, she takes out two large pieces of sticky honeycomb and holds one in each hand above her head. The bees sense her almost immediately and swarm toward her. She holds still as the honey runs down her wrists, reminding herself that she's Immune. The bees aren't interested in her. It's the honeycomb they want.

The room freezes and falls silent as everyone stares at her.

"Please," she says calmly. "Stop hurting each other. Nobody needed to die here. And nobody else has to. This is exactly what Oren wants."

"Oren loves us," Cascade says, stepping forward.

"Oren only loves those who are Immune." Echo keeps her voice level. The bees are gathering on the honeycomb she's holding, dotting the golden cells with their small black bodies. A few have landed on her sticky hands, but not one of them has stung her. They're too busy gorging on the sweet honey.

"You're Immune," Cascade snaps as the Green Borns gather around their new spokesperson. "Does Oren love you?"

Echo almost laughs. "No, Oren doesn't love me. He has exceptions to his rules. Did he love you when he sent you to the Dead Zone after your Confirmation? Did he love Clover when he discovered she wasn't the Sovereign and sent her back to us to die?"

"He was working for the greater good." Cascade crosses her arms as the Green Borns nod.

"*We're* working for the greater good," says Echo. "The Dead Zone and the Extinction Zone have united. We need you to join us. Together, we can create a world without zones. One where everyone's safe."

"Except we can't be safe," Cascade says. "Not without serpentwood. And if you scum don't leave the Sting immediately, it will all be destroyed."

"And who will destroy it?" says a voice Echo knows so well. She turns her head slowly to see River limping toward her. "The person who you say loves you all so much? That doesn't sound like love to me."

River takes two pieces of honeycomb from the jar and climbs carefully onto the table to stand beside Echo. Some bees leave Echo to inspect the new sweet treats on offer, and yet more come through the vents and fly directly to him. Echo's heart swells with love for this guy. He promised to always stand beside her, and it seems he's taking that very seriously.

"Listen to them," Chase calls out as he marches over to stand at their feet. "These two have risked their lives time and time again to save you. They're doing it again right now. Meanwhile, where's the man you claim loves you? He's hiding somewhere safe while he watches his people die. Is that really who you want to follow?"

"You're lying," says Cascade. "Oren protects the Green Borns. The only reason we're at risk now is because you all insisted on coming here. To *our* home."

"And you were one of them," growls Chase. "Since your Confirmation you've been sheltering in the Dead Zone along with all the other Green Born Vulnerables over the years. Are you saying it was okay for you to move zones when you had to, but not the other way around?"

Cascade shrugs as she flicks her blonde hair behind her shoulders. "I can't help where I was born. I'm not like these awful people."

"Well, I was born in the Green Zone, just like you," says Vern. "And I'm proud to say I'm nothing like you."

Lyra comes forward to stand beside Chase. "I was also born in the Green Zone. You forgot me, along with the rest of my people. My own mother forgot me. It's time we remembered everyone. Nobody should be forgotten. Not you. And not me."

Echo smiles down at Lyra, but her attention is quickly stolen by Cascade letting out a cackling laugh.

"Great speech, Iris," she says. "I hate to tell you, but I haven't thought of you once since you left the Green Zone. Nor has anyone else."

"I've thought of her," Reed says quickly.

Cascade doesn't seem to hear him, keeping her focus on Lyra. "I heard someone ask your mother once if she had any children, and I distinctly heard her say no."

Lyra stiffens as a pained growl escapes her. She reaches to the jar of honeycomb on the table beside her. In one quick movement, she takes out a piece and flings it at Cascade. Her aim is perfect. The sticky clump of wax lands in Cascade's long mane of hair.

Cascade screams, trying desperately to remove it. But it's entwined tightly in the strands and the more she tries to get it out, the more it becomes stuck.

"Stay still!" Echo calls out.

But it's too late. Attracted by both Cascade's panicked movements and the sweet scent of the honeycomb, the bees swarm to her.

"Get them off me!" Cascade screeches.

It seems the Green Borns who were so keen to stand by her

side only moments ago have changed their minds. They quickly move back, leaving her to swat at them alone.

"Stay still!" Echo calls again, as loudly as she dares without stirring up the bees further. With Cascade's Vulnerable blood, the insects will be even more frenzied.

"They're stinging me!" Cascade's voice is garbled now as she collapses to the floor.

"Echo, look," says River, directing his eyes upward at Echo's hands.

The bees have left them to go to Cascade, coating her in a thick blanket as more of them come through the vent. There's nothing more that can be done for Cascade now. Everyone in the room knows it.

As she falls silent, Echo glances away, not wanting to witness another death that didn't need to happen.

"You killed her!" a Green Born snarls at Lyra.

Lyra picks up her scythe and waves it at him. "Don't worry. I'll be sure to remember her."

"Smoke!" shouts Makk, running into the eating hall.

Echo hadn't even realized he'd left.

"Smoke!" he shouts again. "There's a fire in the big garden on the balcony!"

"The serpentwood!" Reed gasps. "We have to stop Oren!"

Echo looks at River and they carefully bring down their hands, putting the honeycomb on the table.

"We have to go to Eden," says River.

She nods.

There's no time to unite the people when it's clear they're not ready to listen. Everything they've worked so hard for is at stake.

Including Immunity.

It's time once again...to run.

CHAPTER
TWENTY

RIVER

River takes the stairs two at a time, his breath already sawing in and out of his throat. He desperately wants to believe that Oren wouldn't do something as drastic and deadly as burning the last of the serpentwood. Surely he's not that short-sighted. That determined to cull anyone who's not Immune. Even though there's no Sovereign, they need serpentwood to make adrenacure.

Without it, there's no way for any Vulnerable to survive a bee sting.

"He wouldn't..." River says aloud, as if that can make it true.

"Oren doesn't bluff," Echo pants, shoving open the door that leads to Eden's floor.

River instantly breaks into heaving coughs. A faint haze hangs in the air, the smell of smoke even fainter. But that's all it takes. He realizes two things. He's just as sensitive to smoke as he is to pollen.

And Oren's not bluffing.

"Are you okay?" Echo says, stopping.

River grabs her hand and runs toward the large doors leading into Eden. "I'm fine," he rasps. They don't have time for him not to be. "I'll be even better once we put the fire out."

Because that's what they have to do.

The alternative isn't one he's willing to consider.

They reach the doors and Echo grabs the handle and shoves. It doesn't move. Scowling, she tries again, but the thick white door doesn't even rattle.

"Let me try," River says, taking a few steps back. He runs at the door, ramming his shoulder into it.

It remains tightly closed.

Another wave of coughs explodes from River and he registers the pale tendrils of smoke seeping from underneath it. They feel like they're getting sucked straight into his lungs and sticking there.

"It's locked," Echo says, kicking the door. "Of course it is."

River looks around, knowing there are only two entrances to Eden. This one, and the balcony.

"Quick," he says, ignoring the wheeze in his throat. "We need Nectar."

They sprint back down the stairs, their feet clattering loudly. River focuses on moving as quickly as possible and getting enough oxygen through his tight throat. Leaving the scent of smoke behind has helped, but the mad dash is demanding air.

Echo skids to a stop as they reach the ground floor. "The foyer..." She doesn't finish her sentence, simply glances at the door uneasily.

They have no idea how many bees are still in there. And it's likely still locked.

Even as Immunes, they aren't going to withstand an attack of that magnitude as they try to get out.

But River turns right instead of left. "This way. Through the atrium."

"Yes!" Echo says, sprinting ahead. "Genius!"

The moment they enter the verdant space, River decides it's not as smart as Echo thinks. The sweet scent of flowers seems to reach in and grab him around the throat, making him wheeze again. It's only a matter of time before Echo notices.

When was the last time he had serpentwood seeds? When Clover gave them to him, which feels like a lifetime ago. And the small packet she gave him is long gone. Lost in the constant fight or flight their life has become.

Which means River needs to be careful.

Once they've saved the serpentwood.

He and Echo weave through the atrium, then climb out the window they've escaped through before. River lands on the grass on the other side, then catches Echo to soften her fall. She lands lightly, her hands on his shoulders, then frowns.

"River, your breathing. It's—"

"Fine. Come on," he says, already dragging her around the Sting toward Nectar. "We don't have time."

Nectar is crouched where they left her, her silver disc pulsing softly. "Vigilans," River calls out the moment they're close enough, ignoring how hoarse he sounds.

Nectar powers up, rising to stand on her six legs.

"Thank goodness," Echo puffs.

Without Nectar, they have no way of getting into Eden.

They climb on, Echo at the front, River behind her, then launch into the sky. They direct her with subtle shifts of their bodies, flying on a Worker almost second nature now.

Echo gasps as they round the Sting and the balcony comes into view. River's heart sinks. His lungs constrict at the sight of the smoke pouring into the sky, dark and voluminous.

"Pull your shirt over your mouth," Echo instructs, doing the same with hers.

River does as she says, drawing in a few lungfuls of air beforehand, hoping it'll be enough. There's no time to consider what will happen if it's not.

Nectar just speared straight into the column of smoke.

River holds his breath as she descends and the balcony appears. Flames are visible, dancing along the railing, pumping out the gray smog that's trying to climb down River's throat. He squints as his eyes sting, ignoring the ache as he refuses to draw breath. He holds onto Echo tightly, focusing on doing the one thing he needs to do. Keep her safe.

Nectar turns as she angles down toward the glass wall that separates Eden from the balcony and River registers there's an area of floor untouched by the fire. She lands and they leap off, hunched down as they try to get below the level of the smoke.

"To the Hive," he shouts to Nectar, hoping it'll be safe. It's the easiest place for them to get back to her.

She lifts, swallowed by the plumes of gray, and disappears from sight.

"River!" Echo gasps, pointing to the interior of Eden.

He looks through the glass, his own surprise jolting through him. Eden is green and lush. Untouched by fire.

They look back at the flames devouring the vegetation on the balcony. "Oren's only burned the plants out here," River says.

A puff of smoke hits them just as River draws in a breath. His lungs convulse as smoke coats them and he's wracked by furious coughing.

"Quick, we need to get inside," Echo says, tugging him toward the doors.

To his relief, they slide open, then shut behind them, enclosing them in the untainted air of Eden. River's coughing slows, then peters to sporadic spasms. Echo leans back, relief filling her features. She glances back at the burning balcony.

"Oren only started a fire out there."

River straightens, his breath still a wheeze. He looks over his shoulder at the rows of plants, then out to the balcony. "The adult serpentwood are gone. But the immature plants and the seedbank look untouched."

"He was bluffing," Echo breathes.

River clenches his jaw. "He enjoys manipulating us."

Echo shakes her head. "And keeping us busy. We still need to put that fire out."

"There are hoses," River says, pointing to one on each side of the glass wall. "We use them to water the plants in here."

Echo runs to the one on their left. "Hurry!"

River darts to the hose on the right and grabs the nozzle. "Just pull and it'll extend," he shouts to her. "We'll need enough to reach the doors."

They do it simultaneously, intent on yanking out the length they need.

At the first tug, there's a click, making him freeze. The hoses are practically smooth and silent, like everything else in the Sting. They've never clicked.

"Echo," he shouts. "It's a trap—"

The first explosion detonates near the opposite doors, and the force sends River reeling back and crashing into the wall. He grunts at the painful impact, already pushing himself back. "Echo!" he rasps.

The second explosion hits River like a wall, but he's already braced himself. He weathers the blast of hot air and burning debris as he rushes to Echo. She's sprawled on the ground beside the wall, pale and still.

"Echo," he cries again, falling to his knees. "Echo!"

Her lashes flutter, sending a tsunami of relief through him.

River takes her into his arms, scanning for blood. "Are you okay? Are you hurt?"

Echo shakes her head. "Nothing's broken," she croaks, shifting her body and wincing. She instinctively curls her arms around her stomach. "As far as I can tell."

"Oren knew if someone got in here they'd try to use the hoses," River says, fury flashing through him. "He set us up."

Echo goes to answer, but her gaze is drawn past his shoulder. Her eyes widen. "River..."

He feels the heat before he turns to look over his shoulder, registering the inferno engulfing Eden. His breath evaporates in his lungs. His pulse becomes a frantic rush of adrenaline.

The first rows of plants are nothing more than blackened skeletons as a wall of fire marches forward, finding more and more fuel. Flames climb up the walls and lap at the ceiling, searching for something more tangible. The heat pouring off has River's skin feeling blanched and desiccated.

The smoke has his whole torso seizing.

He leaps to his feet, bringing Echo with him and they both have to raise their arms to shield their faces from the heat.

"Quick, the balcony," Echo shouts over the roar of the flames.

They turn, only to stop.

The fire that started there first is now a living creature feasting on the infrastructure. Whatever plants on there are long incinerated, their ash filling the sky. The floor is a sea of flames, the walls on either side are black and peeling.

"It won't be safe," River says, trying to shout, but it only comes out as a hoarse rasp followed by a deep, hacking cough.

As if to prove him right, the railing on the balcony groans. A second later, the whole thing sags, warped and twisted.

With Nectar gone, the balcony's a dead end.

They turn back to the interior of Eden. River pulls Echo

close to his side, trying to shield her from the heat, assaulted by another set of rib-rattling coughs.

Echo's fingers grip his shirt as she looks up at him. "We have to get out of here. Think River, are there any other doors? Maybe somewhere we can hide?"

He blinks, then looks up, realizing the answer is yes. "The seed bank!" he gasps, once more reduced to spasming lungs.

Echo braces him as he doubles over. "Where?" she shouts as the roar gets louder.

As the flames grow.

He points to their right. "A...door."

Echo squints, tears running down her face as the smoke trapped in the room steadily descends. "I see it!" she cries out. She turns back to River, clasping his face, her hands trembling. "We need to run. It's our only hope."

He nods, no longer able to speak.

A loud crash has them both flinching. A flurry of embers whip around them, one landing on River's cheek and instantly stinging. He slaps it away, his head swimming and vision blurring.

Echo yanks his shirt up over his mouth and onto his nose. "Hold it there."

He does as he's told, trying to think beyond the lack of air getting through the vice around his throat.

Another crash, this one bigger than the last, sends a second wave of heat and embers at them.

"Now!" Echo shouts.

They break into a run, their shirts over the bottom half of their faces, hunching low. River focuses hard on the process of putting one foot in front of the other. He even manages it for a short distance. But then he stumbles. He can barely feel his feet. All he knows is they're weighted with lead.

Echo slips under his arm, bracing him. "Come on. We're almost there."

He shakes his head, wanting to tell her to save herself, but he doesn't have the air. Nor would she listen. So he hobbles, trying to lean on her as little as possible as they beeline for the door only a few feet away.

Except the fire is coming closer. The smoke is thicker. The heat is singeing the very air.

River trips, disentangling himself from Echo so he doesn't take her with him. He hits the ground, registering how warm it is as his hands break his fall. He gasps, trying to breathe, trying to give his body the oxygen it so desperately needs, only to find it's useless. He's not sure he can even feel his chest anymore.

"Oh no you don't," Echo growls.

Hands slip under his arms, hauling him up. And then he's half-staggering, half-dragged toward the door. Echo hisses as she clamps onto the handle, no doubt burning her hand, then shoves it open.

"Thank goodness," she gasps, probably terrified that it was locked.

River's legs give out the moment they enter, once more crashing to the floor. Except this one is cooler. The air's not quite as thick. He hears the door slam closed, muting the sound of the fire on the other side.

He rolls onto his back, finding Echo hovering above him. "You need serpentwood," she whispers, her face agonized.

Except Oren just burned it all in some twisted show of power. The adult plants. The rows of young plants in various stages of growth. The seeds—

River jerks with shock. "The...seeds!"

Echo leans in closer. "What seeds?" She looks around, eyes widening when she realizes where they are.

The seed bank. They're in the room that holds the tiny grains of the future. Thousands of them.

She turns back to River, breathing hard. "There's serpentwood seeds?" She grips his shoulders. "Tell me there are serpentwood seeds in here, River."

He nods, trying to swallow and failing. "Small. Black." He closes his eyes in exhaustion. "Tiny spot...yellow along...edge."

He feels Echo leave, then hears the drawers that line the wall open and closing. "Small. Black," she mutters. "A dot of yellow along the edge."

River focuses on the tiny trickle of air that's still getting into his lungs. Echo's safe for now. And they've inadvertently sheltered in the one place that can save him. He just needs a few seeds. Enough to breathe again.

"No," Echo moans. The sound of drawers opening and closing becomes louder. "Please, no."

Hands press to his cheek a moment later. "River," she whispers. "I'm so sorry."

His eyes flutter open to see her holding a drawer. One labeled *Serpentwood*.

And it's empty.

"Oren must've taken those too," she says, her voice breaking. "He's destroyed everything."

River gazes at her, understanding passing between them.

The serpentwood is gone.

Which means he'll be the first to fall victim to its loss. He'll be the first to die.

He lifts his hand, only able to reach as far as the height of her stomach. He lets it drop onto her, wanting to be touching her, to be as close to their baby as possible.

"No, River," Echo says, grasping his hand. Tears track down her cheeks, smudging the ash on her face. "You're not..." She presses their clasped hands to her belly. "We haven't even discussed names."

River struggles to keep his eyes open. The adrenaline is fading. The air can no longer reach his lungs.

Echo smiles, bringing their joined hands to kiss his fingers. "They'll have your green eyes."

He opens his mouth, wanting to use the last of his air to tell her he loves her. But something strikes him, piercing through the haze of black slowly engulfing him.

Green eyes.

Just like his.

And Flora's.

"If she's a girl..." River wheezes, grimacing as pain rips up his neck. "What if...she's the Sovereign?"

Flora's blood runs through the child's veins. Sovereign blood. It's a long shot, but it's enough to give him hope.

Echo gasps, her eyes opening wide. "Our baby?"

He tries to nod. He really does. But there's no strength left in his body.

His hand goes slack. The fight for air is lost.

And oblivion drags him away from her.

CHAPTER
TWENTY-ONE
ECHO

Echo slips her hand free of River's. She doesn't want his kisses. Or his words. She wants him. All of him. Alive and well and by her side.

"River, don't you dare let go." She clasps her locket, letting the tears run freely down her face. She lost her mother. Then her father. She's not losing River, too.

"I mean it, River," she says sternly. "This isn't the time for a one-off breathing issue."

His eyes remain closed as his breaths come in gasps so shallow they're barely there at all.

"I need you," she whimpers. "Our baby needs you."

River's final words repeat through her mind. *"What if she's the Sovereign?"* Echo doesn't want their daughter to be the Sovereign. Not if River's not here to see it. Nothing will matter if he dies. There's no world without him. Not for her anyway.

A wave of nausea rolls in her gut, reminding her that she must go on. No matter what. Even if...

No! She's not going to accept this. River will be fine. She'll think of something.

Then she looks at his pale face and motionless body, and her brain goes into overdrive, accepting she doesn't have much time. Because neither does he. Soon, without oxygen, his beautiful heart will stop beating.

She needs some serpentwood and she needs it five minutes ago.

Rolling back on her haunches, she lets go of her locket and it catches in her hair. Tugging it free, she goes to tuck it safely into her shirt, then thinks again.

Now it's her father's words playing in her mind. *"What's inside that locket will bring you luck."*

She opens it with shaking hands, never needing luck more than she does right now. Tipping the seeds into her palm, she holds one of them up to the light to inspect it. And she sees something she's never noticed before. On the edge of the tiny seed is a very faint spot.

And it's yellow.

Her heart hammers as she realizes what she's holding. What she's been carrying with her since the day of her Confirmation.

Serpentwood.

River had said they looked like serpentwood seeds and she'd dismissed the idea as crazy. But he was right! And now it's the last of this precious plant in existence in the entire world.

Which means she's faced with an impossible choice.

Does she use the seeds to save River, the father of her unborn child and the only guy she'll ever love? Or does she use them to save humanity from its inevitable extinction?

And that's not even taking into consideration the promise she made to her father to plant them in the Dead Zone.

"You've got to be kidding me," she groans as the gravity of the outcome of her next action slides over her.

How can it all come down to this? To her? An ordinary girl from the Dead Zone who asked for none of this yet has somehow ended up being the one who gets to choose if everyone lives or dies. Flora had the same power. And she turned her back on humanity, deciding it wasn't worth saving. Echo can't possibly follow in those footsteps. She's witnessed the beauty of the world. Seen it in the delicate petals of a daisy. The loving gaze of a mother. The intricate patterns of a spider's web. She's felt it, too. Every time River touches her. Holds her. Kisses her. He proved to her that love exists. And love can only continue if life goes on.

She can't possibly choose one person over humanity. Even if he's the most incredible person she could ever dream up.

And River wouldn't make that choice either.

He'd let her go. Just like she needs to.

Still clutching the serpentwood seeds, she watches as River's body gives up its fight and his gentle wheezing slips into a terrifying silence.

"I'm so sorry," she whimpers, unable to accept what she knows she must.

Closing her eyes, she's flooded with memories of River and all the sacrifices he's made for her. She sees him running into the Betadome to drag her away when she was caught in a swarm of bees. She sees him giving her the water they found in the Extinction Zone when he was so thirsty himself. She sees him diving in front of her to take a bullet filled with venom...

Every time they've faced danger, River's put Echo before himself.

Her eyes spring open as she's struck with one undeniable thought. River *wouldn't* make that choice. He would never choose humanity over Echo. Even when he thought she was the Sovereign, he protected her from further harvests. And that was for nobody's benefit except her own.

He's been her protector. Her savior. Her champion.

He chose her. Again. And again. And again.

Which means now she gets to choose him. Whether he likes it or not.

Her hand moves to River. Parting his lips, she tips the seeds into his mouth and works his jaw to crunch them up.

"Come on, River," she pleads. "Chew the seeds. It's serpentwood. It'll help you breathe."

Each second that River doesn't move shatters Echo's hopes into smaller and smaller fragments as she realizes she hadn't acted fast enough.

She made the impossible choice.

She chose him over all of humanity.

And because she hesitated, now nobody will survive. Not River. Not anyone.

Even if their child is the Sovereign, the future is bleak. Without serpentwood, the Code is useless. They can't make Immunity. They can't save anyone.

She chose wrong.

But she also knows she chose right.

She followed her heart. Which means when it's her turn to leave this tragic world, she can do so knowing she stayed true to everything she and River worked to build together.

Because when it came down to it, in the choice of life versus love, she chose love. And there's nothing and no-one she loves more than River. The decision she was forced to make was no decision at all. If she had her time again, she'd still choose River.

Yesterday. Today. Tomorrow.

It was always going to be him. It always will be.

There's a crackling noise that has Echo leaping back in fright, until she realizes where it came from.

River.

He draws in another sharp breath and his lungs wheeze.

"That's it, River!" Echo scrambles forward and puts her hand to his cheek, hardly daring to believe it. "Do it again!"

His eyes open and he looks up at her with a vacant stare. Then recognition lights his emerald irises, and they flood with warmth.

"Breathe," she tells him. "Don't try to talk. Just breathe."

He takes in more air, each breath sounding smoother than the one that came before.

Her tears turn to open sobs as she lets out the sea of grief she was storing.

"You found the seeds." He blinks up at her.

"I said don't talk." She runs her fingertips down his cheek, marveling at every tiny detail. The line of his jaw. The darkness of his lashes. The curve of his cheek. But most of all, the rise and fall of his chest.

His eyes graze her face then lower to see the open locket hanging from her neck. She snaps it closed and tucks it in her shirt.

"Your seeds," he whispers.

"That's right." She nods. "My seeds. Turns out you were right. They were serpentwood."

"But..." The realization of what she did washes over him, and she can see his mind reeling in protest.

She quickly presses her index finger to his lips. "Don't. Talk."

"Ech—"

"You really are very stubborn, aren't you?" she scolds, unable to wipe the smile from her face. He may be upset with her, but at least he's alive to feel that way. She'd accept him being angry with her every day for the rest of her life just as long as he continues to draw breath.

"They were the last," he says, still too weak to sit up.

"And you were my last," she snaps. "And my first. And my everything in between. I wasn't going to lose you, River."

"But—"

"But nothing." She sighs. "Don't you dare protest unless you can put your hand on your heart and swear to me that you wouldn't have done the same for me."

His lips tip up into a guilty smile. "I love you, Echo."

"Oh, River." She leans forward and presses her forehead to his. "I love you, too."

They remain frozen in that position for precious minutes. She knows as soon as he's strong enough they have to deal with whatever's waiting for them outside that door, including the ramifications of her decision.

But that can wait.

Because right now, the world contains only two people.

Echo.

And River.

Alive and well and by her side.

TWENTY-TWO

RIVER

River feels like he's been frozen. His body calcified by cold, everything hard and inert. Thawing out is far slower and more painful than he'd like.

His heart thuds as it pumps blood to every cell. His lungs gorge oxygen like a starved Dead Born.

And his mind struggles to process Echo's decision.

She used the last serpentwood seeds in existence to save him. They'll never make adrenacure again. Even if by some remote possibility she's carrying the Sovereign, they'll never make Immunity.

She chose him over every last soul in existence.

He reaches up to brush a stray hair that's escaped her braid, his arm feeling like stone. He has no words for what she did. The emotions are choking him just as completely as his allergic reaction did.

He's astounded. Humbled. Scared what all of this will mean.

And in a moment of clarity, he realizes if the roles were reversed, he would've done the same.

Sacrificing one in the name of many is where Oren went wrong. Where the line between the greater good and heartlessness was blurred. How one person got to decide who lives and who dies.

Echo was right.

Choosing their humanity, choosing love, is the answer.

And that choice means he's lying here, looking at her. Touching her. Loving her with every shred of his being.

Wondering if their child is the Sovereign.

River groans, knowing he needs to get up. That this fight is far from over. Echo moves closer, prepared to help him, no doubt conscious of the same.

"Whoa. That was..."

They both startle as Reed's voice fills the room. Echo spins around to look at the speaker in the ceiling it just tumbled from. "What the..."

"You two are going to be the stuff of legend, you know that?"

"Reed?" Echo says, even though it's clear who it is. "You can see us?"

"It's how Oren's known all of our movements since we entered the Sting. He has secret cameras everywhere."

River's lips press together in a tight line. Oren's always felt one step ahead of them.

"Not anymore, though. I've locked myself in his office. I shut down any other access to the camera feeds."

River and Echo glance at each other, knowing this is significant. Oren's all-seeing eyes have just been closed. He's working blind.

"We need to get back to the others," River says, not surprised to find his voice is croaky. His throat feels bruised after the invisible vice that almost killed him.

"You need to get to the Hive," Reed says flatly. "There's something you have to see."

Reed's words send foreboding shooting through River.

He glances at Echo, seeing the same emotion darkening her eyes. The sense that this war just deepened is undeniable. River pushes himself up with a groan, every muscle aching. He feels like he's been run over by a pod.

Echo's hands slip behind his shoulders. "Are you okay to do this?"

"Never better," River grunts. Echo frowns and he plants a quick kiss on her lips. "Figured I should do something with this second chance at life I've been gifted."

Her face softens even as the concern doesn't fade from her eyes. Drawing more precious air into his lungs, River gets to his feet, using a nearby chair for support as Echo slips under his arm. His head swims and the room multiplies as he stands upright, forcing himself not to sway with his surroundings.

"Maybe we should—"

"Get to the Hive," he finishes for her.

Echo's mouth clamps shut as she frowns. They shuffle toward the door and although nausea has his stomach doing somersaults, the room actually steadies.

"I didn't save you just for you to collapse on me," she mutters grouchily under her breath.

"You saved me because you love me," River says, pressing a kiss to her temple. "And I want to fight for that."

Echo looks up at him, the tenderness in her dark gaze taking his breath away. Another quick kiss is all he allows himself. Echo's gifted him more time with her. The battle is now to make sure that will be a lifetime, with their loved ones around them.

They reach the door and Echo places her hand on it, her body tensing. They don't know what's on the other side. An out-of-control fire? A collapsed floor that's compromised the entirety of the Sting?

"By the way," Reed says from above. "You're about to get wet."

Frowning in confusion, Echo pulls open the door. A torrent of rain hits them in the face, instantly soaking them. She sputters, looking up and registering what River noticed when they first arrived in Eden. The sprinkler system that waters the plants. The very same plants that are now puddles of ash on the floor.

Reed turned it on remotely, dousing the fire before it could do any more damage.

Although not before the serpentwood was destroyed.

River pushes away the distressing thought. Continuing to move forward is all they can do right now.

"The door's unlocked," Reed says, his voice above and behind them. "So you can make your way straight here."

River and Echo step into the deluge, their feet splashing in the ashen puddles as they make their way out. Everything around them is melted or incinerated. The screen on the wall that used to project the morning announcements is warped and cracked and River looks away. Those messages were just another way Oren spread his propaganda. How he secured his control.

At least they've managed to use the technology to their advantage. Reed can now communicate with them.

Water streams down River's face, his back, his whole body, and the coolness invigorates him. Washes away the remnants of death and fear that were clinging to his consciousness. He opens his mouth to catch some of the wetness, using it to fuel the body that feels like it just aged a few decades.

Just as Reed said, the door's unlocked and they step through into a dry space, the elevators in front of them.

"Getting those going will take a bit more time," Reed says, his voice coming from another speaker above them. "Oren did a number on their programming."

River nods as he suppresses a sigh. No amount of water is going to give him the energy he needs to get to the Hive. He's going to have to dredge up reserves somewhere from the body that was dying less than an hour ago.

Echo pats his soggy chest as she settles more securely into his side. "We'll take it slow."

"Guys!" Reed shouts, alarmed. "You need to get out—"

His warning is cut off as the door to the stairwell bursts open. Adrenaline fires through River, injecting him with the fuel to protect Echo. The final reckoning with Oren has come.

Except it's not Oren who runs into the corridor. It's Roark. And he's holding a venom gun.

River stares at the man who threatened Makk by holding a knife to his throat. The man he knocked to the ground then let free in the hope he'd see that hate and violence isn't the way forward.

Turns out he was wrong.

Roark grins darkly, aiming the venom gun at them as he steps forward. "You're not going anywhere."

River and Echo stop, slowly raising their hands to show they're not a threat. "We're on your side, Roark," River says, his voice low.

"You've never been on my side," Roark spits. "Or any Dead Born's."

River remembers what fueled Roark's hatred—the loss of his brother, Trid, the Dead Born who was killed when they were trying to retrieve adrenacure from the Sting. Back when they were testing for the Sovereign. When they believed it was Echo, when Flora was still hiding her ultimate betrayal. It feels like a lifetime ago, yet the fury on Roark's face is undeniably fresh.

Echo lifts her hands an inch higher. "We're fighting for everyone, Roark. So we can have peace."

"And look where it's got us! We're dying quicker than we did in the Dead Zone!"

"And Oren will keep going if we don't stop him," River says.

Roark lifts the gun until it's aimed at their chests. "Oren would've stopped by now if you didn't bring this all on us."

River realizes there's no point arguing that Oren was no doubt working to exterminate every last Vulnerable, Dead or Green Born. Roark's mind has been twisted by hatred. He won't consider another option.

Echo shakes her head. "We're Immune, Roark. That gun can't kill us."

His lip curls up. "You may be able to withstand one shot, but several?" He takes a step forward. "And even if you do, you'll be incapacitated long enough for me to finish this."

River's pulse thuds heavily in his veins. Roark's right. And his intent to kill is clear. He brushes Echo's hand, pulling it back slightly as he hopes to communicate they need to run back into Eden. Right now, the seed bank is the safest place for them.

Her chin lowers infinitesimally, indicating she understands.

Simultaneously, they spin, ducking as they run back to the door.

Except it shoves open before they reach it, another person stepping through.

Also holding a venom gun.

"Oh no you don't," says a hard voice.

River's eyes widen as he recognizes Grove, the Green Born who shot him in the eating hall.

Grove steps through, registers Roark on the other side, a slow smile spreading across his face. "You were about to lose them, huh, Dead Born?"

Roark angles his venom gun at Grove. "I was about to finish them."

Now caught between the two sides of the war he never wanted, River tries to understand how this has happened. How did Grove just appear in Eden?

He must see the confusion on River's face, because he grins. "Oren saw the sprinklers come on right before the screens went black." He sneers then adjusts his clothes. "He had a Worker drop me off. You're not the only ones who can ride them, you know." He raises the gun he's holding. "And this time I have a queen bee gun."

River's eyes dart to the weapon he's holding, registering the six gold lines circling the barrel. Grove's telling the truth. He has a weapon that can kill River.

"Oren's using you to do his dirty work," Echo says, stepping so she can keep both men in sight. "He probably did the same with Cascade."

River realizes she's right. Cascade was never a leader. Someone must've given her the idea. And given the Green Borns the venom guns.

"Oren knows I'm loyal to him, he told me so," Grove says. "It doesn't matter that I'm Vulnerable."

River has to resist shaking his head. Oren told Grove exactly what he wanted to hear—that he'll survive this despite not being Immune. He probably told Cascade the same.

And she's dead.

Grove moves further into the corridor, his gun unwavering in its aim on River and Echo. "He also told me you're not his real son, River. No wonder you turned your back on everything he's tried to build."

"Ha!" Roark spits. "That's why he wants you dead."

River fights the very core of his being as he takes a small step away from Echo. Right now, protecting her involves spreading out the target they've become. Hoping to draw the attention of the two men and their guns on him.

"Now you're working together?" he asks. "A Dead Born and a Green born uniting? Isn't that everything you've fought against?"

"We both want the same thing."

Roark and Grove speak simultaneously, eyes darting to the other in surprise. They've been brought together by a common goal. A common enemy.

River and Echo.

Unity has been achieved.

"Then who's going to be the one to steal the glory?" Echo snaps.

River almost gasps. She's goading them?

She closes the distance between them, her hand wrapping around his, tugging lightly. At first, he has no idea what that means, but then it dawns on him. He just hopes he's right...

River slides a glance at Roark. "Dead Borns love their violence. Killing's their pastime. You'll be first, Roark."

He sneers as he adjusts his aim. "You think you can make me second guess this? As if I care what anyone thinks of Dead Borns?"

Echo barks out a harsh laugh, glancing at Grove. "A Green Born wouldn't have the guts. They pretend death doesn't exist."

"I fired the first shot in the eating hall!" Grove screams, his face flushing bright red as his hand clenches around his gun.

"No! They're mine!" Roark roars.

River and Echo are already dropping, hitting the floor hard as they throw themselves down. The faint pops are simultaneous, puncturing the hatred pouring out of the two men's lungs.

River draws Echo in close, trying to shield her with his body even as she does the same with him. He braces himself, waiting for the sting of venom entering his body, waiting to discover if it will be from a queen bee.

Yet it doesn't come.

Nor does Echo jerk in his arms as if she was hit.

They pull apart, confirming the other is okay, before looking around. Both men have fallen where they stood. Both a distended, purple version of themselves.

River and Echo get to their feet, registering Roark is far more bloated, his death no doubt faster thanks to the queen bee venom. But Grove is just as lifeless. Equally as dead.

And although it meant they survived, although their demise was fueled by hatred and short-sightedness, River feels their loss like any of the others.

Roark and Grove were simply two more victims of an evil manipulator.

"Yep," Reed says from above. "The stuff of legend."

River and Echo both huff, half in amusement, half in relief. They clasp hands, squeezing tightly, grateful to be able to touch. To have the other by their side.

"Now, you *really* need to get to the Hive," Reed adds.

This time, River and Echo don't hesitate. They break into a run, yank open the door, then stop to survey the stairwell. It's empty. No more revenge-fueled Dead Borns. No brain washed Green Borns.

"We're on our way, Reed," Echo says as they ascend the first flight.

Except there's no answer.

River frowns. "There mustn't be any cameras in the stairwells," he says, already out of breath.

The other possibility is that Oren's got to Reed, and that's not one River wants to contemplate.

River's already slowing by the second set of stairs. Echo doesn't say anything, simply moving in closer and slipping an arm around his back. He leans against her gratefully even as he tries to not put too much weight on her. She's carrying his child.

Who may be the Sovereign.

By the time they reach the Hive, River's feet are scuffing the stairs as it takes effort to lift each one and he's breathing hard. Yet he doesn't falter, doesn't slow. With each heaving inhale and exhale he reminds himself he's grateful to be breathing at all.

He and Echo stumble inside and he leans against the wall as she looks around, panting but on high alert. But the Hive is empty, just like it was before.

"Look." Echo points.

Where there used to be the glass wall to Oren's office that Nectar had crashed through, there's now a solid opaque glass one.

"Reed said he was in Oren's office, didn't he?" River checks.

Echo nods, pushing open a door in the wall, revealing a smiling Reed. He waves. "Glad you could make it."

River shakes his head as he and Echo make their way over. They enter and Reed presses a button from behind the desk. The door instantly shuts and River has no doubt it's now securely locked.

Echo shifts protectively closer to River. "What's going on? Where did this wall come from? I thought this place was destroyed."

"So did I. I came up here to see if I could access the sprinklers to put out the fire," Reed explains as he takes a seat behind the desk. The very same desk Oren has sat at for years, lording over every life in the Green Zone and Dead Zone. Even the Moon Zone, a zone few knew existed. "Then I went digging. And found some stuff. Including a button that made this glass wall rise right out of the floor."

River turns to look at the other side of the opaque wall and Reed presses another button. One by one, square screens come alive, rows and rows of them every image revealing some new snapshot of the Sting.

This is how Oren's watched everything, from the comfort of his office!

Reed's hand moves again and twelve of the small rectangles contract together, making one large screen. It fills with an image that has River blinking and stilling.

It's not like the others. It's not an image of the present.

They're looking at times that have passed.

At a history that brought them to this very moment.

CHAPTER
TWENTY-THREE

ECHO

Echo stares at the screen that was once nothing more than a wall of glass. On it is an image of her standing in the Betadome. Her face is caked in dirt, which does nothing to hide her expression.

She's confused.

She's angry.

She's hurt.

She's afraid.

"That's our Confirmation," she whispers to River as she realizes when the footage was taken. "That's us."

She sees them standing together, distrust and resentment shimmering between them like a heavy fog.

Oren's words ring out in the background. *"Two Immunes are joining us this year."*

The memory of that moment is still clear, but seeing herself living it brings it into even sharper focus. And it's a focus she's not sure she wants to revisit.

River urges her to follow him out of the Betadome, but she shakes her head, and they argue. Then she's running to the net.

To the guy she thought she loved, each step taking her directly away from the guy she was destined to love so much more.

She cringes as she sees herself press her hands to Chase's, the silver net separating them physically, his betrayal creating a deep chasm that would never be fully bridged. Because Echo's life was about to take a turn that this previous version of herself would never have been able to imagine.

The River of today shifts uncomfortably beside her as they watch her go back to him. He leads her out of the Betadome.

Two strangers.

Two enemies.

Two people who were never supposed to meet.

But now that they have, they can never be parted.

She remembers how she'd felt about River in that moment. That he was rude. Superior. Arrogant. And she'd been so very wrong. Looking at him on the screen now, she sees a different River. A broken young man struggling to hold himself together. One who'd just lost his twin and had his future shattered. She wants to shout at herself to be kinder to him. To have some compassion for the loss he was suffering alongside her own.

Reed presses another button and the screen goes black before dividing into the smaller rectangles they saw earlier. Each one shows a different scene as Echo and River walk away from the Betadome.

Daphne holds a white suit in her arms and a false smile on her face.

Clover clasps her hands together in glee, her eyes fixed on River.

Reed studies Echo with a look of fascination and puzzlement.

Rose claps silently as she bites her bottom lip.

But it's the screen at the very bottom right corner that has

Echo gasping. There's an image of the Dead Borns gathered at the net.

"He has cameras in the Dead Zone," she says, hardly able to believe it.

Reed nods. "Although, from what I've been able to figure out, there's only one at the black door. He must have it hidden in the frame."

"Look." River points. "It's Flora."

Sure enough, Flora is in the corner of the screen embracing Chase. Echo flushes to remember how she'd asked him to look after Flora, with no idea how much they already meant to each other. That was just the start of a long list of things she'd been naïve about.

Then something else catches Echo's attention. She steps closer to be sure she's not imagining it. Reed taps a button and the entire wall is filled with the scene in the Dead Zone.

"Dad," she whispers, holding back her tears. "You came."

Her father is standing at the back of the crowd with his palm pressed over his heart and wet streaks of pride snaking their way down his cheeks. He said he could feel her future was as an Immune. Now she'll never know if there was more to his hunch or if perhaps every parent felt like that when sending their child into the Betadome.

If she knew he was watching, it would have been so much harder to walk away from him. Which is why he kept out of sight. Just like River, her father always put her first.

Her dad's knees wobble and Chase races from Flora's side to catch him. He'd promised to look after him and it seems he kept true to that. It also seems he hadn't lied when he'd said her father was far sicker than he'd let Echo know.

"I've seen enough," she tells Reed, turning away from the screen, sadness welling in her every pore. "This has to stop. We have to find a way to unite the people. It's gone on too long already."

Reed pulls back his shoulders. "And I know exactly how to do it."

"How?" River steps forward.

"Do you trust me?" Reed asks.

"Yes," River says without hesitation.

Echo nods, realizing that while it's taken a long time, she *does* trust Reed.

"Is everyone still in the eating hall?" Reed starts tapping on the keyboard, his focus sharp.

Echo looks at River and shrugs, realizing she isn't sure where everyone went after they left in their failed attempt to save the serpentwood.

"Ah yes," says Reed, finding the camera he needs. "They're still there. You'd better join them. It's better you're there when they see what I have to show them."

"And what is that exactly?" Echo asks.

Reed doesn't answer. He's too busy tapping buttons. But that's all part of the concept of trust, she supposes. He'll choose the right footage to get their point across.

"Come on." River puts a hand on Echo's back. "We'd better hurry."

They exit through the LaB and head for the stairwell. Echo's stomach contracts at the thought of what they might find in the eating hall. It had been mayhem when they'd left. Her only hope is that the shock of the thought of losing their last remaining serpentwood had brought everyone to their senses. Maybe they're united already?

By the time they reach the door to the eating hall, Echo and River are both panting.

"Are you okay?" she asks him, wondering if they should have moved slower. "Can you breathe?"

He nods, tilting his head toward the door. "It's quiet in there."

"Is that good?" Echo asks, listening hard.

River cringes. "I don't think so."

Echo pushes open the door and immediately reels back at the scene that greets them.

The Dead Borns and Moon Workers are huddled in a corner. The Green Borns are standing guard with their venom guns. A quick scan of the terrified faces confirms Echo's worst fear. Everyone she cares about is there. Makk. Nola. Vern. Chase. Jupiter. Goldie. Lyra...

Tables have been set up to block anyone from escaping. Each one has an oozing piece of honeycomb sitting on it, coated in bees. As long as the people stay still, they're safe. It's a prison wall even more effective than iron bars.

"Glad you could join us," sneers a female Green Born, who seems to have taken over from Grove as the leader.

"Let them go, Daisy," says River, his face full of distress. "They're not going to hurt you."

"They're eating all our food," Daisy snaps, flicking her long dark braid over her shoulder. "We need it. We'll starve."

River steps forward with his palms held in front of him to show he's no threat. Echo keeps close behind him.

"Daisy," he says. "This isn't how you were raised. The Green Borns value peace above everything else. What you're doing to these people isn't peaceful."

"They're not people." Daisy looks to the corner of the room. "They're either Dead Born or Forgotten."

Echo's eyes flare as she steps out from behind River. "It could so easily have been you over there. These *people* are no different to anyone else."

Daisy raises her venom gun with a shaking hand and points it at Echo.

"I'm Immune." Echo instinctively puts her hands in front of her stomach as River edges closer, preparing to dive in front of her again if he needs to. "You'll be wasting your bullet."

The wall at the end of the eating hall lights up, revealing itself as a screen.

Daisy turns when Oren's image appears, and River immediately puts himself in front of Echo. If it weren't for the fact she's carrying his baby, she'd protest. He's weaker than she is right now.

"Is that live or a recording?" Echo whispers, hoping Oren hasn't somehow gotten to Reed and prevented him from showing whatever it was that he had planned.

Daphne strides onto the screen answering Echo's question with her mere presence. Memories of her bloated body lying on the floor of the bunker hit her with a thud. No matter how awful Daphne was, Echo's still not sure anyone deserved to die in such a brutal way.

There's a strangled moan from the corner as Lyra stares up at the woman who gave birth to her, then later abandoned her when she wasn't Immune.

Turning back to the screen, Echo sees Oren open his arms. Daphne slides into them, holding herself at enough distance that she can gaze lovingly into his eyes.

"What happened?" she asks. "I thought you added Immunity to Flora's water."

"I did." He nods. "It seems she had other ideas."

Echo realizes this must have been filmed right after their Confirmation. That's one downside of covering the Sting with cameras. Oren inadvertently filmed himself.

"The filthy Razer." Daphne's face fills with hate. "Flora chose him over her own father, which means she wasn't nearly as clever as we gave her credit for."

Chase leaps up, sending bees rising from the honeycomb. Tuff holds him back as the bees settle.

"Flora was smarter than all of you scum put together," Chase growls.

"Flora *is* clever," Oren says to Daphne, almost as if he'd heard Chase's protest. "Which is why it's for the best that she left us today. She was getting too close to the truth."

"She won't be able to do much from the Dead Zone." Daphne lifts a finger and runs it down Oren's face in a way that makes Echo's stomach turn.

"What did you make of the Dead Born?" Oren asks. "I was sure Immunity had been bred out by those animals."

"Animals?" Echo repeats out loud, a bitter taste forming on her tongue.

Daphne shrugs. "We'll need to watch her. Keep her close. It was wise to have her assigned to the LaB. And to River. He's loyal to you."

"She's connected to the filthy Razer," says Oren. "I suspect Flora somehow faked the Dead Born's Immunity so she could have him to herself. We'll need a sample of her blood."

"I'll talk to Reed." Daphne flutters her eyelashes as Oren gives her an approving smile.

Echo shifts her feet, wondering how this conversation is going to unite the zones. So far, all it's done is make Flora seem like a traitor. What is Reed up to?

"These are only minor interruptions, my love." Oren kisses Daphne's forehead. "Our plan is still on track."

Daphne smiles up at him. "Only the Immune shall survive."

"That's right." He lets go of Daphne to stretch his arms out wide. "One day the entire world will be ours to rule over. No more nets. No more giving away rations. We'll wipe out all the

Dead Borns along with any Green Born who's not truly Immune."

There's a gasp from Daisy's direction as she lets her gun fall to her side. The Dead Borns and Moon Workers remain silent, including Chase. This attitude of Oren's is no shock to them. But each Green Born in the room looks like they just saw a ghost. No, worse than that. They saw a demon. And it has every one of them in its sights.

"A perfect race of perfect humans," says Daphne. "With you as their King."

"And you as my Queen." Oren takes Daphne and spins her around.

The video cuts to black, then a new image appears. A glowing, golden image that tells Echo they're looking at the Hive.

Blossom is being carried in by Tuff and placed on the floor. He steps away from her unconscious body to join Oren, and a glass screen rises.

Echo grimaces, knowing what's coming. She'd underestimated Reed. He was wise to choose this particular scene. The Green Borns need to see where their false Immunity came from.

The giant mechanical Worker emerges from the hatch, and Echo decides she's seen enough harvests to last her a lifetime. She turns to watch the Green Borns' reaction instead as Blossom's terrified screams fill the room.

Their faces tell the story. Horror mingles with shock. Realization morphs into betrayal. And anguish sits right there beside deep sorrow.

Blossom's a Green Born, which makes her one of their own. And Oren was treating her like nothing more than a science experiment, all so he could rule over his perfect race of Immunes.

"It's over," River whispers.

Echo looks back at the screen which is now showing the Sovereign graveyard. There are hundreds of corpses. Row after row of them.

Dead Born and Green Born.

Segregated in life.

Identical in death.

All human. All taken before their time. And all at Oren's hand.

The screen goes black again and now a younger version of Lyra is staring back at them.

"Come along, Iris," says Daphne's familiar voice. "Hurry now."

"Where are you taking me, Mom?" Lyra asks. "Will I be safe?"

"You're Vulnerable," Daphne says coolly. "You'll never be safe."

Lyra weeps as she's marched down a dark tunnel and pushed out a hatch into the bright sunlight.

"Mom!" Lyra turns around, looking directly into the camera positioned over the hatch as she bangs on the hot metal surface. "Mom! Where are you?"

Echo looks across at the horrified Green Borns. Then she looks at Lyra, the girl who would survive this ordeal only to refuse ever to be called Iris again. She's standing at the edge of the group, her entire body visibly shaking.

"Please don't leave me out here!" the younger version of Lyra begs as she collapses into a heap on the hot ground of the Extinction Zone. "I'm all alone. Mom! I'm so frightened. Help me!"

The footage cuts away from Lyra and shows Daphne walking back down the tunnel.

Alone.

And smiling.

It's a look Echo's very familiar with. And it makes her feel ill. Perhaps the brutality of her death had been warranted in some small way.

The screen fades to black and silence hangs over the room. The only sound is the beating of their hearts and the humming of the feasting bees.

"I'm so sorry," says Daisy, letting her venom gun fall to the floor. "I didn't know."

The other Green Borns gather at her side, all visibly distressed. "None of us knew."

"I didn't know either," says River. "But ever since I found out, I've worked to make things right. You can do that, too. Starting right now."

"One zone," says Echo, hope lighting in her chest. "One people."

"One zone," Daisy repeats. "One people."

"One people!" comes Oren's furious voice through the speakers, making everyone still. "That's what I've wanted all along. One people. *My* people!"

"We're not your people!" Daisy shouts back. "You lied to us!"

"What you were just shown is the lie," says Oren. "That footage was edited together to paint me as the villain. You know I'd never hurt you. I care for my people. I always have."

"You want us dead," another Green Born calls out.

"Any one of you could still be Immune," says Oren. "I tried to give you all a chance to find out."

"By releasing bees in the Sting," sneers Daisy. "That's not keeping us safe."

"I said I care for *my people,*" Oren clarifies. "And my people are Immune."

"I'm Immune," Echo calls out. "And I'm not one of your people. I never will be."

"Nor will I," River says.

"In that case, I'm afraid the time has come," says Oren calmly. "I've been so very patient with all of you, but even someone as forgiving as me has a limit."

Echo shakes her head as anger continues to build inside her. They'd only just managed to achieve the impossible. Unity. And now Oren's going to undo everything with his sweet talking.

"What are you up to, Oren?" River growls.

"You never did call me Dad, did you?" says Oren. "Maybe if you'd accepted me as your father in the same way I accepted you as my son things might have worked out differently between us."

"He's *my* son," Vern growls. "Always was. Always will be."

"I asked what you're up to," River says, trying to deflect attention away from Vern to keep him safe. "You said the time has come. The time for what? Nobody's going to follow you now. Not after what they just saw."

"Oh, I think they will," says Oren, his voice bouncing around the stark walls of the eating hall.

"Don't listen to him!" shouts Echo, refusing to allow Oren to send them a single step backward. "Whatever he's up to, we're not buying into it!"

The room fills with nodding heads, followed by the sound of Oren's laughter.

"Be in peace," he says.

The vent in the ceiling where the bees had come through drops open and a fresh army of queens emerges in a wave, each of them fitted with a flashing red light.

Reed's face appears on the giant screen, his eyes wide behind his glasses and his jaw hanging open.

"Everyone!" he shouts. "You need to run. Now!"

CHAPTER
TWENTY-FOUR
RIVER

R iver can't drag his gaze away from the threat pouring down the vent in a torrent of black and gold. He subtly moves so his body is between the swarm and Echo as he tries to figure out what Oren's strategy is. Stinging everyone with queen bees won't identify the Immune and cull the Vulnerables. That was never his plan. He wants to keep Immunes to build his new humanity.

Right now, everyone will die.

Unless his father's mind has snapped... Unless Oren has decided to kill every last soul who defied him.

The queen bees become a cloud hovering close to the ceiling, their tiny red lights looking like hundreds of eyes blinking at their prey.

Yet, they don't move.

Don't attack.

Everyone in the eating hall is frozen with fear. Someone muffles a sob somewhere to River's left. He moves slowly, carefully, never taking his eyes off the tiny insects that can end every life in this room. All the Green Borns. Every last Dead Born.

Surely this isn't what Oren wants.

Well, they're not going to stay here and find out.

"Split up," River says, keeping his voice low but forceful as his gaze darts around the pale, frozen faces. "Every Green Born take a Dead Born and hide."

"As quietly and smoothly as possible," Echo adds, her own voice a little more controlled.

River draws in a steadying breath, realizing she's right. The moment he spoke, the bees feasting on the honey had also raised their sound level. Now their humming is louder. Tenser.

There's a double threat in this room. The super bees, who are quick to attack. And the queen bees, programmed to attack.

"Kill any bees that follow you," River instructs.

To his surprise, Daisy's the first one to move toward the Dead Borns. She carefully weaves her way around the upturned tables with the honeycomb and bees, then takes Fray's hand and strides to the rear of the eating hall. Sledge leaps to join them, then ducks and slows as the bees closest to them hum with annoyance.

"There's a back door," Daisy hisses, ignoring the threat. "This way."

Several other Green Borns move, claiming a Dead Born as they follow. Some whisper they'll go to their room, others have plans to get to different floors such as the classrooms where there are more places to hide. They disappear into the kitchen area where River knows is a rear door used for delivering supplies.

River's mother points toward the front entrance to the eating hall, encouraging others to go that way. More Green Borns collect Dead Borns as they quickly make their way there.

Vern helps her usher the people, and River wishes there was a moment to tell him he's proud to know he's his son.

But there's not.

River glances up, registering the queen bees still haven't moved. They're a hovering, buzzing cloud. Although it's a blessing, the mystery of why has the air drawing tight with tension. Everyone in the room keeps glancing between them and the other bees, trying to predict which they'll have to fight off first.

"River," Echo says quietly, indicating a nearby table with honeycomb and bees perched on it.

He realizes what she's asking, and they move over to it, carefully lifting it up and then moving it to the side, steadily and slowly so the flow of people can continue.

Throughout it all, the queen bees remain where they are, buzzing as they simply watch.

"What's Oren doing?" Echo hisses.

River shakes his head, as clueless and worried as she is. None of this is making sense, but if they can get everyone out before it does, then he'll take it.

He and Echo have just placed the table carefully down when a muffled cry has River spinning around. Daisy rushes back from the kitchens, her eyes as wide as those right behind her.

"What is it?" Echo asks in a concerned whisper.

Daisy shakes her head, her hand still clamped over her mouth. Fray slips an arm around her shoulders. "There were more queen bees. On the other side of the back door. They attacked."

"Escape through the front door," River tells them as he breaks into a run.

Echo's right beside him. "There are more," she frowning.

Of course there are. Oren's planning something. River can feel it.

They burst into the kitchen area, River grabbing a pot lid on the way as Echo snatches a plate. They stop, trying to contain their breathing as they listen out for the queen bees.

Except the kitchen is quiet.

"The door's still open," Echo gasps.

River realizes she's right. The others failed to close it in their terror. One glance at each other and they run toward it, knowing they need to contain this threat as much as possible. The buzzing of the queens becomes audible as they approach, and River's pulse rises with it. Running toward queen bees under Oren's control is the definition of foolishness.

Yet it's the only way to keep everyone safe.

River extends his strides so he overtakes Echo and reaches the door first. He expects to see a swarm of queens coming at them, so when he registers the cloud of black, gold and man-made red, he grabs the handle to the door and slams it. It shuts with a loud thud, making him simultaneously wince and huff with relief.

Echo skids to a halt beside him, breathing just as hard as he is. The run wasn't far, but it was an adrenaline-injected one. River grabs her and presses a quick kiss to her forehead. He hates that she has to put her life on the line like this. Especially when she's carrying their child. Yet, he understands that she can't sit by and watch. That's not the Echo he fell in love with.

She leans into him for a brief second, as if she's allowing herself just that moment of connection in this desperate battle to save themselves and everyone else, then leans back, frowning.

"They weren't moving," she says, looking at the closed door. "The queens were hovering, just like the ones in the eating hall."

River glances back, working to slow his heart rate. All he registered was the threat before he slammed the door shut, but now he has time to process it, he realizes Echo's right. The swarm was suspended mid-air. They weren't attacking.

"Let's think and run," River says, placing his pot lid on a nearby bench and breaking into a jog as they head back to the eating hall. "Oren's up to something."

His parting words float through River's mind.

Be in peace.

They were said with derision. Almost with dark humor.

As if Oren's in on a joke the rest of them have yet to figure out.

They discover most of the Green and Dead Borns have evacuated the eating hall when they arrive. River's mother and Vern are funneling the last of them toward the door. River and Echo slow as they weave their way through the overturned tables and chairs, keeping a careful eye on the bees devouring the honeycomb.

"We'll go to the Hive," River says to Echo. "We'll figure something out with Reed."

She nods. "And we'll be able to see if there's anyone still out in the open."

Goldie, Tuff, and Makk are the last to pass through the door, Tuff's hand firmly planted on Makk's shoulder as he keeps glancing back, clearly wanting to be with River and Echo. They exit and River's mom and dad glance at each other. He pulls her in to press a sound kiss on her temple and she leans in for the briefest moment, taking comfort in the touch. In the very same touch that River and Echo just allowed themselves.

River's heart swells even as his chest tightens with the determination that they'll all live through this nightmare. His mother and father deserve it.

A movement above him catches River's attention. He looks up and his blood turns to ice.

"No!" he gasps. He wants to shout the word. Scream it. Tell his parents to get out.

But he can't raise his voice.

He can't bring the super bees down on his parents. Not when the queen bees just contracted and speared toward them.

"Nola!" Echo groans. "Vern!"

Although their names are little more than a pained whisper, River's parents turn around. Their eyes widen as their faces drain of color.

"Run!" River begs.

His father spins around, pushing River's mother in front of him as he ushers her through the door. The queens fly at them faster, but it's clear they won't get there in time.

They turn in the doorway, looking back at them, River's dad's hand on the handle.

"Shut it!" River shouts, no longer bothering to be quiet. He and Echo are Immune. It's far more essential that his parents are safe.

Except his father doesn't move. Instead, River's mother indicates furiously with her hand for Echo and River to join them.

They're waiting for them, unwilling for them to be trapped in the eating hall with the queen bees.

It's the opening the queens were looking for. They descend on River's mom and dad, a cannonball of venom.

"Shut the door!" Echo cries.

But River's father stubbornly shakes his head. "Hurry!"

River and Echo inject every drop of adrenaline coursing through them into their legs, running as fast as they can. But the queens are faster. They arc down, coming even closer together, now an arrow of death.

One aiming straight for River's dad.

"No!" River shouts, picking up a nearby chair and throwing it with all his might.

It sails through the air, smashing straight into the swarm, crashing into the wall on the other side. The queens scatter as a handful drop to the ground, their red lights extinguished. Beside River, Echo sidesteps to knock over a table decorated with the honeycomb. It crashes and honey splats over the floor. Any bees behind them who were triggered by the noise are instantly diverted.

River draws Echo back to his side, lifting his other arm to protect his face as they power through the remaining queens flying in random directions. The blow must've messed with Oren's ability to control them. It's an advantage they have to make the most of.

River and Echo shoot past his parents into the stairwell. "Now will you shut the door?" River asks as they pass through.

His father grins as he shoves it closed. "Took your time—"

"They're coming!" River's mother cries out.

River spins to see a handful of queens flying straight for them in a tight formation. River leaps at the door as his father shoves it, propelling it shut.

Except they're not quick enough. Three queens slip through, moving so fast their tiny red lights are a blur.

"To the Hive!" Echo calls out, leaping up the stairs.

River's father grabs his mother's hand and yanks her up after Echo. River comes up the rear, his gaze over his shoulder as he watches the queens close in on them. At least the stairwell is empty, which he's glad for. It means the others have escaped throughout the Sting.

Above them, Echo abruptly stops, bracing herself against

the walls as River's mother crashes into her back. "More queens!" she gasps.

River looks up, registering another swarm hovering halfway up the next flight of stairs. "Back down!" he shouts.

He spins, swiping at the queens who were chasing them. The bees lift high into the air to escape his flailing hands, probably not wanting to be struck again. "Go!" he tells his parents and Echo, propelling them past him then coming up the rear.

They run back down, their panting breaths loud in the narrow stairwell.

Echo tries the door two floors down, only to find it's locked. So is the one below it.

"Keep going!" she pants, skipping the next and descending another flight.

They can't afford to slow down. The trio of queens is right behind them.

They burst out into the foyer, finding it empty of bees, the floor scattered with shards of glass. It crunches under River's newly toughened feet as he looks around, wondering how they're going to escape the queens.

The airlock is still firmly closed.

River's dad throws himself at the nearest elevator doors, hitting the buttons, slamming his fists against them. The queen bees drop into the foyer, forming a triangle. One that points at their four victims. There may only be three of them, but they have more than enough venom to end all of them. One could easily sting Echo enough times to kill her alone.

"Reed!" River shouts. "The elevators!"

It's their only hope.

To his surprise, the doors open. River and the others hurl themselves into the elevator. Echo slams her hands on the hexagonal buttons to close the doors.

They stay open.

"Reed!" she shouts. "Shut the doors!"

"I told you," comes the panicked response through the speakers. "I'm still figuring the elevators out!"

The queen bees shoot forward, small in size, monstrous in threat. River takes a step in front of the others, wishing he had something to throw at them or use as a shield.

With a sharp shove, his father steps around him, and before River can stop him from sacrificing himself, his dad swipes his fingers up the hexagonal buttons in reverse order. To River's shock, they light up. The doors to the elevator slide shut.

Closing them in, and shutting out the queens.

River's mom turns to his dad. "How did you—" she gasps, looking as astounded as River feels.

River's father grins crookedly. "I was messing around once, playing Sting roulette. I did that and it started going down. Freaked me out when it didn't stop at the processing center, so I quickly pressed the buttons to go up."

Echo blinks. "It was an override command." She shakes her head. "Oren always has one."

River thinks of when Daphne was able to override Nectar out in the Extinction Zone. Echo's right. Oren always has a contingency plan.

Their heavy breathing sounds harsh and loud in the elevator as it silently descends. River's hand brushes Echo's and their fingers entwine. They got away. Alive.

"What the..." comes Reed's voice from the speaker above.

River tenses, feeling Echo do the same behind him. "What?"

The elevator comes to a stop and the doors slide open, answering the question for them.

The Sovereign graveyard is teeming with Green Borns,

Dead Borns and Moon Workers. River recognizes Makk, Goldie, Tuff, Sledge, Fray, Lyra, Daisy.

Everyone's here.

"Guys…" Reed says, his voice low and tense. "Something's going on."

River steps out, Echo beside him and his parents right behind. Reed's words are an understatement. Yet a heavy sense of foreboding tells River they're also prophetic.

The whole frantic run here, the queens never stung them. They went after River's father, but that was no doubt Oren's personal grudge against the man who Magnolia chose over him. Then there were the swarms that were placed to stop them going up. The locked doors.

The queens were programmed to round them up.

To bring them all to the Sovereign graveyard.

For Oren's ultimate plan.

TWENTY-FIVE

ECHO

The moment Echo steps out of the elevator, every cell of her body screams at her to get back in. This is a trap. And it's been set by Oren, which makes it the most dangerous kind of all.

There are traumatized faces wherever she looks. Yet no queens. Not even so much as a humble bumblebee. The people have been herded into the Sovereign graveyard then abandoned.

But why?

A small group surges into the elevator, trying to get away from this dungeon of death. But none of the buttons work and they remain where they are. Vern tries the override combination, but even that fails.

"There are dead bodies everywhere," one of the women sobs. "So many of them. I can't handle it."

"What are we going to do?" someone else asks, directing the question at River.

River holds out his hands. "We're going to stay calm and figure this out."

"And we're going to stay united," Echo adds. "Just like we did when we left the eating hall."

The people step out of the elevator, their eyes cast down.

"It's okay," says Echo, unable to blame them for wanting to escape. "I was terrified the first time I saw this place. But there's safety in numbers. We need to stick together."

River puts his arm around her. "We're all on the same team now."

"Except for one," Vern growls, scanning the ceiling for one of Oren's hidden cameras. "Are you watching us, you evil bastard? I'll never be on your team."

"Vern," says Nola firmly. "River said to stay calm."

Vern draws a breath and nods obediently. "Yeah, okay."

Echo loves the dynamic between these two. It's such a shame they missed out on so much time together. She can only hope they still have years ahead to make up for it.

"Hey, where's Chase?" Makk asks, still clutching his whip, ready to take down any queen or bee that dares to come near.

Echo scans the faces in the crowd as concern beats at her temples. "Did he make it down here?"

"Yeah, I saw him earlier." Makk hops from foot to foot, looking for his hero. "He was definitely here."

"He went down there." Lyra points to one of the tunnels. "He said he wanted to look for something."

Echo peers down the dark corridor, certain Chase wasn't looking for something.

It was *someone*.

Nola slips her hand into Vern's as she realizes the same.

"Do you think Flora could be down here?" she asks.

River shrugs, his brows pulled down. "Maybe? If Oren brought her into the graveyard. Although he's usually more interested in testing the living than the..." He swallows, unable to say the last word.

"I'll go after Chase," says Echo. Whatever Oren has planned for them, they need to be ready for it. And Chase is one of their best fighters. It's not like him to leave his Razers at such a crucial moment.

"I'll come with you," says River, dashing her hopes of going alone. If Flora's down here, her body's not likely to be in great shape. River went through enough seeing his twin jump from the Sting. He doesn't need more painful memories to haunt his dreams.

"You can't go, Echo!" says Makk. "We need to stick together. You just said so yourself."

"That's right," Echo agrees, wondering if that kid ever misses a trick. "Which is why I'm getting Chase."

"No, Echo." River puts a hand on her back. "Chase made his choice."

Reluctantly, she has to agree. And maybe he's not looking for Flora. Maybe he's looking for a way out of here.

The elevator doors slide closed and there's a hum as it heads back up into the Sting with its empty cargo.

"Where's it going?" Echo asks, rushing forward.

"More to the point, who's it going to bring back?" River urges her to stand away from the doors.

"Reed!" Echo calls out. "Can you hear us?"

Silence is their answer, leaving them no choice but to wait. Oren must've blocked Reed's signal. Hopefully that's all he's done to him... But Echo doesn't have time to worry about Reed now. He's proven he's capable of looking after himself.

"We've got this covered!" shouts Lyra as the Moon Workers surge toward the elevator doors with their scythes held in front of them like spears. "Nobody gets out of that thing alive, you hear me?"

Echo finds herself hoping it's Oren who appears when those doors inevitably open. It would be a fitting end for him to die at the hands of the people he sent into the nothingness, declaring them Forgotten.

Taking two steps back, Echo stands with River, readying herself for whatever terror Oren will rain down on them next.

"This is where we take control," Sledge growls to the crowd. "Gather together. We're one unit. We'll face this together."

The seconds tick by like excruciating minutes, but they hold their formation, determined to fight whatever horror Oren unleashes on them next.

"What if it's full of queens?" Jupiter asks from somewhere behind Echo.

"He could just send them through the vents," says Nola. "It won't be queens."

"Maybe it's nothing," a Green Born says hopefully.

"It won't be nothing," someone else replies before Echo gets the chance.

There's a creak, and the doors open a crack, even though Echo was certain she hadn't heard the elevator return.

"Hold steady!" Lyra calls.

The doors slide back in a rush, revealing an empty space. The elevator car is missing, leaving only the steel cables that run the length of the Sting.

A bearded Moon Worker steps forward and turns to look up into the shaft while his companions remain poised, ready to strike. The man makes a sudden garbled noise, then flies upwards in a blur, and disappears.

"What happened?" River gasps.

"I don't know." Echo's heart thumps. "He was there one second and gone the next."

"Ojai!" Lyra shouts, leaning forward. "Are you okay?"

"Watch out!" shouts Echo, just as Ojai's scythe clatters down the elevator shaft, landing with a clang at the base.

Lyra jumps back, clutching her own weapon in her shaking hands.

"Ojai!" one of the other Moon Workers shouts, his voice echoing back at them in the empty shaft. "Where are you?"

An eerie silence envelops them, every one of the frightened people in the graveyard doing their best to still their beating hearts as they wait.

"I'm going to look up there," Lyra says eventually. "I didn't come this far just to stand here."

"Wait," says the other Moon Worker. "I'll hold onto you."

"No," says Tuff, stepping forward. "I will."

Tuff is easily the tallest and strongest person here, well used to hefting people around the Green Zone, whether they were dead or alive. He's the best person for this job and he knows it.

Lyra eyes Tuff suspiciously as he grips her around the waist.

"We're all on the same team," River reminds her. "You can trust him."

Makk winds his whip around his wrist and grabs the back of Tuff's shirt. "I'll hold onto Dad."

"No, you won't," says Goldie, slipping between father and son. "I'll hold him. You can hold me."

Lyra turns back to the elevator shaft and cautiously leans forward.

"Can't see anything yet." Her voice quavers. "Or n—"

Lyra's feet lift from the floor and Tuff grabs on tight. River dashes forward to help Goldie keep hold of Tuff, and Echo sees two metal pincers on the end of long spindly legs gripping Lyra by the shoulders.

"It's a Worker," she gasps.

Lyra lets out a scream as she thrashes, fighting against the metallic beast trying to drag her into the elevator shaft. There's the clanking of metal as her scythe hits at the Worker. Tuff grunts as he holds on tight and more people surge forward as they form a human chain, all determined not to let the Worker claim another life.

"Aim for the disc on her back!" River shouts at Lyra. "It's the only way to kill her!"

Lyra swings her scythe upward, while the others hold her down.

Echo goes to help River, but a set of strong arms pull her back.

"Keep the baby safe," pants Nola. "There are enough people helping already."

Echo grits her teeth. She's pregnant, not useless. But Nola's also right, so she stays back, making no promises to remain that way.

There's more screaming and thrashing, then an almighty clatter as a Worker drops in the elevator shaft and crashes to the base. The killing machine lapses into seizures, sending her long legs into tremors as her glowing disc blinks, fades, then extinguishes.

"Got you!" Lyra shouts as she collapses back into the people who'd been holding her down. She rights herself and waves her scythe at the Worker. "Take that, you evil creep!"

But no sooner has she said these words, another Worker emerges from above. This one drops smoothly and scurries forward, sending everyone scattering backward.

"Get it!" shouts Lyra as the Moon Workers swing their scythes. "Do not retreat!"

There's a frenzy of movement, punctuated by a series of grunts and crashes. The Moon Workers dispose of the giant bee with surprising speed, lighting everyone's souls with hope.

"Bring it on, Oren!" calls Sledge, who's now holding a scythe. "Send us anoth—"

"Look out!" someone screams, and Echo spins around to see a third Worker scurrying down the elevator cable with amazing dexterity for a metallic beast of such enormous size.

"Get it!" cries Lyra.

"Wait!" shouts River. "It's Nectar! It's the friendly one!"

The people freeze, trusting River completely as Nectar emerges from the elevator shaft and makes her way peacefully through the people to come to a stand beside River. He pats her head in the way Flora used to and her silver disc glows softly.

Relief whooshes out of Echo. Nectar won't let anything happen to River. She'll protect everyone here, but she'll protect River first.

"Stay on guard," Sledge growls, his focus firmly on the empty space before them. "Oren's not finished with us yet."

The people form a barrier at the elevator with Nectar at the front. River's right behind her, ready to issue whatever command is needed to keep them safe.

Everyone holds still. Waiting to see what Oren's going to throw at them next.

Unable to stay back for another moment, Echo's just about to join River when she hears a movement behind her.

She spins around to see Chase standing at the end of one of the tunnels with a bundle of fabric in his arms. He looks so broken that for a moment Echo questions if it's even him. He's perfectly still, frozen in time, and it tears at Echo to see her friend like this.

Chase needs her. And there's no doubt they need him in this war. But she's afraid the moment she leaves the group gathered at the elevator Oren will strike.

Knowing she has no choice, she runs to Chase, quickly realizing it's not fabric he's holding.

It's Flora.

Her body's been preserved by Oren's Workers and wrapped in cloth.

Chase collapses to his knees and looks up at Echo, tears streaming down his handsome face.

"I didn't search for her, Echo," he sobs. "She disappeared and I didn't go after her."

"You were trying to do what was right," says Echo, wishing he'd chosen another time to give in to his grief. "You always do."

He shakes his head. "It wasn't right. She thought I didn't love her. But I did. I loved her so much."

"I know." Echo glances over her shoulder to make sure another Worker hasn't emerged. Everyone remains still, apart from Nola and Vern who are running across to them.

Nola gets to Chase and kneels in front of him, reaching out to touch her daughter's lifeless face.

"My Flora," she whispers as Vern crouches beside her. "My beautiful, clever girl."

Chase carefully places Flora's remains in her mother's arms and Nola draws her to her chest while Vern puts a steadying arm around her. It's a scene that breaks Echo's heart and she finds herself with her palm pressed to her stomach, trying to protect her child in a way she knows she won't be able to once they're no longer cocooned in her belly.

"I loved her so much," Chase repeats as he stands. "I wasn't there when she needed me."

"I know, Chase." Echo looks over her shoulder again, relieved that nothing has happened just yet. "But right now, the Razers are the ones who need you. You've worked all your life for this moment."

Chase looks toward the crowd gathered at the elevator, seeming confused. Echo's not sure what's caused this snap in his sanity, but it could be any number of things.

Grief.

Guilt.

Malnutrition.

Dehydration.

Exhaustion.

Seeing so many of his people die after dedicating his entire life to saving them...

That would be more than enough to break even the strongest person.

She takes his hand and drags him away from Flora, hoping he can hold onto enough of himself to find the fight she knows burns inside him.

Makk spots them and dashes over.

"There you are!" he cries. "Come on! The Razers need you."

Chase gives Makk a half smile and lets go of Echo to allow Makk to lead him to the front of the group beside Nectar and River. He plants his feet and raises his fists, and Echo lets out a breath.

Chase is back.

River glances at Echo and she gives him a nod to let him know she's okay. She makes her way forward, refusing to face this threat from the back of the crowd. This has been her fight from the start, and she intends to finish it standing by River's side.

Lyra lets out a battle cry from the front row and Echo braces herself. There's the sound of whirring and the clanking of metal on metal and a Worker drops to the base of the elevator, filling the entire space as she balances herself expertly on the broken remains of the beast Lyra killed. There are several more sets of pincers holding onto the elevator cables as the shaft flashes with colorful lights.

"There's more of them!" Lyra cries. "Don't let a single one of them out!"

The Worker at the base of the shaft leaps forward and Lyra brings down her scythe. She misses and the giant beast swipes at her, knocking her backward. Sledge brings down his weapon, shattering the red disc and disabling the threat as the Worker collapses, joining her fallen comrade.

"Two down!" cries Lyra as she scrambles forward with blood running down one side of her face.

Nobody has time to recover, let alone take a breath as the next Worker emerges. Nectar shoots ahead with River shouting commands as she swipes and thrashes at their attacker. Backing the Worker into a corner, Nectar drives her stinger forward, piercing the beast's belly just like she did in the Hive. The giant queen squeals and clatters to the floor as Lyra smashes her scythe into the red disc.

The next Worker drops down before this one is even dead, quickly pinning Lyra to the wall. But the beast has little hope. She may be larger and stronger than the army she's facing, but she's nowhere near as angry.

The people are in a frenzy and everyone here knows they have nothing to lose. They surge forward, pulling the beast away from Lyra and clawing at it. It attacks back, sending people flying.

Echo picks up a scythe that's fallen to the floor and swings it at the Worker, using all the fury she's built up inside her at the injustice of the world. She pretends each of the metallic beasts that continue to emerge is Oren and this fuels her further.

It's hard to know how many people they're losing in this battle, but not a single Worker has made it out of the elevator shaft.

"The elevator!" River shouts from inside the shaft. "It's coming down!"

Echo's eyes fly wide as she pants, trying to feed her starving lungs. "Reed must've worked it out!"

Nectar picks up River with her front legs and scurries out of the shaft as more Workers drop down, landing on top of each other as the elevator car knocks them from their positions clinging to the cables. The result is a mess of metal with the Workers' legs entangling with each other as they do their best to separate themselves and get on their feet.

"Get back!" River cries, extending his arms to try to force the line of people away from danger.

The base of the elevator car appears and the Workers scramble harder to free themselves. But the more they thrash, the more tangled they become.

"Watch out!" Echo screams as one of the beasts manages to wrench herself free. Her long front leg darts out and grabs Makk's whip, which is still wrapped around his wrist. He flies into the shaft, landing on the pile of twisted metal, and screams as the elevator continues to come down.

"Stop!" Echo cries, hoping Reed can hear her. "Stop the elevator!

River shouts something at Nectar but before she can process the command and react, Chase has launched himself into the elevator shaft. He unravels Makk's hand and pushes the boy toward Tuff, who passes him to his hysterical mother and turns around.

Just as the elevator completes its journey.

Crushing every last Worker.

And Chase.

Amidst the sound of metal bending and twisting, there's one noticeable sound that's missing. Chase doesn't so much as mutter a word, let alone scream.

"Chase!" Makk whimpers from his mother's arms. "Is he okay? Where's Chase? Chase!"

Echo goes to Makk, squatting in front of the boy who just lost his hero.

"He's gone," she says, her own heart aching at the loss of her friend.

"It's my fault," Makk sobs.

"It's what Chase wanted." Echo shakes her head. "He died like a true Razer. And he's with Flora now."

"But I didn't even like Flora," Makk whines as his mother hugs him closer.

"Echo." River says her name in such a way it has her standing and going to him without hesitation.

"What is it?" she asks as their hands automatically find each other.

"The doors are opening." River turns to the elevator as everyone who's still standing contracts around them.

"What next?" Lyra groans.

As the doors begin to slide apart, Echo instinctively draws closer to River, certain of one thing.

Whatever's inside, it's not going to be good.

CHAPTER
TWENTY-SIX
RIVER

R iver braces himself, the adrenaline that had barely faded flashing hot and fast again. He tugs Echo a little behind him, and surprisingly, she lets him. Admittedly, not as far back or behind as she'd like, but enough that part of her is obscured. The fact that his bold fighter allowed the compromise is a testament to how high the stakes are.

Every life in this room is hanging by a gossamer thread.

Including their unborn child's.

The seconds before the elevator doors fully open feel like minutes. Too long for every eye to be unblinking. For every lung to be frozen. As they wait, everyone's as silent and breathless as the corpses lining the tunnels around them.

The white doors slide open, uncaring of the time it takes to do so. Far slower than River's thundering heart wishes. Far faster than the dread in his gut can process.

The first thing that's visible is a wall of black and gold, tiny red lights flashing within.

"Queens again," Echo gasps.

The people behind them collectively shudder and contract,

children tucked in amongst the adults, scythes and chair legs and whatever else they could snatch to use as a weapon clutched in white-knuckled hands.

River takes an involuntary step back, bringing Echo with him. The same thought from the eating hall is pummeling his mind.

Killing everyone can't be Oren's plan.

Not unless he's finally snapped...

The queens move as one as they float through the open doors, then expand to create a shimmering veil. Revealing what's behind.

Oren's smile twists the skin molded by fire as he steps through, the queens moving so they form a hovering, buzzing cloud around him. The faint, cumulative light from their backs illuminates his melted features in a sick, crimson glow.

The first collective breath of the people he's regarding is a horrified intake.

Their reaction only makes him smile wider.

Oren stops, then glances back at the elevator. It sits a few inches off the ground, the crushed metal of the Workers beneath it.

Along with Chase.

River's chest tightens at the loss. Ultimately, Chase's sacrifice to save Makk proved how far he'd go for those who need protecting and defending. River respects that. Honors that. Chase just didn't realize Flora, with her smarts and her show of strength, was one of them. River hopes that somehow, now that they're both gone, Flora knows that.

Oren snorts. "When will you people learn?" His gaze steadily turns back to River, Echo and the others. "I crushed the so-called leader of the Razers, just like anyone else who's foolish enough to defy me."

"And the Workers were just collateral," River spits. "Like every life in this graveyard."

Oren's eyes flare as his mangled lip twists. "You saw what happens when you try to save everyone." His gaze flickers to Lyra, then back. "I'm the only one strong enough to do what needs to be done."

"You're a cold-blooded murderer," Echo shouts, her voice hard with conviction. "Nothing more."

"Murderer!" River's father cries.

"Killer!" someone else shouts.

Several people stomp their feet, a few Moon Workers rap their scythes against the cement floor as a growl of agreement fills the air.

Oren simply glares at them in disgust. "Short-sighted idiots," he spits. "I'm the one being humane. By fighting for your Vulnerable lives, you're selfishly signing everyone's death warrant. A slow death by disease and starvation."

"That's not the way it has to be," River calls out, rejecting Oren's words. "We don't have to choose."

Oren takes a step forward and the crowd instinctively retreats, maintaining the distance between them. The queens move with him, a humming, deadly barrier if anyone were to try and get close to him.

"They haven't told you, have they?" His gaze flickers to River, glowing with triumph. "There is no Sovereign."

Shock ripples through the crowd as River's hands clench. Oren's weaving a narrative of hopelessness. One where he's some twisted hero fighting to save humanity, one strong enough to make the hard choices.

"That doesn't mean—" River starts, only to be interrupted.

"Flora was the Sovereign," Oren shouts, the queen bees surrounding him twitching at the elevated noise. "And she chose to die rather than save you." He levels his gaze to River.

"You call me murderer and killer, but what does that make her?"

River's mouth clamps shut as he's rendered mute by the pain and betrayal of his twin's loss.

"She was broken by you," Echo says, her voice low, yet carrying through the room as she steps beside River. "Her death is a testament to the darkness you've sown, Oren, long before we reached this moment. She believed you were her father. And you rejected her, over and over. You broke the Sovereign years before we knew who she was."

Realization dawns through River. Echo's right. Oren broke the very thing he killed so many searching for.

"You're not the voice of hope," River says, each word stronger and louder than the ones before it. "You're the destroyer of faith. Of dreams. Of souls. Of everything humanity needs to survive."

Flora was the Sovereign, but she was also a symbol of the fragility of the human heart. Of what it needs to thrive.

Silence once more reigns, and River has no idea what the people behind him are thinking. Have Oren's words fractured the fragile peace between Green Born and Dead Born, the one they worked so hard for?

Or have they realized what they're really fighting for here?

Not Immunity.

But the core of humanity itself.

The power of unity.

Oren lifts his arms and the queens move with him, a hazy, dark cloud outlining his every move. "Those who are Immune, step forward," he booms, clearly having realized that's where the threat lies. "You will be spared from what's coming."

The promise of death drips from every word. Oren's cold smile only reinforces it.

227

This is their last chance for his precious Immunes to choose him.

River remains still, as does Echo. She realizes, just as he does, that it's time for each person here to make their choice. To decide what they're going to live for.

A heartbeat passes.

Then another.

No one moves.

For the first time since they entered the Sting, River's heart swells. Pride infuses it. Gratitude fills it. A sense of purpose encloses it.

While a small amount of glee sparks deep inside it.

No one is willing to side with Oren. Even if they're Immune. No matter what he plans.

River holds the gaze of the man who was once his father, smiles a little, then takes a deliberate step backward. Echo comes with him, her chin high. It's a small movement.

But a significant one.

They merge with the people around them, Green Born, Dead Born, Moon Worker. Someone grips his other hand while another hand lands on his shoulder. Others close around Echo, forming their own protective barrier.

A human one.

One there by choice, not the small red lights on their back, controlling them.

Fury fractures across Oren's face, flushing it a deep, dark red. His scarred, mangled skin almost looks pale in comparison. "Then so be it," he screams.

The words are so loud, so infused with vitriol, that the queens around him ripple as the shockwaves move through them. Their humming increases. Their movements become agitated.

River and Echo step back along with the crowd, watching

as the queens contract around Oren. His rage has irritated them.

His hatred could be the very thing that ends him.

Except he pushes up his sleeve as he unclenches his hand, revealing a small controller in his palm. The moment his muscles ease, so do the queens. They expand around him once more, although their agitated humming still fills the air. They're unable to fight the technology attached to their back.

"They're under my complete control," Oren says, a smug smile playing at the edges of his melted lips.

River braces himself. If this final act of rebellion has sent Oren over the edge, they're about to fight a swarm of queen bees in the same way they did in the Dead Zone.

But Oren's gaze moves over the crowd, to the back of the large room, then to each side. "Just like they are."

The clattering of metal legs on cement, the humming that grows exponentially, has ice clawing up River's spine. Each gasp that follows is like an adrenaline shot for his pulse.

From the corner of his eye, a Worker appears at the mouth of a tunnel. Then another in the one beside it.

Lyra gasps, stepping further into the crowd as yet another mechanical bee appears on the other side. River's eyes dart all around as each tunnel fills with a metal body, the blue and red discs on the back illuminating their impassive faces.

Within seconds, each tunnel has a Worker standing before it. As one, they enter the large room, their legs on the hard floor sounding like a death rattle.

The doors slamming closed behind them, shutting off the tunnels, only solidifies it.

They're trapped in here.

With over a dozen Workers.

The low chuckle that slices through the silence has River spinning back. Oren's stepping into the elevator, his queens framing him. He mouths one word as the doors close on his triumphant face.

"Proelium."

The Workers move as one, lifting into the air, then spearing down.

"Fight!" River roars, breaking into a run.

"Smash their discs!" Echo shouts, right beside him.

The Worker closest to their right darts down and grabs a Dead Born at the edge of the crowd. A Moon Worker leaps up, slashing with his scythe, but she's too quick. The scythe clangs against her legs as she flies up out of reach.

She hovers there, curls her abdomen in and stings the Dead Born, the needle-like tip impaling his back. She's already descending, impervious to his screams of agony as she drops him and snatches her next victim. A woman falls on the man's already swollen body, wailing.

Horror slices through River. The Workers are identifying the Immune.

And culling everyone else.

"Don't let them grab you," he shouts. "Avoid their stingers!"

The people scatter, screaming with both fear and fury. The chair legs and pieces of timber they'd snatched to protect themselves against the queens become their weapons as the Workers hunt them down.

One dips, trying to grab Tuff, but he ducks and lashes out with the length of metal he's holding. There's a loud clang and the Worker retreats. Only to drop down and take a Green Born next to him.

With lightning-fast movements, she stings the woman then drops her, already scanning for more prey.

River stops, tugging Echo close to him. They're Immune, so would survive. But the majority of the people here won't.

And there's nowhere to hide.

A scream has River spinning around. He knows that voice. It's one far too close to his heart.

Just as he dreaded, a Worker has picked up his mother. She screams again as she flails, her legs thrashing through the air. A roar follows as River's father leaps and grabs the legs wrapped around River's mother's torso. His face contorts as he drags himself up, a short piece of wood in his hand.

River's running as his own denial explodes from his lungs. "Mom! No!"

The Worker folds in on herself, ignoring Vern as if he's the insect as her stinger arcs in. It jams into River's mother's back, making her arch and cry out. Vern's wail of pain joins her.

The Worker drops her and River's mother falls to the ground in a heap. His father leaps after her, folding over her protectively. But the Worker's already moved on. She's done what she was programmed to do.

"Magnolia," River's father screams, hands fluttering as he knows there's nothing he can do. "My beautiful Magnolia!"

River leaps over a swollen, lifeless Moon Worker, his heart already aching as it pounds against his ribs. Not his mother. Please, not his mother. He can't lose her too!

A shadow appears overhead, but River never slows as he continues the desperate run to his parents. He ducks, wildly thrashing out with his arm. It hits hard metal as she tries to grapple him.

"River!" Echo screams.

He looks up to see the Worker coming down on him, lights flashing with excitement behind the glass of her eyes. He puts up his hand although it's no use. He's next to be taken and stung.

The Worker barrels out of his line of sight as another monstrous metal machine crashes into her. River reels back and as the people around him scatter. Two Workers just crashed?

"Nectar!" River gasps as he realizes what's happened.

She's been programmed to protect him!

The attacking Worker reels sideways, trying to right herself, but Nectar is already aiming at her with her stinger. River turns away, knowing his very own knight in shining armor will take care of the threat.

Right now, his mom is dying.

Except when his gaze falls on his parents, he sees his mother blink up at his dad, then lift a shaking hand to cup his cheek as a smile fills her green eyes.

River stops, shocked and relieved. His mother's Immune.

Echo appears beside him, breathing hard. "Thank goodness," she breathes as she registers what River did. But then she looks around, her body going tense. "River, we have to do something..."

He scans the mayhem around them. People are screaming and running, shouting and fighting. But no matter what they do, the Workers are picking them off one by one and stinging them.

Already the crowd is thinning. Bloated bodies litter the ground.

Oren's ultimate plan is working.

"Nectar!" River shouts.

She rises from the carnage of the Worker she just demolished, shooting straight for him. River glances at Echo. "Get ready."

She nods, looking around and grabbing a nearby scythe. A dead Moon Worker lies not far away, her sightless eyes staring up at machines trying to exterminate them.

Nectar drops low as he runs toward her, grasps her harness and leaps on. Urging her forward, he aims for Echo. The moment they're close, he swoops down and reaches a hand out. Echo grabs it and he hauls her up behind him.

"That one!" Echo shouts.

River angles Nectar, aiming for the nearest Worker. They fly high over her then spear down. The moment they're close enough, Echo jabs the scythe, fracturing the glass of the disc. But not breaking it. The Worker angles away with an angry hum, dipping dangerously, but not losing control.

"We can finish her," Echo yells.

River chases the Worker, ducking past another as she catches a Green Born. One slam into her side and she drops her prey. Daisy runs away, throwing herself at the nearest tunnel as she desperately tries to open the door. Tears stream down her cheeks as she pulls and heaves, but it doesn't move.

"Up, River!"

He instinctively follows Echo's command, angling Nectar high. They fly over another Worker, narrowly missing her, then straight toward the damaged one.

"Hold on," River says, gripping Nectar's metal body more tightly with his legs. Echo's arm tightens around his waist.

They dip fast, then angle sharply.

The moment they're in reach, Echo slams the scythe down on the broken glass. It shatters completely, the blue light flaring bright then dying out just as fast.

"Look out!" River shouts as the Worker crashes to the ground.

Green Born and Dead Born sprint to get out of the way. All but one body that lies prone on the ground.

River almost groans as he realizes who it is.

In the time it took to kill the Worker, Daisy was attacked again. And killed.

The dead Worker collapses on top of her, crumpling into a heap of lifeless metal.

As Nectar rights herself, no doubt waiting for the next instruction, River scans the tidal wave of destruction they're trying to stop.

They won't be able to end all of the Workers. Not before far too many die.

"We need somewhere to hide," Echo says, her voice thick with emotion.

River's own throat is tight with the pain of having to watch this unfold. Oren's trapped them underground. There's nowhere to go.

Except Echo's words give him an idea.

He angles Nectar down, aiming for the nearest tunnel. The moment they touch hard ground, he says one word.

"Aperta."

Nectar walks forward and taps out a combination on the nearby pad, just like she did the time Vern was trapped in one of the tunnels.

The doors instantly slide open.

"Yes!" Echo gasps as she leaps down.

River joins her, staring into the darkness that's waiting. The darkness that may be their salvation.

It seems Flora's parting gift could turn the tide, after all.

"Everyone in here!" he screams. "Hurry!"

"This way," Echo shouts. "We can get away!"

As pale faces turn and realize there's a sliver of hope of surviving this, River realizes they've uncovered more than just a place to hide.

They were able to fight off the Workers when they were bottlenecked in the elevator. Maybe the tunnel will allow them to do the same.

As a tide of people come at them, he glances at Echo, finding the same knowledge settling in her dark gaze.

It's their only hope.

TWENTY-SEVEN

ECHO

Echo waits beside River as the people run past them into the dimly lit tunnel.

"Let the Vulnerables go first!" River calls after them.

"If you have a weapon, give it to an Immune," Echo adds, willing everyone to move faster.

A Worker charges forward and swipes at a Dead Born at the rear of the group, sending them sliding. Nectar screeches and immediately attacks. A Green Born seizes the chance to help the terrified Dead Born, dragging them into the tunnel. It's a scene Echo never thought she'd see, and if she weren't in such a panic, she'd take a moment to feel proud.

Nectar rears up on her back legs and strikes the other Worker with her front pincers, stabbing her giant stinger forward as she tries to impale her opponent. Another Worker joins the fight and Nectar swings around seeming to have already anticipated this.

Echo and River back down the tunnel, knowing there's nothing they can do to help Nectar. They've seen her face similar situations before and come out victorious. They just have to hope she can succeed once more.

They turn around so they can move faster, and see Nola, Makk and Tuff running at the back of the group. Maybe Echo should have thought through her request for the Vulnerables to go first. Nola may be Immune but she's weak from her recent attack. And Makk's only a kid—one who Chase just gave his life to save. But Tuff's running a little slower and Echo has no doubt he'll do whatever it takes to keep them both safe. As a Vulnerable, Lyra is further ahead, shouting at everyone to keep moving no matter what.

"Will Nectar be okay?" Echo pants, hating that they left her to fight for them.

"Flora programmed her to be smart," says River, glancing over his shoulder as they run. "She can do it."

There's the sound of clashing metal and the familiar screeching of a Worker succumbing to death and Echo gasps, hoping it wasn't Nectar. Every one of their lives is depending on her right now.

Looking back, she sees a Worker flying into the tunnel.

"River!" she screams, grabbing his arm. "Look!"

River spins around, then pauses. "It's Nectar!"

Echo pants hard beside him as she tries to feed her lungs with oxygen. Nectar also comes to a stop and is working furiously at the roof of the tunnel. But she's too far away for Echo to see what she's doing.

"She's digging!" River gasps. "She's collapsing the tunnel."

Echo hadn't heard River call out a command. "Did you tell her to do that?"

He shakes his head. "Told you Flora made her smart."

"She's helping us, even now," says Echo. Flora may have believed humanity wasn't worth saving, but she left behind a legacy to help them on their way. Chase did too. Half the Dead

Borns in this tunnel are here because he recruited them to his cause.

A bubble of grief builds in Echo's chest, and she pushes it down. There will be time to mourn the loss of her friend later. Right now, she needs to make sure she doesn't lose any more.

Nectar works quickly, caving in the roof of the tunnel to build a wall. It's even darker in the enclosed space now without the glow from the main chamber of the graveyard filtering in. The way Nectar continues to move, it's clear the other Workers have found her and are trying to break their way through. But she's determined to fight them off.

"We need to move!" River shouts, pulling her further into the tunnel.

They run, trying to close the gap between the rest of the group.

"Where do you think it leads?" Echo asks.

"I don't know." River's voice is laced with worry. "I haven't been down here before."

"How can you tell?" All the tunnels look the same to Echo, although she hasn't spent as much time down here as River.

"The others were lined with cement," he pants. "And this one smells different."

Echo draws in the earthy scent to realize River's right. It's fresher somehow. Could it be too much to hope that there's a door to the outside world? Echo would be happy if it were the Extinction Zone. Anywhere other than this crypt will do. She imagines a life raising her child by the moonlight in the Moon Zone and decides she'd be perfectly fine with that. If she'd known she was pregnant when she was there, she may never have left at all. The only thing that matters now is making sure her child has the chance to draw breath.

They catch up to the others whose energy seems to be flagging.

"One zone!" River calls out, doing his best to keep them motivated to move. "One people!"

And with those words, Echo knows she needs more for her child than just the chance to live. She needs to be able to provide them with a life worth living. Which means she has to fight. This isn't over until they put an end to Oren. Because he's proven that while he's still breathing, he's never going to stop.

"We do it for Chase!" calls Makk, picking up his pace.

"And Daisy!" shouts someone else.

"And Ojai," growls Lyra.

Everyone here is missing someone they cared about. This isn't just a battle for their lives, it's a fight for everyone who's already lost.

"There's a door!" shouts Jupiter, grinding to a halt.

The group of people stop, panting hard as they gather around Jupiter. Echo moves behind River as they work their way to the front. They're nowhere near the end of the tunnel. It seems unlikely there'd be a door.

"Where is it?" asks Echo, struggling to see anything in the dim light.

"I felt it as my fingertips brushed past," says Jupiter. "Just here."

River runs his hands over the wall.

"You're right," he says. "There's an opening here. A metal panel. And this part of the wall's made from stone."

A screech of Workers rattles down the tunnel and Echo hopes with every shred of her battered soul that Nectar is keeping Oren's army at bay. It seems inevitable they'll eventually break their way through.

"We have to hurry," Echo says, her heart beating fast. "If we can't open it, we need to keep running."

"I can't keep running," an exhausted Dead Born sobs.

"We can open it." Lyra steps forward in the shadows with her scythe raised. "Get out of the way."

They all step back as Lyra swings at the door. Sledge joins her and they take it in turns to beat at the metal opening. Each thud echoes down the tunnel to join the screeching of the Workers.

"Nearly there," grunts Sledge as he abandons his scythe and kicks at the panel. The door buckles, then flies off its hinges leaving an opening the size of Nola's half door in her hut back home. Which right now feels a million miles away.

Golden light pours into the tunnel and Echo blinks, trying to understand what could possibly be behind this wall. Surely not another Hive...

There's the sound of Workers screeching, then a loud whirr.

"They're coming!" Echo gasps. "Get inside."

The people crouch as they move quickly into whatever strange place is on the other side of the small door. If it's another one of Oren's traps, then they've fallen for it. But there's really no other choice.

"Hurry!" says River, ushering as many people in as fast as he can.

A Worker flies down the tunnel and Echo holds her breath, unable to see the color of the disc glowing on her back. River puts a hand on Echo's head and pushes her through the door now that everyone else is inside, and dives in behind her.

Echo blinks in the bright light, struggling to find her focus amongst the horde of people. She turns back to the doorway to see Tuff slide in the piece of metal, working with Lyra to use their scythes to secure it in place. There's a loud clang as the Worker beats at it from the other side.

"What if it doesn't hold?" Goldie asks, pulling Makk to her.

"The Workers are too big," says River. "They'll never fit through the opening."

A sadness passes over Echo to realize that includes Nectar. Hopefully wherever she is, she's not too badly damaged.

Reminding herself that Nectar is made from metal and not from flesh, she turns around to see where they are.

"River," she whispers, all other words failing her as she takes in what she's looking at.

They're standing on the edge of a large underground field. Golden light is streaming from lamps that line the ceiling, along with dripping hoses to water the long rows of crops that stretch out before them. The water droplets catch the light and sparkle like an upside-down night's sky.

People are already scurrying down the rows of plants. Some are finding places to hide. Others are picking off leaves and holding them to their nose, trying to work out whether they can eat them. Jupiter has found a hose and is filling buckets and passing them around for people to drink.

Echo glances at River to see if he's noticed what she has. Because every plant here is exactly the same species. And it's the one thing Echo never expected to see again. Surely, this is too good to be true.

"Serpentwood," they say in unison as their hands interlink.

"Oren didn't destroy it." River squeezes her tightly. "He just wanted us to believe he did."

"It was all for show." Echo shakes her head, barely able to take in the vast quantity of serpentwood before them. It's not even close to being endangered. She would no longer even call it rare. "He was keeping it all for himself."

"We should have known," growls River. "He'd never leave himself without a backup plan."

Always one step ahead, it seems Oren had gone to great

lengths to ensure he could continue to manufacture adrenacure, along with his false Immunity.

Jupiter comes over with a bucket of water. "You need to drink."

"Thanks." River takes the bucket and passes it to Echo.

She takes long gulps of the cool liquid, then passes it to River as she wipes her mouth with the back of her hand.

"We also need to get out of here," says Jupiter, keeping their voice low.

Echo nods. "We definitely can't go out the way we came."

There's another loud crash at the metal door and Echo jumps. Even though the Workers can't get in, they haven't given up trying. Tuff and Lyra hold onto the scythes, making sure the door stays in place.

Jupiter takes the bucket of water over to them, ensuring they get their fill.

"River!" shouts Makk. "Echo!"

Echo scans the field but can't spot Makk's small frame amongst the rows of serpentwood.

"Up here!"

She looks up and sees Makk near the ceiling, halfway down the field.

"There's a ladder!" he calls, answering the question she didn't get time to ask.

They run down between two rows of serpentwood and Echo's aware if she didn't look up, it would feel exactly like she's outside. The lamps are throwing off heat making it feel like a warm sunny day. Without the blue sky, which she can only hope she'll live to see again one day.

Goldie is halfway up the ladder behind Makk, not prepared to let her determined son get too far away.

"There's a hatch up here!" Makk pushes on a panel. It

opens and he moves it out of the way and climbs further up, disappearing into the roof.

"Get back down here!" Goldie shouts, climbing faster to reach him.

River is the next up the ladder and Echo follows with a little distance, not wanting to put too much weight on the ladder at once.

As Goldie reaches the top, Makk's face appears.

"It's another tunnel," he calls down. "It goes up. I think it leads outside."

Hope lights in Echo's chest. She's tired of running. With every twist that Oren throws at them, they're losing more people. They can't go on much longer before they'll be forced to admit defeat.

There's more crashing at the metal door and Echo looks down to see Tuff fall backward as it caves in. Long metal legs swipe through the open space as he and Lyra shuffle away from danger.

"It's no use!" Lyra calls. "We can't keep it closed."

The Workers claw at the edges of the doorway, trying to widen it. Going anywhere near it now is far too risky.

"Over here!" Echo calls back. "We think we can get out!"

People emerge from their hiding places and gather at the base of the ladder as they wait their turn to climb.

Goldie disappears into the ceiling, followed by River, then Echo climbs through. The tight space she finds herself in reminds her of the tunnel from the bunker that led to the Green Zone. She crawls through, dragging herself upward, telling herself that each gulp of air she's drawing in is fresher than the one before.

Just as her skin feels like it's going to tear from her knees, she sees daylight. River hauls himself out of the tunnel and spins around to help drag Echo up onto solid ground. She's out of breath and falls onto her back and looks up to see something miraculous.

Blue sky.

It's the most beautiful sight in all the world. Other than River's face, of course. Turning her head, she sees he's still working to help others from the tunnel one by one.

"We got out." She breathes in the fresh air, hoping there's enough time for everyone else to make it out, too.

"I did it," says Makk, hopping around beside Echo as she struggles to her feet. "I really did it."

"You sure did." She reaches out to touch his arm.

"I think that's why Chase saved me," says Makk quietly.

"What do you mean?" Echo asks.

"He saved me so I could find a way out and save all these people." Makk pulls back his shoulders. "I'm a real Razer now."

Echo smiles. "You always were, Makk."

Liking the sound of that, Makk goes to help River, giving his aunt Nola a big hug when she emerges.

Echo's proud her child will be related to Makk. And Vern and Nola. Her family may no longer be around, but her child will grow up loved.

Looking around, she sees they're in the Extinction Zone. The Sting looms in the distance, telling her they're not too far away from the edge of the Green Zone. She doesn't really care where they are, just as long as they're not in the Sovereign graveyard. Because now they have a chance to make this right in a way they couldn't when they were in Oren's domain with him calling all the shots.

Tuff emerges last from the tunnel and goes directly to Makk and Goldie, drawing them into a hug.

"Is that the last of everyone?" River asks, peering down into the darkness.

Sledge has Fray tucked into his side, but he turns to River and nods.

A quiet sadness crosses over Echo as she thinks of all the people who didn't make it. So many either gave their lives for the cause or had it snatched away against their will. Only one person has been getting what they want out of this. And he's somewhere in that tall building they nearly lost their lives escaping from.

River comes to Echo and wraps his arms around her. She snuggles into his chest, grateful for the chance to do this when there were so many moments she thought it would never happen again.

"We have to go back," she whispers, surprising even herself with how firmly she believes this.

Oren can't get what he wants. He can't win. Not after all the death and misery he's caused. They have to put a stop to him, or they'll never be able to live without looking over their shoulders as they wait for him to play his next move.

"I know," River says.

Two simple words that have enormous ramifications.

Two words that could spell life.

Or death.

But both of them know there's no choice.

There's a whirring sound and Echo and River let go of each other and look to the sky.

"Nectar," says River, his face lighting up. "But how?"

"She's smart, remember." Echo beams up at the mechanical beast who's become both their savior and friend. "Flora made her smart."

Nectar lands in front of them and dips her head. She's covered in dirt, looking more brown than silver. One of her middle legs is missing and while her disc is cracked, it remains intact.

"She must've dug her way out," says Echo, reaching out to pat her.

"You clever queen." River climbs onto Nectar's back and puts out his hand to help Echo up.

"Can I come too?" Makk asks.

Goldie pins her son to her chest as her answer.

"Not this time." River smiles at his cousin.

"Where are you going?" Nola asks, equally as concerned about her own son.

"To finish what we started," says Echo.

River gives the command and Nectar extends her wings and launches her battered body into the air.

It's time for Oren to taste his own venom.

It's time for this war to end.

CHAPTER
TWENTY-EIGHT
RIVER

River tears his gaze away from the pale faces growing smaller as they fly higher. His mother looks terrified that she's about to lose her remaining child. His father is clutching her hand, although it's not clear whether he's offering support or seeking it. The Green Borns and Dead Borns may be wearing different clothes, but their faces hold the same mixture of hope and fear.

Makk is grinning as he punches a fist into the air.

River turns back to face the wind, squeezing Echo's hands as they tighten around his waist. The Sting is straight ahead, a shimmering spire reaching for the sky. Oren's in there. Probably still thinking he's won.

And in some ways, he has.

They may have escaped, but they're not free.

They won't be until he's dead.

River glances back, his heart thundering even though his resolve is steady. The people below are now just a blurred crowd. There's no way to tell the difference between Green

Born and Dead Born. They're simply a huddle of people wanting to live in peace.

In unity.

"River," Echo whispers, lifting a hand to point to their right.

He turns the other way, gasping when he registers what she has.

The Dead Zone is…gone.

There's no net. No haphazard huts. Nothing.

"The fires must've spread," he says, his eyes roaming as he takes in the scale of the devastation.

Before, the Dead Zone was derelict and decrepit, but it held homes. It was a testament to the human fight for survival.

But the flames of the bonfires they lit to keep the queen bees away found a village of dry tinder and unattended fuel.

Now it's just a sea of ash and desolation. There's nothing left.

"We can't go back," Echo says, her voice a mix of sadness and determination.

River faces the Sting once more. "No, we can't."

That's what facing Oren is all about. Turning their back on the way it was. Then forging the way it should be.

"The Hive?" Echo asks.

River nods. They can't go back through the Sovereign graveyard. And the front foyer is probably still locked, as is any other door as Oren seals himself in his fortress. The hole in the Hive is their only way in.

Once there, they can work their way down.

There will be nowhere for Oren to run.

Angling Nectar up, River and Echo rise higher and higher. They circle the narrowing Sting, feeling like they're heading to the sun. The hole appears, a gaping wound in the side of the blazing white as it reflects the light.

Nectar lands, staggering a little now that she's missing one of her legs, and River reaches back to steady Echo. The cracked, silver disc flickers as Nectar crouches and he wonders how much further she can go.

River slides down, helping Echo even though he knows she doesn't need it. They're all tired. Battered. Dredging up the last of their reserves.

He brushes the side of Nectar's head with his palm. "Thanks." She doesn't move, and his lips soften as he switches to Latin. "Gratias."

Nectar hums in response, nuzzling his hand. River almost smiles. Nectar is all he has left of Flora. The small gesture of affection, no matter how programmed, is welcome.

River glances at Echo. "Let's find Reed. He has eyes everywhere, he'll know where Oren is."

"Reed's dead."

The words slice through the air, making River's pulse jackknife. He spins, angry. No, furious.

The finale to this war that's taken too many has come.

Oren continues to stroll into the Hive, any semblance of his twisted smile gone. His eyes are hard, his features solidified in the melted, warped landscape that is now his face. "The ten queens I sent in would've taken care of him."

River's gut clenches. One would've been enough.

"Another death on your conscience," Echo spits.

Oren angles his head, the movement condescending rather than a show of agreement. "Hopefully I'll be able to sleep tonight."

River takes a step forward, leaving the ledge and Nectar behind. Echo's right there with him. "You'll be answering for your crimes long before then," River promises.

Oren's lip twitches. "You never understood. Even though I spent your whole life showing you."

He raises his hand in front of him, then uncurls it. Inside is the controller River noticed in the Sovereign graveyard.

"The queens," Echo breathes, also realizing what it means.

The wall to their right slides down, revealing the hundreds of tiny cells containing the queen bees. They twitch restlessly, creating a patchwork of black and gold movement.

Then the glass containing them is dropping, releasing them.

"You won't be jamming it this time," Oren says, his voice full of dark glee.

River glances at Echo, at the sky behind them, conscious of the deadly drop below. His gaze falls on Nectar. Even damaged and unsteady, she's the only one who can't be killed by the queens.

"Proelium!" River cries, even as he knows this might be the last attack Nectar ever makes.

She whirrs to life, coming up on her five legs as her wings snap out.

"I was just thinking the same thing," Oren snarls.

He shoots his arm forward and the queens spear ahead in a tight formation.

River shoves Echo behind him, his pulse frantic as he looks from Oren to the fast-approaching bees, to the open expanse behind them, even as he knows there's no time to fight or flee.

The queens are an arrow that's already upon them.

Except they fly straight past, swarming over Nectar. They amass on her silver disc, the faint scraping of jaws on glass rasping through the air.

"No," River gasps. He's about to move when a hand clamps on his arm.

"There's nothing you can do," Echo tells him, her dark eyes full of sorrow.

"Unless you want to hasten your death," Oren adds.

An audible crack sounds, followed by a flash of silver light. Nectar crashes to the ground as her disc goes dark.

River turns to Oren, hatred boiling in his veins. This man has taken so much from him. From everyone.

All in some twisted thirst for power.

"Excellent. She was starting to annoy me," Oren says as he twists his hand. The queens return, dutifully hovering around him. "See what can be done when one's willing to make difficult choices?"

River glances at the queens, then back at Oren, unsure what he's trying to convey. "More death?" he spits.

Oren sighs. "Or have I ensured life?"

Echo gasps, realization dawning over her face. "You're going to do the same to the super bees!"

A cold smile curls up Oren's twisted features. "You were always a smart one." He turns his hand one way and the queens tumble in a wave, then twists his palm the other way. The queens roll in the opposite direction, hundreds of tiny puppets under his command. "With this, we won't need Immunity."

Horror slithers up River's spine. "Because you'll control the bees."

Oren draws in a deep breath, his eyes flashing with pride. "They'll be mine. Pollinating where I say. A threat to no one." He licks the edges of his lipless mouth. "Unless I say so."

Even as denial roars through River, he knows with cold, hard certainty that this is Oren's plan. One he refuses to accept. "This isn't the solution."

"It's the only way," Oren shouts, making the queens buzz in agitation. "I'll be the one who saves humanity!"

"Until someone decides to weaponize the bees, like you did," Echo says, waving her arm in the direction of the queens. "Then it'll be a war no one can win."

Oren glares at her. "I'll be in control. That won't happen."

He'll kill anyone who defies him, as many times as he needs to.

"You're sick," River whispers. "Twisted."

Addicted to power.

"I'm the one strong enough to do what needs to be done," Oren snaps, as if saying it so many times will make it true. He lifts his arms, the queens rising with them. "And the last thing standing in the way is you two."

River glances at Echo, knowing what he has to do. There's nowhere to run. No way to fight.

And there's one thing they came here to do.

Without Oren, there are no queen bees under human control. No battle for power. No hatred festering beneath the veneer of civility.

River's heart beats hard inside his tight chest. Maybe this is what he was always supposed to do.

Echo's pregnant. She may carry the Sovereign.

He's the one who has to make sure there's a world for their child to save.

Echo shakes her head, tears shimmering in her eyes. "No, River. It's not the solution."

He wonders if she realizes she just repeated the same words he threw at Oren.

River doesn't respond, his silence saying everything.

It's the only way.

With a maniacal laugh, Oren brings both hands together to point them at River and Echo. The queens shoot forward, mindless killing machines thanks to one man's greed. They fly fast and straight. Their target understood.

River digs his feet into the floor, his hands hot fists at his side. He only needs to get close enough to grab Oren. They're the only weapon he has. All he'll need.

Suddenly, the queen bees explode outward, dispersing like fireworks. River straightens, trying to understand what's happening. Echo grips his hand and plants herself beside him, letting him know he won't be going anywhere.

Together, they watch as the queens come together again, then stop, hovering mid-air, halfway between them and Oren.

"No one's power is absolute," snaps a new voice.

"Reed!" Echo gasps as they watch him enter the Hive.

Oren snarls as he leaps toward him, but Reed lifts his hand, unafraid. The queens dart closer, their humming increasing. The controller sitting in his palm has Oren freezing, fury spitting from his eyes.

Reed skirts around him, flashing a grin at River and Echo as he comes to stand beside them. "By the way, I found the code for controlling the queens."

Echo huffs out a breath, an exhale of relief, but also an almost-laugh. The same two emotions are making River's muscles weak.

Oren's lost.

His own queens will be his undoing.

"Shall I?" Reed asks, arching a brow over his glasses.

Echo smiles. "Don't hold back on our account."

They all turn to the man glaring at them across the room.

"Goodbye, Oren," River says.

Reed throws his fist forward and the queens burst into movement again, but this time in the opposite direction. They shoot straight toward Oren, a deadly mass of black, gold and red.

Except Oren doesn't look terrified.

His own grin twists his features. "Magnolia!"

The queens instantly stop, their red lights flashing furiously. Oren lifts his hand and crooks his finger as his grin impossibly grows.

The queens calmly fly to him in a coordinated mass, hovering in front of him. Waiting for their next order.

The color drops from Reed's face. "He…"

"Yes, I do," Oren booms. "I always have a backup plan."

Using River's mother's name. As if she's Oren's secret weapon.

River and Echo shift closer together, their fingers entwining as the knowledge they've lost closes around them.

Oren was one step ahead.

Like he always has been.

He bursts into laughter, reveling in the moment. Glorying in his victory.

He throws his head back, his cackles growing in volume. "My power is absolute!" he crows. "I am the Sovereign!"

River can't breathe. His heart is frozen behind his ribs. His soul is weeping.

They've lost, even though Oren's claim is most certainly a lie.

And the moment Oren finishes celebrating, they'll be dead.

A faint sound has them instinctively ducking when they realize what it is. The tiny insect floats over them, entering the Hive as if it's curious. As if it's wanting to see what all the fuss is about.

And there's no red light on its back.

It's a simple bee.

No doubt released from the glass column in the foyer, one of the many now buzzing through the Sting.

River watches it, now grieving for the tiny life he grew up worshiping. Their failure means these mighty insects will pay the price for bringing humanity to its knees. The war between man and nature will continue. The fight for dominance will be never ending.

"I am the Sovereign!" Oren roars, his arms out wide, throwing his words out to the world. "Kneel before me!"

The bee twitches with agitation, moving further into the room.

"Now!" Oren screeches.

Reed goes to move but River grabs him by the shoulder. "Never," he says, his voice low and hard.

Oren's hands tighten into fists, making the queens contract. "Kneel before your Sovereign!"

"You will never be the Sovereign," Echo promises.

Oren roars with rage, the sound ricocheting around the room. "Then die!"

The words are ejected like a bullet, agitating the swarm hovering beside him. The queens can't do anything about the noise that's always signaled threat.

But the single bee in the room can.

Drawn to Oren's vitriol, it shoots straight for him and lands just below his jaw.

He freezes, eyes shooting wide open. Then gasps.

His hand lands on his neck with a slap as his eyes bulge.

River's seen the death knell that happens next far too often, yet for the first time, he welcomes it. Oren drops to his knees as his body swells and inflates, his skin turning the color of a bruise.

"He's Vulnerable," Reed says, his eyes wide behind his glasses. "Oren was Vulnerable all along."

Oren gargles out an objection, but nature's already decided his fate, weaving it into his DNA. Making it absolute.

His eyes become slits. His lips turn blue. The scars on his face stretch in grotesque patterns, splitting and bleeding.

He falls forward, slamming into the floor face first.

Dead.

River approaches him slowly, stopping to stand over the

man he called father, the man arrogant enough to crown himself Sovereign.

Echo stands beside him, entwining their fingers like they have so many times before.

But this time is different.

It's symbolic. Monumental.

"Be in peace," River mutters to Oren.

Echo looks up at River. "I know we will be."

He turns to her, unsure whether he's breathing. His chest is too full of love and wonder and disbelief.

Then they're moving, pulling each other into a tight embrace, coming together.

They're crying. They're smiling.

They're...alive.

And although Immunity has remained elusive, they found something just as powerful.

Unity.

A third body crashes into them. "Yep," Reed says, throwing his arms around both of them and clasping tight. "You two are legendary."

5 YEARS LATER

CHAPTER
TWENTY-NINE

ECHO

E cho scans the landscape, glorying in the many gifts of mother nature. The warm sun beats down on rows of lush crops that stretch to the horizon. The sound of laughter floats through the air, mingling with the sweet scent of honey. And a small hand clutches her own.

She squats down and her daughter lets go of her to mimic her position, wobbling a little as she balances on her heels.

"Maggie," Echo scolds, unable to keep the amusement from her voice.

Her daughter grins back at her with the same lively spirit as the grandmother she was named after.

Echo sits on the soft grass, folding her hands on her knees, waiting as Maggie does the same. She scratches her nose, wiggles her toes and claps, giggling as her sweet shadow diligently copies her. It's a game that started when Maggie was only small, and it warms Echo's heart. There'll come a time when her daughter will want to walk her own unique path, but for now all she wants is to be like her mom.

"Are there any bees, Mommy?" Maggie looks around nervously.

"Not here, darling," she replies. "The net keeps us safe."

Rather than living inside a giant net, there's now one that stretches across the fields. It means the bees are trapped, rather than the humans. As much as Echo would love every creature to be free, without Immunity, there's really no other choice. The bees are still deadly to countless numbers of their population. Maybe even Maggie. They can't afford to take any risks.

There are footsteps behind them, and Echo turns to see River approaching.

"Daddy!" Maggie squeals, getting up to run to him.

Echo sighs contentedly. Maggie may follow her every movement, but it's her father she looks like. With a tangle of unruly dark hair and big emerald green eyes, Maggie is a smaller, more feminine version of River. Which makes her a little like Flora, the clever aunt she's growing up hearing so much about. And that's not where the similarities stop. While the other children play in the protected gardens, Maggie spends as much time in the LaB as she's allowed. She's already taken over an entire corner where she conducts her own experiments as she peppers Reed with questions.

Maggie reaches River and he scoops her up, kissing her once on each cheek then swinging her onto his shoulders where she rides proudly like a queen surveying her land. Echo's not sure which is a more beautiful sight. River and Maggie—the two people she loves with all her heart. Or the magical world they're trying to create.

Echo stands, stretching up to kiss River. Their lips connect and a jolt of excitement lights her soul. She wonders if he'll always have this effect on her. Every kiss feels like their first.

Maggie leans over River and taps Echo on the head. "Are you two kissing *again?*"

"Maybe." Echo pulls back and smiles up at their daughter. She hopes one day Maggie will understand just how important she is. Not just to them, but to the future that's being carved out right here. Finding out she was pregnant was what gave her the determination she needed when the zones were at war. River, too. Maggie was their inspiration to fight. To build a better world than the one they'd grown up in.

Turning to look out across the landscape bursting with food and life, Echo has no doubt they're on their way to achieving exactly that.

Because it's not the Green Zone she's looking at.

It's the expanse of dirt that was once called the Dead Zone. Only there's nothing dead about it now.

"The Sun Lands are so pretty, Mommy," says Maggie, noticing her gaze.

Echo smiles, loving that the new name for this slice of the world comes so naturally to her daughter. The ash from the fires that destroyed the village Echo had grown up in had regenerated the land, and it wasn't long until crops could be planted. Nobody was keen to retain the name that had been given to them in a world that treated them as less, so it became the Sun Lands. And as Echo looks across at it now, she decides the name's perfect. It's a name that speaks of hope, just like the people who work hard to cultivate it. People who have enough food to fill their bellies, leaving the scurge behind as nothing more than a painful memory.

For a time, the Green Zone remained, although when it became almost impossible to find the border that distinguished the two zones, they merged into one.

As they should always have been.

Just like Echo and River had always said.

One people. One zone.

Even the Moon Zone is now considered part of the Sun Lands, affectionately known simply as the Moon. As for the Extinction Zone—that's now referred to as the Future. It's a place of promise, because who knows how far the Sun Lands could stretch now there's peace between the people.

River lifts Maggie from his shoulders and settles her on the grass. They sit either side of her in their little family of three, keeping her close just in case a curious bee has managed to escape the net. There are adrenacure stations dotted all over the Sun Lands, accessible to all who might need them. Reed's been able to keep producing the precious canisters, with thanks to Oren's secret field of serpentwood. He even figured out a way to harvest adrenaline from donors using excitement rather than fear. All Echo needs is one lingering kiss from River. Makk prepares for his donation by jumping from the top of the Sting in a parachute instead. As for Goldie, all she has to do is watch Makk jump.

The process produces less adrenaline than Oren's methods, but Reed's figured out a way to use what he collects to manufacture artificial adrenaline, which is as effective. Still, Echo wishes the process wasn't necessary. The extraction itself is painful and she dreads the day Maggie has to make her first donation. But she knows everyone must contribute, because the bees are as deadly as they've ever been, and without Immunity the adrenacure is a necessary part of life. As are the suits the people wear when tending the fields. Many even choose to work at night when they feel safer, reminding Echo of the Moon Workers.

If only they had the Sovereign, life would be so much easier.

But Flora made her decision, and they have no choice but to work around it. And it's not all bad. With no Sovereign, lines between the zones became blurred, then eventually extinguished. People had to find a way to live together, along with the bees.

Maybe that's how it was always supposed to be.

Maybe that's the lesson humanity was supposed to learn.

"What's a birthday?" Maggie asks.

Echo laughs at the random way her daughter's busy mind works. "Where did you hear that word?"

"Reed said it to me." Maggie frowns. "This morning. He said it was my birthday and that I've had five of them."

"Then I guess it's your birthday," says River, chuckling. "We're better at keeping track of seasons than days around here. But Reed would know."

Maggie groans. "But what is it? What's a birthday?"

"It's the day you were born," says Echo. "Five years ago today, you came into the world."

"And it was the best day of our lives," River adds.

"Yes," Echo says. "Once your dad stopped fussing and worrying about both of us, he had a great day."

"Were you happy to meet me?" Maggie asks.

"Oh, you have no idea." Echo shuffles a little closer to this precious child they'd fought so hard for.

"I was happy to meet you, too," says Maggie, matter-of-factly, even though she couldn't possibly remember any such thing.

"Do you want to know something else about birthdays?" Echo asks as she's struck with an idea.

Maggie tilts up her head and rolls her eyes dramatically. "I want to know *everything* about birthdays."

"You're just like your Aunt Flora," says River. "She wanted to know everything as well."

"About birthdays?" Maggie asks.

"About *everything*." River squeezes Maggie tightly and she giggles.

"So, what is it?" Maggie turns her attention to Echo, who's busy removing the locket she still wears around her neck.

"People used to give presents on birthdays," says Echo. "On the day I turned seventeen, my father gave me this special locket."

"But I'm not seventeen," says Maggie. "That's a very big number. Reed said I only have five birthdays."

"Do you want the present or not?" Echo laughs.

"I want it," Maggie says quickly, her green eyes wide as she stares at the locket Echo's dangling in front of her. "Please, Mommy."

Echo slips it over her daughter's head, wishing she'd had this idea earlier so she could have put something special inside it like her father had.

"I like birthdays." Maggie holds out the locket and studies it closely. "Does it open?"

Echo nods. "It does. But there's nothing in there."

"We'll find something special to put in it," says River as Maggie carefully opens it. "Your grandfather put serpentwood seeds in there for your mom. She used them to save my life."

"There's still one in here," says Maggie.

"No, there's not." Echo leans in closer. "It's empty."

"There really is." Maggie taps the open locket on the palm of her small hand. "It's stuck in the bit where it closes."

"That's probably just a bit of dirt," says Echo, unable to stop her heart from beating a little bit faster. She'd promised her father she'd plant the seeds in the Dead Zone. After she used them to save River, it was a promise she never expected to be able to keep.

"See!" Maggie says triumphantly, holding out her hand. "It's a seed. With a little yellow spot."

Echo gasps to see it's true. Maggie unmistakably has a serpentwood seed in the palm of her hand.

"Daddy," says Maggie. "Do you need your life saved?"

"Not right now, thanks." River smiles at his daughter, then looks at Echo, knowing exactly how much this means to her. "Maybe we can plant it instead?"

Maggie's eyes light up. "We could have our very own serpentwood bush."

"You know we always share what we have," River says gently.

Maggie nods. "But I don't have to share my locket, do I?"

"No," Echo says. "Although, one day you might like to give it to your child."

Maggie nods, even though she doesn't seem entirely on board with this idea. But that attitude will change in time. Maggie didn't just inherit River's looks. She inherited the kindness in his heart.

"Where should we plant it?" Maggie squirms out from between her parents and jiggles in front of them.

"Hmm." Echo looks around, not wanting to take Maggie too close to the netted crops. She can hear the humming of the bees from here. They won't know if Maggie's Immune until she's seventeen. Oren was right about one thing, Immunity isn't truly established until late adolescence. Given both her parents are, there's every reason to hope. She might even be the Sovereign they were searching for. But that will be an answer they'll have to wait for.

"I think we should plant it over there." Maggie points to the adrenacure station several yards from the net. "That way if Daddy has a one-off breathing issue, we can easily find some seeds to help him."

Echo snorts, which makes River burst out laughing. It seems she may have used that phrase a few too many times.

"Well?" Maggie taps a foot impatiently. "Is it a good spot?"

"It's a perfect spot," says Echo as they follow Maggie over to the station.

River stoops to pick up a sturdy twig, which he then uses to carve out some dirt in the exact spot Maggie selects. The soil is dark and rich, so unlike the dust that had once coated these lands.

"Can I do it, Mommy?" Maggie holds out her hand with the seed. "Can I plant the special seed?"

Echo nods. Having her daughter fulfill her promise is even more special than her doing it herself.

Maggie squats down and drops the seed into the hole, instructing River on how she wants it filled back in. Echo takes a water bottle from the adrenacure station and dampens the soil while River inserts the stick like a little flagpole so they can find the spot again.

"Will it grow big and strong like me?" Maggie asks.

"I hope so." Echo looks briefly to the sky, hoping that her father can see them. Tears sting her eyes as her heart fills with both joy and grief. Then she sees a shadow move out from behind a cloud as a familiar hum buzzes through the air.

"Nectar!" Maggie squeals. "Reed fixed her up! It must be for my birthday! I really love birthdays!"

Nectar sustained a lot of damage in the final days of their war with Oren. And without Flora to repair her, she had to be taken to the LaB. Reed tries to find time to spend on her—usually with Maggie by his side nagging at him to hurry up. It seems he finally succeeded.

"Reed!" Maggie calls, jumping up and down to see him riding on Nectar's back.

The giant Worker swoops in a large circle, taking Reed soaring across the Sun Lands.

"Reed!" Maggie waves her little arms wildly. "I'm right here!"

Reed flies low over the netted fields and the people lift their heads in amazement, peering up from the visors in their suits.

"Can I have a turn on her?" Maggie asks, her jaw hanging open.

"Definitely not," River and Echo say in unison.

"But it's my birthday," says Maggie. "It's a very special day."

"No," they both say again.

They look across at each other and their hands automatically entwine.

Always in sync.

Always together.

They may not have found everything they need.

But they found so much more.

CHAPTER

THIRTY

RIVER

River's pretty used to smiling. In this new world where he's surrounded by so much—peace, family, love—smiling is like breathing. Easy. Unconscious.

And for someone like him, who's learned not to take the ability to inhale and exhale for granted, smiling is something he's grateful for each and every day.

Reed sweeps out wide, throwing his arms in the air. River's smile fades as he watches it, registering the expanse of green and stone that Reed's now above.

They have so much.

But not everything.

The scoring grounds are now the shining grounds. It's where every soul who was lost to Oren's society and the fight to end it is now buried. Moving all the bodies from the Sovereign graveyard took months, but with the help of the re-programmed Workers carrying and digging, the task was completed.

Too many lives lie deep in the rejuvenated soil, a riot of vegetation that would rival the Betadome covering it. Each one has a large stone to mark their final resting place, and in that stone a line has been etched. Each groove has been filled with molten metal, and it's that sea of silver marks that catches the light and glitters, honoring the new name.

River's hand holds Echo's a little tighter. So many aren't here to breathe the green scent, to smell the rich earth, to taste satiation day after day, to see the shades of green that stretch far further than any of them thought possible.

Chase. Trid. Navy. Rose. Cascade and Clover. Daisy. So many. Including Flora.

Echo leans against him, following his line of sight and gazing at the shining grounds. "They would've been proud."

River nods, his chest tight. "Yes, they would have been."

He wonders what Flora would think of all this. She died believing it wasn't possible. That it wasn't worth fighting for. She took the promise of a Sovereign to her grave, now buried deep in the shining grounds.

The knowledge has always tinged his grief. Flora was a beautiful, fragile soul. Her legacy will never reflect that.

"Are you sure I can't have a ride on Nectar?" Maggie asks, pouting.

River's smile returns, always bigger and sweeter when it comes to his daughter. He bends down to scoop her up, holding her as they watch Reed approach. "Very sure. You know no one's allowed to ride the Workers until we know whether they're Immune."

Maggie's pout grows, her bottom lip almost swallowing her top one.

River chuckles, jostling her. "But Nectar's special. She'll be around a lot more than the other Workers."

"She will?" Maggie asks, tilting her head as if trying to understand why that would be.

River doesn't get a chance to reply because Reed's descending. He wonders how much of Nectar's programming has remained intact. How much of Flora is still a part of her…

The sun glistens on Nectar's sleek metal body as Reed lands several feet away. "Flying is always cool, but there's something special about doing it on this old girl," he says, swinging a leg over so he can slide off.

Except Nectar's glass eyes land on River, then light up. With an excited whirr, she rushes toward him. Reed yelps as he tries to leap off, only to be bumped by one of her wings. He lands on the soft grass in a tangle of limbs.

Maggie squeals with delight as Nectar barrels at them, stopping only inches away. The giant metal bee whirrs even louder as her jaws work, clacking and clicking.

"She's talking to me!" Maggie gasps.

Echo smiles, leaning her head against River's shoulder. "She likes you."

Maggie wriggles, urging River to take her closer to Nectar. "Hi Nectar," she says, reaching out to brush her head. "Wanna go for a fly?"

Echo shakes her head, a smile hovering at the edges of her lips. "Cheeky girl," she admonishes.

"She only speaks Latin," River adds, glad for that.

"Then learning about birthdays is going to have to wait," Maggie says, her brow puckering. "I need to know *everything* about Latin."

River catches Reed's gaze as he dusts himself off, and Reed nods, answering the silent question. Nectar is still programmed to only respond to a handful of people's voices. River has no doubt learning Latin is exactly what his daughter will do.

The sound of pounding feet has River and Echo spinning,

his arms tightening around his daughter. No one moves that fast or loud in the Sun Lands, not unless something's wrong.

"It's Nola and Vern," Echo says, sounding relieved.

River lets out a breath. Seems the threat of danger still lingers in his nervous system.

Reed steps up beside them, squinting. "And everyone else in the Sting," he points out.

River realizes he's right. A crowd is assembling along the edge of the field, every face angled toward them, silent and tense.

He and Echo move closer, tightening around Maggie protectively as the relief is short-lived. River wonders whether Maggie's about to fly on Nectar after all. Keeping their daughter safe is their first priority.

His mother and father reach them, worry twisting their features. "Is everything okay?" his mother asks, eyes darting over the four of them.

River's father scowls as he pants after the frantic run. "We saw Reed on a Worker heading your way, when all the others are in the fields. We were worried something was wrong."

"It's Nectar," Echo says. "Reed fixed her."

Reed flushes, shifting his weight. "Surprise," he says weakly.

River's mother's gaze snaps to the metal bee, registering the silver glow emanating from her disc. "Oh."

River's father chuckles as he shakes his head. "That makes sense." He turns toward the crowd who are watching this all anxiously, lifting both arms up to create a circle over his head. He was the one to suggest using large body signals to communicate across longer distances, reducing the need to shout.

The crowd takes a second to register the message, or maybe they just take a moment to believe it.

River scans the throng of people, shocked at the number of

bodies. Reed's right, it looks like everyone in the colony is here. Tuff and Goldie, the only reason Makk's beside them is he's holding onto the shoulders of his younger sister as she tries to wriggle free. Jupiter and Lyra, even though they tend to work the night shifts. Sledge and Fray, their son wrapped in a tiny white suit.

Slowly, arms rise up to send back the "okay" message. Their bodies relaxing is visible even at a distance as their heads sink an inch, as smiles reveal flashes of teeth. Turning, they filter back to whatever they were doing before the call of alarm disturbed them.

River blinks, touched by the show of support.

Every one of them came running. They were all ready to fight. To defend.

River's mother brushes her graying hair out of her face, sighing. "I suppose it's going to take a little longer for everyone to trust this." She sweeps her arm to encompass the Sun Lands.

River's father wraps an arm around her shoulders. "Some things you don't take for granted," he murmurs, pressing a kiss to her temple.

River's heart warms, just like it always does when he sees his parents like this, which is often. They're rarely apart, touching frequently, always looking a little younger when the other is by their side.

Maggie wriggles in River's arms, letting him know she wants to be put down. The moment her feet hit the grass, she runs to River's father, grabbing his hand and tugging.

"Grandpa, will you teach me Latin?"

His brows shoot up. "What happened to learning about the different types of adjuvants?"

Maggie waves a dismissive hand, sending a mischievous grin at her parents. "This is more important."

"Go on, Vern," River's mother cajoles.

River's father grins. "Anything for the two Mag—" he wiggles his brows "—nificent girls in my life."

Giggling, Maggie claps her hands as River's mother beams. She cried when Echo told her what they were naming their daughter.

River reflexively gives Echo a squeeze. Watching his parents and his daughter together always tugs a chord deep in his chest. She squeezes him back, just as conscious of the gift family is, possibly more so.

"Shall we start now?" River's mom asks.

"Yes!" Maggie squeals, already taking each of her grandparents in a hand. "Hurry, before Mommy and Daddy figure out I'm trying to steal Nectar!"

River's father ducks his head as he breaks into a run, dragging his two Mag-nificent girls with him. "Quick! Just in case they heard you."

Maggie and River's mom giggle and skip as they follow, their laughter carrying over the green ocean, Reed shouting to them to wait up. Ahead, Lyra steps from the edge of the crowd, and River knows who she's waiting for. The romance between her and Reed was a slow burn, but still a beautiful one.

River and Echo glance at each other, their love for one another and the amazing child it created shining in their eyes. Realizing they have a rare moment alone, he pulls her close and presses a kiss to the tip of her nose.

"When I fell in love with you, I had no idea what it would mean," he murmurs.

Echo smiles up at him, tenderly placing her hand on his chest, right over his heart. "Neither of us did."

River grins. "To be honest, I could never have pictured this. You. Maggie. The Sun Lands."

"Turns out reality can surpass dreams," Echo says, her soft

eyes roaming his face. "Although in all of them, I was loving you."

His heart swells as his chest tightens. "That was a given," he whispers, emotion clogging his throat.

He turns her in his arms so her back is pressing against his front. "And that meant we have this."

They gaze at the Sun Lands. At the ever-growing, ever-evolving horizon. At the infinite layers of height and depth and beauty. At the shades of green within green.

"Viridescent," River breathes.

He hasn't allowed himself to say that word since Flora's death. It was too painful. But saying it now feels right. Like he can let the hurt and anger go, and allow the sweet memories and feelings to fill the space left behind.

Nectar whirrs, grabbing their attention as she rises up. River watches in shock as the small plate in her forehead pulls back, revealing the camera. Beams of light shoot out, creating an image.

One that has River clinging to Echo as his knees go weak.

"It can't be," he gasps.

Echo glances up at him, her shock already morphing to a smile. "It is." She untangles herself from his numb arms, then wraps her own around his waist. "It's a message."

From Flora.

His twin hovers just above the grass, a shimmering image being projected by Nectar. She looks just like she did five years ago, beautiful, strong. Yet...breakable.

With a small nudge from Echo, River moves so he can face his sister. His heartbeat is present in every inch of his body, yet achingly absent at the same time.

"Flora," he whispers, and he realizes he can feel something.

Warm, wet tears are trekking down his cheeks.

Flora smiles, looking in his direction, but not quite at him.

TAMAR SLOAN & HEIDI CATHERINE

"If you're watching this River, then you've found a reason to say our special word." She presses her hands to her stomach. "And for that, I'm glad."

River swallows as Echo tucks herself tightly into his side, telling him without words she's here for him.

"It also means I get to tell you one more time that I love you," Flora continues, her green eyes shimmering. "And to say I'm sorry that I wasn't stronger."

"Oh, Flora," River whispers.

"If all this failed, I didn't want to be around to see it." She smiles a little. "If you succeeded, then I have no doubt it's as beautiful as your soul."

Echo squeezes River's waist. "It is, Flora. It really is."

His twin straightens a little. "And it also means there's one last thing you should know."

River stills, noting Echo does the same.

"I figured out why Echo was immune to queen bee venom, even though I knew all along she wasn't the Sovereign." Flora smiles. "Her Immunity was gifted by the child she was carrying."

"Maggie," Echo says, sounding astounded as River feels.

"It's called fetal-maternal microchimerism," Flora says, slipping into scientist mode. "When a woman's pregnant, the cells of her baby migrate into her bloodstream, leaving a permanent imprint. It's beautiful, actually. The baby protected Echo as much as Echo protected the baby."

Matching tears are now slipping down Echo's cheeks. "My beautiful baby girl."

"And yes, that does mean your child is a Sovereign, River." Flora angles her head. "Whether you had a son or a daughter."

He frowns. "But—"

Flora lifts her hand as if she knew that was coming. "The Sovereign Code was never only linked to the female chromosome." Her face hardens. "Although the moment I discovered that, I deleted any trace of it. It was one piece of information Oren would never have."

"River..." Echo breathes. "That means..."

Flora's image flickers, and when it sharpens again, her gaze seems to settle right on him. "You're the Sovereign, River," she says, a sweet, beautiful smile climbing up her face. "As is your child, and possibly any others you have, just like we're both Sovereigns. Your children's children could be Sovereigns as well."

His mouth pops open, then just hangs there. His heart jolts to a standstill, then just sits in suspended animation.

His twin had one last secret.

One last truth that will save them all.

"Thank you, River." Flora's gaze flickers from side to side as if she's looking for someone. "And you too, Echo. Thank you for being the ones strong enough to fight for everything you have now."

Flora's image disappears, leaving behind stunned silence.

Echo moves around so she's facing River. Her hands come up to frame his face as she smiles. "Turns out I was the one making out with the Sovereign all along."

He blinks. Blinks again.

Then blinks one more time, just for good measure.

Echo grins, her eyes twinkling with the mischief that always reminds him of Maggie. "I knew I was doing the right thing when I gave you those serpentwood seeds."

River huffs out a laugh, the first sound he's made since he learned the truth he never saw coming. When Echo chose to give him what they believed were the final serpentwood seeds as Eden burned around them, she didn't choose him over humanity.

She chose the person who could save every last soul.

"I..." River's voice fades away. There are no words for this moment. In fact, he's not sure it needs them.

Instead, he mirrors Echo's actions and cups her face. He leans down as she reaches up. Their lips tenderly brush. Their breaths mingle.

Their hearts thud out the future that's now theirs.

Reality has certainly outdone their dreams.

They have unity.

Along with the one thing they fought for from the very beginning.

Immunity.

THE END

Ready for a new series by Tamar Sloan and Heidi Catherine?

Check out Elemental Games now!

http://mybook.to/ElementalGames

ELEMENTAL GAMES

When Aura and Hayze wake up with six others in a place they've never seen, they know three things.

They're childhood enemies.
No one remembers how they got here.
And there's no way out.

In a world with no rules or reason, there's so much they don't know. Why they're so drawn to each other. Why they can bend an element to their will. And why each day is deadlier than the last.

Aura and Hayze need answers because one thing is certain.

Their lives depend on uncovering what is truth and what is reality.

An intoxicating thrill ride packed with twists, romance and nail-biting action! Lovers of Maze Runner and The Hunger Games will devour Elemental Games.

Grab your copy now.

https://mybook.to/ElementalGames

THE THAW CHRONICLES

Tamar Sloan and Heidi Catherine are the authors of the bestselling series, The Thaw Chronicles.

Get your free prequel now!
http://mybook.to/BurningThaw

WANT TO STAY IN TOUCH?

If you'd like to be the first for to hear all the news from Tamar and Heidi, be sure to sign up to our newsletter. Subscribers receive bonus content, early cover reveals and sneaky snippets of upcoming books. We'd love you to join us!

SIGN UP HERE:

https://sendfox.com/tamarandheidi

About the Authors

Tamar Sloan hasn't decided whether she's a psychologist who loves writing, or a writer with a lifelong fascination with psychology. She must have been someone pretty awesome in a previous life (past life regression indicated a Care Bear), because she gets to do both. When not reading, writing or working with teens, Tamar can be found with her husband and two children enjoying country life in their small slice of the Australian bush.

Heidi Catherine loves the way her books give her the opportunity to escape into worlds vastly different to her own life in the burbs. While she quite enjoys killing her characters (especially the awful ones), she promises she's far better behaved in real life. Other than writing and reading, Heidi's current obsessions include watching far too much reality TV with the excuse that it's research for her books.

MORE SERIES TO FALL IN LOVE WITH...

ALSO BY TAMAR SLOAN AND HEIDI CATHERINE

The Thaw Chronicles

Elemental Games

ALSO BY TAMAR SLOAN

Keepers of the Grail

Keepers of the Light

Keepers of the Chalice

Keepers of Excalibur

Zodiac Guardians

Descendants of the Gods

Prime Prophecy

ALSO BY HEIDI CATHERINE

The Kingdoms of Evernow

The Soulweaver